Shawn Maureen McKelvie

ISBN: 1468137549
ISBN-13: 9781468137545

PREFACE

It was probably more than a decade ago that I developed the title *Ice Within the Soul.* At that time the phrase represented the pure evil of serial killers, murderers, and pedophiles—those who went into murderous rages with no remorse for those they inflicted pain upon. It was a time when horrible, senseless crimes seemed to fill the evening news and pages of the daily paper. All too often I cringed traumatized, while processing such reprehensible violence against human beings.

During those times I wondered how the world seemed to breed so many cruel, twisted human beings. Sadly, not every serial killer, pedophile, murderer, or bully looks like a monster. Some are quite attractive and may even exhibit a respectable façade. Their looks are used as a tool to lure their unsuspecting prey into their deceptive, wicked web. Slowly, a dark evil core and the ice within the soul would become another's tragic reality.

My fascination in observing the dynamics of friendships, families, and people in general started in childhood. What made some families grow closer throughout devastating hardships, while others fell apart over minor miscommunications? I came to realize that there are varying degrees of emotions like good and evil in all of us. That's when I developed the phrase "situational ice." It's my homegrown definition of "ice" that forms in the souls of everyday people. I'm referring to the cold resentment that slowly brews for weeks, months, and years. Unfortunately, we all know someone whose soul was filled with anger, rage, jealousy, and even evil...that lasted a lifetime.

This is not a horror story, but one person's journey through the first four decades of her life. Moe Bender arrived in this world wide-eyed and wondrous. As a five-year-old, Moe Bender relied on her intuition and quickly learned you shouldn't *always* obey adults. Moe's ability to sense concealed evil, passive-aggressiveness, or emotions such as resentment and anger were felt as a palpable internal alarm! Her story is one of a young life that wasn't always carefree or painless. It shows that good, everyday people can also have varying degrees of "ice" within their souls, that mass murderers were just one extreme end of the spectrum.

Moe Bender was one of six siblings with a special bond that was slowly falling apart. The flashes of the young girl's destiny came as visions. She followed those visions and tried to decipher the gift of feeling the emotions of those around her. It wasn't always a gift—sometimes it was more of a curse. To a young child, it was confusing to see a smile on someone's face while feeling the intense hostility from across the room. Many of us have witnessed firsthand how harboring anger or resentment over a period of years can cause great destruction, especially to a family. It's like a contagious disease that can spread quickly to every member. When you see a vision of what is to come years from now...how do you stop it? How do you melt the ice within the souls of those you love, and even within your own soul?

Ice Within the Soul is a novel loosely based on my own life. I incorporated many of my rich experiences as one of six siblings. Those were the years we thought were more simple and carefree. The book spans more than four decades of the character Moe Bender's life. Her journey is sprinkled with lighthearted comedy, complicated family issues, paranormal and embellished events. The names of the characters are fictitious. The dramatizations and some supernatural occurrences were added for pure reading enjoyment. Any resemblances to persons living or dead are purely coincidental.

My sweet husband, Dr. Milt McKelvie, was my sounding board as I developed my content for *Ice Within the Soul*. He had faith that I had a unique story to tell and encouraged me to finally make my dream a reality. He was my master critic, rather harsh at times—but I went back to rewrite, revise, and then rewrite all over again! I slowly started to witness firsthand that my husband could actually feel my story. When he read it for the last time, he looked at me and in a sweet voice shared that there were many times he laughed out loud and many pages that brought tears to his eyes. Most of all, he wanted to keep turning the pages. Milt, it was your strength, patience, encouragement, and love that inspired me to put all the words on paper.

There were also several family members and friends that were my eternal cheerleaders and voices of encouragement. Thanks to my early proofreaders: daughter, Lauren Corrigan, son, Chad Tenge, friends; Crispin Melloh, Kathy Stephens-Williams, Candy Johnson, Susan Ellison and Ella Nayor. A special thanks to my sister, Cheryl Marlin. I will forever appreciate your help, wisdom, editing and sharing our rich history as siblings.

CHAPTER 1

I ran around the field, arms outstretched, while taking in the beauty of a Southern California spring. In the eyes of this young girl, the small grassy lot by the alley was an open mountain range, like the one in the *Sound of Music*. I looked up at the blue sky and twirled round and round in a patch of flowers. There was an invigorating scent of honeysuckle and the green of newly mowed lawns that filled the air. Yes, I took great delight in nature, animals, and the great outdoors...it made me happy! The morning routine was for my four siblings and me to be scooted out of the house shortly after breakfast. This was so my mother could enjoy a few cigarettes, a cup of coffee, and an hour of two of quiet time. I didn't mind, for I was at peace in a field that was full of friends...ladybugs. According to history, ladybugs derived their name in the middle ages when plant lice were devouring the precious crops. The local farmers gathered and prayed to the Virgin Mary to help protect their vital source of food. Amazingly, soon afterward, the ladybugs came in swarms and ate the pest destroying the crops. Hence, the name, "The Beetles of Our Lady," shortened to ladybugs.

Whatever the history, I knew the red-shelled ladybugs were so adorable, they surely must be good! To my delight, I felt a tickle on my arm and saw a mother ladybug carrying her tiny, red-cloaked baby on her back. To me this was a rare and endearing moment. It was like watching a mother holding her infant child. "So sweet!" My eyes were wide with fascination!

I smiled at these amazing tiny creatures on my arms. Needless to say, I wasn't surprised to see and smell a pungent yellow substance on my arm. This, of course, was Momma Ladybug's defense against the big gentle giant holding her now, me...Moe Bender.

I continued to twirl around and around with the ladybug duo on my arm. Surely they must be having as much fun as I was! Out of the corner of my eye, I saw the new girl, Leslie Ward. She lived across the ally and was now watching me enthusiastically play in the field. Of course it was selfish of me to not share this incredible site. I called out her name.

"Leslie, come and see what I have!"

Leslie was shoeless but stopped to pull up her stretched-out, dirty socks. She waved as she scrambled over to see the cause of my excitement. My friend was a disheveled six-year-old with dirty blonde hair. I momentarily wondered if the new girl was playing unsupervised beauty parlor. As she ran toward me, her unevenly chopped coif blew in the wind. She huffed and puffed, using my shoulder to halt the momentum of her short sprint. The remains of grape jelly clung precariously to Leslie's chin. It was my nature to be observant; I wondered if the dried food on her T-shirt was a combination of oatmeal and toast. In between panting to regain her breath, she excitedly searched to see what I was holding.

"What is it?"

Her eyes zeroed in on baby ladybug on the momma's back..."Ohhhh!"

Leslie gingerly placed her fingers under the ladybugs, slowly redirecting them from my arm to hers. Leslie's eyes widened and seemed amused, watching the ladybugs crawl on her forearm. I grew concerned with the sudden change in her tone of the deepening of her voice. In a split second, Leslie's lips went from smiling to thin and tight while she gritted her teeth. Before I could react, she released an eerie primal growl. Leslie seemed crazed as she forcefully squished the unsuspecting duo between her fingers!

The intense shock of what I just witnessed stunned me, and I gasped! Seconds later I came to my senses screaming, "Stop, Stop it!"

I quickly pushed Leslie to stop her from smashing the defenseless ladybugs. A yellow juice remained on my arm, emitting a strong pungent odor. The scattered flecks of the ladybugs' grand red cloak were now falling gracefully to the ground. It sadly represented momma and baby ladybug's flag of defeat.

Leslie's eyebrows remained furrowed as she clenched her teeth in hatred. It was as if someone had turned on Leslie's psycho button! Had this girl gone absolutely mad? We both now stared at the scattered remains on the blades of grass. My heart sank as I mourned the loss of my two little friends. Slowly I looked up and my eyes met Leslie's devious, calculating stare. Suddenly, a chill went right up my spine and hairs raised on the back of my neck. It was obvious she enjoyed my pain and smiled now at my bewildered face. I mustered up enough courage to yell,

"Leslie! Why? Why did you kill my ladybugs? They weren't hurting you!"

My heart was pounding so hard and fast that it was almost audible. Could she hear it too? I angrily gritted my teeth, glaring while I waited for an answer. Leslie was as cool as a cucumber. Her piercing blue eyes seemed to bore a hole in my head. No answer from her...just a victorious, smug smirk. Just as quickly as it started, Leslie's monster-like facade faded, and her demeanor returned to that of a child. The tiny girl innocently started to wipe away the evidence on her clothes. The speckled yellow juices now dotted Leslie's T-shirt. She hummed a tune as she cheerfully skipped towards home.

My hands covered my eyes in disbelief as I knelt above the remains. What in the world just happened? That day I learned this world could be a confusing place. I previously assumed all children were good, that they, too, loved and were fascinated by God's creatures. How could a six-year-old release such unprovoked rage on innocent little ladybugs? I felt Leslie's unpredictable nature contained a dark, evil seed. It made me wonder what or who else was she capable of hurting. Yes, Leslie most certainly frightened me.

I avoided Leslie like the plague for several weeks. I opted instead to hang with my two older brothers and my sister, Charlee. Her name was pronounced "Charlie" by us kids; however, she gave herself a new stage name each week. Heck, we lived in Southern California, and everyone wanted to be an actress! We even set up a stage made of boxes and put on plays for the neighborhood kids. Charlee the Big Ham loved an adoring audience. Her favorite song was *My Boy Lollipop*. The song had a catchy tune that was initially was sung by Barbie Gaye in the '50s. My sister Charlee would toss her honey-brown curls to and fro as she skipped on the stage. Yes, Charlee was an act herself, singing at the top of her lungs...

"You're my sugar dandy, Ho-Ho my lollipop, My Boy Lollipop...."

I admired her confidence and wished I had a big dose of it too. No doubt Charlee would be a famous movie star someday. Charlee actually looked more like Shirley Temple than Barbie Gaye. She prided herself on having the same ringlet curls and deep dimples.

We Bender kids were responsible for recruiting an audience for Charlee's performance. If no one was available, then my brothers Sam and T-Mac and I were the official "clappers." Yes, it was our job to applaud Charlee's act. Charlee would even prompt and encourage us to whistle and yell, "More! More!" That made Charlee happy, and she would blow kisses as she retreated backstage.

There were times we all took turns as "the Star." Personally, I cringed at the thought of performing in front of people. I was shy and awkward and needed some prodding to get up on the stage. That is, unless I was telling a joke or doing something goofy like imitating the Three Stooges.

I'd look cross-eyed, start snapping my fingers, and go, "Nyuk, nyuk, nyuk!"

Just like Curly Howard. Another favorite stooge character was Moe Howard. I'd gruffly bark commands at an imaginary Curly and Larry. As Moe, my slap shtick would include forehead slaps, nose tweaks, and double-cheek slapping. The big finale was taking my two fingers and acting like I was going to poke out the eyes of those in the front row. I could see my mom peering out the window, laughing. That was better than any applause!

My brothers had the same act, which would always begin and end the same way. They were sumo wrestlers. They would lunge at each other, growling, with outstretched arms and grisly sneers. Unfortunately, the sumo-demo would always lead to a real fist fight. That's when the show really started, and kids would come out of the woodwork! The spectators would cheer loudly for their favorite towheaded Bender boy. Charlee would look at the influx of spectators and scream.

"Moe! Moe! Make sure they all paid their quarters!"

Sam was powerful and built like a thick brick shithouse. Sam's angry face would turn a bright shade of crimson as he glared at T-Mac's silly boxing shuffle. That crazy dance step always made the kids howl and eight-year-old Sam growl.

"Fight like a *man*, you sissy!"

T-Mac was short, athletic, and quick as lightning. He took delight in making his older brother mad. T-Mac smiled as he ducked to escape Sam's punch. T-Mac wouldn't be laughing, though, if Sam got hold of him. Both would topple over, rolling around on the floor of our stage. In the process they sometimes tipped over my Kool-Aid stand! In all honesty, I didn't like to see my brothers fight. Fortunately, the battle never lasted too long before Mom broke it up. Usually, it was only seconds later when a frazzled June would run out the back door.

"Sam, T-Mac! Knock it off right now!"

My mom pulled Sam off of T-Mac. She then would point to the gate yelling, "Show's over, kids! It's time to head on home!"

We had a colorful family, for sure—especially Charlee with her vivid imagination. I was with a friend one day at Pan American Park. Yes, I was five and allowed to walk to the park or most anywhere by myself. Heck, most kids did back in 1962. Anyway, Charlee came up and asked us if we had seen Priscilla. I had a look of absolute confusion and thought, "What in the heck do you have up your sleeve now?" My young, pig-tailed friend asked, "Who is Priscilla?"

Charlee, in her best performance as concerned sister, moaned,

"Why, Prissy is my identical twin sister! I can't find her anywhere! Can you please help me find her?"

I knew from past experience that it was best to go along with Charlie, or else pay later. My friend and I search the whole dang Pan American Park, calling, "Prissy!" Of course we never found "the twin," because she didn't exist. Charlee was always creating pseudo people in her life. Maybe it was to confuse me, practice her acting skills, or both. Many years later, Charlee confessed about her white lies. Charlee knew that by the time the other kids found out, our family would have moved.

During our childhood, we lived in Wisconsin; St. Simons Island, Georgia; Alameda, California; San Diego, California; Bremerton, Washington; and now Long Beach, California. It was a lot of change for us kids. We would make friends, whom we would grow close to, then never see again. We'd sometimes relocate mid-semester and have to catch up with a new teacher's program. It was hard to try to fit in with new kids and classrooms all the time. Oh well, that was our life, and I truly believe it made us siblings close. Our lives may change month to month or year after year, but we always had each other.

Now, there was a fifth child, too—three-year-old Alan. Alan was the only boy that had dark brown hair like our dad. Alan could be a real thorn in our sides, with his nonstop talking—and tattling. I guess I shouldn't talk about being a tattletale. There were just times, though, when I needed to report my lazy older brothers' antics. T-Mac would hastily wash dishes, leaving lots of mushy breakfast crumbs on the plates. I'd say, "Ewww—yuck! Mom, T-Mac's just dipping the dishes in the water and not scrubbing!" In our household, if you didn't do a chore right the *first* time, you'd be punished with a week of washing and drying dishes.

The wheeling and dealing started, "Hey, if you don't squeal, I'll give you three of my best Purie marbles! I countered with five Purie marbles, and T-Mac counter offered four. It would go on and on until we reached an agreement. I would then place all the dirty dishes back in the sink for T-Mac to wash—or, if he gave me enough Purie marbles, I would do his job too. As much as I hate to say it, being a part of a large family taught me the importance of working as a team and the art of negotiation.

One busy Saturday, I tried to charm my way into less work by striking up a conversation with Mom. She was hastily scurrying around the kitchen to finish her chores. She grimaced as she thumbed through the thick stack of household bills. I carefully watched for the right opportunity to start flattering my beautiful blonde mother.

"Mom, your lipstick is pretty!"

"Thank you, dear," My mother replied in a flat impatient tone. After all, her favorite saying (then *and* now) was, "Kids should be seen and not heard." Mom gave me a raised eyebrow, completely aware of my strategy.

"Mom, what was I like as a baby? Was I good, or did I cry a lot?"

Mom shook her head. She gave an exasperated lengthy sigh and paused before she spoke.

"Geez, I don't know, it was too long ago!" Mom was now tapping her finger on the counter with a pen in her mouth. It was now only seconds before I would be shooed away. I needed to find another topic, and fast!

"Okay, Mom, how about school, did you like it?"

That particular question stirred some interest in June. She momentarily paused to reflect and dig something out of her memory bank. Her reply caught me off guard.

"Well, Moe, I definitely should have gone to college and not had so many children."

My ears perked up at this unexpected revelation. What the heck? I sighed a deep, impatient sigh and tried again...details, details, I need more details!

"Okay, now, Mom, would you have stopped *before* or *after* me?"

I was anxiously tapping my toe, awaiting an answer. Geez, it better be the right one! Heck, maybe if June *had* a college degree, I wouldn't be here doing chores!

"Hmmm." June's lingering deep reflection on college life made her smile.

"Yes, I would have had *maybe* one or two kids."

Still a noncommittal answer! For Pete's sake! I quickly brushed my unruly bangs out of my eyes and impatiently crossed my arms. I needed to find out which two out of the five Bender siblings would be "*the Keepers.*"

I stood in the kitchen still dressed in my Japanese kimono pj's. My long dark ashy blonde hair still had evidence of bedhead. As I scratched my scalp in wonder, my bangs once again fell forward into my eyes. Heck, no more hinting around! I needed to just be straight and ask her.

"Okay, now, Mom, *if* you *had* to pick two children, who would they be?"

My mom threw her head back and gave a hearty chuckle. She raised her hands, palm side up.

"Who knows? Maybe I wouldn't have had any at all!"

My mom was born June Lily McKinley, the eldest of six in a small town in southern Wisconsin. She was a beautiful, petite woman with blonde waves that bordered her glamorous face. I wanted to look just like Mom when I grew up! June was the prettiest mom in the neighborhood, hands-down. June was quite talkative around her friends but much more introverted around us kids. When Mom and Dad had company on weekends, they played cards until the wee hours of the morning. Long after I was supposed to be in bed, I'd sneak around the corner to listen. It made me smile to hear my mom's cheerful, animated voice. And the big belly laughs made me put my hand over my mouth and laugh too! It would be fun if she were like that all the time. The next day we would have the mom who was far away, deeply immersed in books or busy catching up on housework or bills. It seemed like she had a story to tell, and I wanted to hear it! But my mom's history was a mystery.

I wanted to know more about her as a person and not as my mother. I was always wide-eyed and anxious to know what life was life for her as a child. The exchange of information would have made her seem more human—knowing she also had many ups and downs in life, that she also made mistakes! But when I would ask her, time after time, year after year, I got the same response "Moe, I don't remember; it was just too long ago."

My dad used to tell us all lengthy stories about growing up in Wisconsin with his two brothers and his dog named Doodie. Dad would go on and on about all the antics he and his brothers got into—like the time he added mixed vegetables to dog food. My dad, "Big Al," told his younger brother it was beef stew!

Dad chuckled as he imitated his brother gulping it all down and then scraping the bowl for more.

"My brother Billy said it was the BEST he'd ever had!

Dad slapped the table as he bent over to laugh.

"Can you imagine the look on his face when I told him it was Doodie's food?"

Someday, when I have children, they won't have to work so darn hard to find out about me, my life. Now, we feisty Bender kids had no problem communicating with each other. When we were upset and feeling sad, we could easily share those feelings. If it was due to someone picking on us at school, either Charlee or Sam would offer to beat them up. Of course, fighting wasn't the answer. But it was a sibling's way to show they cared. We were basically a happy family. What definitely made us all thrilled, though, were the rare times Mom let her hair down to be silly. When Mom was happy, we were *all* happy!

Like the times we'd catch Mom singing "Zip-A-Dee Doo-Dah," from Walt Disney's *Song of the South*. My four siblings and I would look at each other and laugh as Mom snapped her fingers and gleefully danced around the room. It thrilled us all to see her so carefree and smiling, we'd start jumping around and singing too! We were never quite sure what triggered the sudden burst of cheer; maybe it was the thought of getting her caffeine and nicotine level up, or maybe Dad coming home from overseas..."Mr. Bluebird's on my shoulder, it's the truth, it's actual, everything is actual, everything is satisfactual...." At the time I thought it was a goofy song. Little did I know that I, too, would continue to sing this catchy tune for more than half a century. The song "Zip-A-Dee Doo-Dah" became a ritual to sing in the morning myself after a good night's sleep, to sing to my own children, or even, years later, to sing to my grandchildren. It seemed to soothe them as babies, cheer them as grumpy toddlers, and make them laugh as teens. So when I think of "Zip-A-Dee Doo-Dah," it brings back fond memories of the moments when my mom would finally relax, smile, and enjoy life, even if it was only for a short while.

June and Big Al, my father, met in their freshman year of high school. Big Al was tall, dark, and handsome. To me, he looked like Gregory Peck, who played Atticus Finch in the movie *To Kill a Mockingbird*. Big Al was also quite an intellectual, with goals of becoming a physician someday. Mom and Dad's courtship continued throughout high school, and they married soon after graduation. Her dream was to go to college after high school, maybe go into nursing school or become an accountant.

To everyone's surprise, my sister Charlee was born a year after Mom and Dad were married. It was Big Al who was college bound, while Mom stayed home to raise us kids. Dad attended school full-time and managed to work almost full-time, too. Dad came home from school, worked on his homework and passed it to Mom before leaving for work. Mom would proofread, make corrections, and type it up so Dad could turn it in the next day.

Somewhere along the line, my dad decided to enter the navy as an officer once he graduated with his degree in chemistry. My father grew to love the navy, especially the travel, and slowly pushed the thought of medical school into the distant past. That was the second big disappointment for my mom, June. The first was that she didn't attend college or have a career herself. In those days, it was expected that a women marry, stay home, and raise a family. June was from a large Catholic family and wasn't anxious to have one of her own, but that's what happened. Five little feisty Benders came into this world, almost one right after another. It was an exhausting blur of multiple pregnancies. A couple deliveries occurred while Big Al was overseas. How sad it must have been to be alone during the birth of a child.

There was no doubt Big Al loved June Lily McKinley, though. When my dad met my mom, he said it was love at first sight. Well, that was the case for my dad. It took my mom awhile to feel that way about Big Al. I don't recall many displays of affection by my mom. However, I knew that she cared about my father, in her own way. It wasn't expressed openly, though, until sometime after Dad's funeral in 2003. It was then that my mother shared how much she always loved my father and knew how much he loved her, too.

There were times when Big Al spent months overseas, so we would pack up and visit our grandparents in Wisconsin. Those were the times when

June was absolutely overwhelmed and needed to be the child again. Yes, in the loving household of Grandma and Grandpa McKinley, there were some pretty special memories for all of us! Both Grandma and Grandpa were wonderfully nurturing and had a great sense of humor.

I remember bringing a "fart bag" on one of our trips to see them. I was so anxious to put it under Grandpa's favorite cushion. Nothing really got past Grandpa, though. Grandpa had a crooked nose from his old boxing days and always wore a hat that made him look like a mobster. He looked tough on the outside but was a big old cream puff on the inside. He played along and acted like he didn't know the fart bag was under his chair cushion. As he seated himself, a loud release of bubbly gas was expelled from the fart bag. Grandpa raises his hands up in the air and exclaimed, "Oh my gulley, did I do that?

He then repeated the performance again and again, saying, "Excuse me! It must've been the beans!"

All of us kids were rolling on the floor, laughing. Grandpa smoked his pipe and winked at my Grandma. My jovial Swedish Grandma said, "Herman, don't you blame it on my chili! You're just full of hot air!"

Often, we would huddle around Grandma and plead with her to tell our fortunes on the Tarot cards. She had learned to read cards from her own great-grandmother. When it was my turn, Grandma said, "Moe, you have a very bright future ahead of you!" I excitedly grew close to hear every word.

"Really Grandma? What will I be when I grow up?"

"Hmm, let me look through your cards," Grandma said, carefully analyzing the cards. "Looks like you're going to become a nurse or anything you want to be! Moe, you are like a duck on a June bug. You just grab on and don't let go until you get what you want!" Grandma smiled as she reached up to pinch my cheek.

We all enjoyed the visits to Wisconsin to see our grandparents, aunts, uncles, and all the cousins. We had so much to learn from them but so little time, as our visits became less frequent. I'm not sure why.

We started out making trips twice a year, then every year, and soon just maybe every two years. It just wasn't enough time! You can never have enough people love you in this world, and we all felt so loved by our extended family up north. Our world involved multiple moves from state to state, where nothing was the same; in Wisconsin, our large, cohesive family offered us stability and comfort. That was not in the Bender cards, though. We soon piled in the station wagon, all waving good-bye to our grandparents. We all blew kisses until their silhouettes were like ants on the horizon.

When we got back to California, we counted the days before Big Al returned from overseas. Unfortunately, the first thing he'd do after kissing my mom was take out the clippers. In the days of Beatle-mania, a crew cut was the only acceptable hairstyle for Big Al's boys. I'm not just talking about a crew cut—but a *very* short one! Sam and T-Mac used to cry whenever Dad would take out the clippers.

"Noooo! Noooo!"

I stood there, supervising, trying to coax Big Al into letting Sam and T-Mac have longer hair.

Soon I would be sharing an empathy wail with my brothers.

"Noooo, Dad, it's too short! Sam and T-Mac look bald!"

In my mind, they looked like Curly Howard from the Three Stooges! Charlee would make matters worse by running up to the boys later and rubbing their heads, as if it were crystal balls. "Wish I had a watermelon, wish I had a watermelon!" she'd say.

Oh, geez, Sam and T-Mac would get *so* mad! One time T-Mac got one of Big Al's short crew cuts before his birthday party. Mom had a pony and professional photographer who took pictures of T-Mac on it. Later, T-Mac showed his dislike for his party cut by drawing a mustache on the eight-by-ten photo. Needless to say, T-Mac's little stunt didn't go over well with Big Al. Yeah, I'm sure someone went to bed with a red fanny that night!

The boys weren't the only ones subjected to bad cuts. If my mom had her way, I'd sleep on sponge curlers each night and run around with banana curls and inch-long bangs. Mom trimmed them so short at times that I'd run a strip of scotch tape across my forehead. It was the only thing that held down the nub for bangs! In elementary school, I already felt like a gawky girl, with my long legs and short waist. I'm not sure I considered myself pretty, but I did love my long hair. I also wanted long bangs...like the older kids were wearing!

It had been a couple months now since I last saw Leslie. The trauma of seeing the momma and baby ladybugs tortured by Leslie's bare hands was still vivid in my memory. Leslie waved hello as I walked by her house.

"Moe! Moe, come on over!"

I shook my head. "Not today, Leslie, not today."

I just wasn't ready to face her again. Maybe I'd give it a day or so. In the meantime, I would pass time by running around the green grassy field. *I won't stop running until a lady bug lands on my arm!* Little did I know that Leslie had followed me to the corner lot.

"Moe, you ain't doin' nuttin' but runnin' like a fool! Why don't you play with me?"

I continued to run, yelling,

"Go away, Leslie, I'm trying to catch a ladybug!"

My legs were always restless, and running soothed my soul. So I ran around the field full of knee-high weeds, my arms outstretched in the hope a ladybug would use one as a perch. Leslie soon left and walked home. Whirling, running, now singing my made-up tune...

Ladybug, ladybug, come out and play.
Ladybug, ladybug, Leslie's gone away.
Ladybug, ladybug, don't be blue.
Ladybug, ladybug, I'll protect you.

I now thought of myself as the savior of the ladybugs. I was on a mission to keep them safe from Leslie's rage. No more will I allow her to kill them, at least in my presence.

My siblings were growing tired of having me around as a third wheel. Charlee literally fired me from being her audience when we played "Stage." She said I was an unenthusiastic clapper! Geez, you can only applaud so many times to "My Boy Lollipop" or the "Good Ship Lollipop"! Yes, guilty, my hands hurt after clapping to the twentieth song! What is this with lollipops and songs, anyway?

One way I'd pass the time was to pick to flowers for the altar in my room. I felt it was important to make an altar; after all, I wanted to be a nun when I grew up. Mom gave me an old shipping box, and I placed a crisp, white pillowcase on top. A large cross was placed in the center, surrounded by fresh flowers from our garden. I gingerly placed my rosary and a Saint Joseph statue, alongside my homemade alter.

I also had this fascination, not with the Virgin Mary, but with Mary Magdalene. Unfortunately, we didn't have her statue in the house. In a book of saints, I recalled a picture of beautiful Mary Magdalene was praying on her knees and asking for forgiveness. I once heard someone say that she suffered such a loss with her "defamation of character." *Whoa*, I thought, *that must've been an awful disease!* I wasn't quite sure what she did that needed forgiving, though. It must not have been too bad, as she still became a saint. Charlee later told me that Mary Magdalene was a prostitute and that she had "Demons with her sexuality."

"Hmmm," I replied. My young mind wasn't able to comprehend exactly what that meant, and frankly, I was bit afraid to ask. To me it meant that a person could make mistakes and still be forgiven. How does that work, though? Does God give you three strikes and you're out, like in baseball? I thought I'd ask that question in Nun College!

We Benders weren't considered rich. However, we had more community pride on this side of the alley. The homes were landscaped and well maintained, with fresh coats of paint every now and then. The ones behind us were more worn and neglected. That was where Leslie resided with her father, grandma, and brother. As I closed the gate and walked into the alley, Leslie called my name.

"Moe, come on over and see my new Chatty Cathy!"

I finally decided to take Leslie up on her offer to play. Leslie opened the door, accompanied by a German Shepherd. Heck, I didn't even know she had a dog! It turned out to be Leslie's grandma's dog that barked and intermittently nipped at my backside. I nervously said, "Owww, Leslie, your dog is biting me!" From another room, the older woman yelled defensively, "Dex doesn't bite!"

"Yes, ma'am," I said. "I can feel his teeth pinch my skin!"

The woman then opened up the bathroom door. I don't know what frightened me more, Big Dex or Leslie's grandma exposing her bare naked body, with breasts the size of big Southern melons! Grandma was apparently giving herself a sponge bath in the sink! (Years later in nursing school, we girls in the dorm called that a TPA bath...Tits, Pits, and Ass. That was an expedited means of cleaning our bodies when late for class.)

Leslie's grandma insisted,

Honey, I tell you, Dex doesn't bite...let me see where he bit you!"

I stood there with my mouth open, my mind in a frenzy. I hesitated about going near this naked woman, but then she walked toward me. Dex was still jumping and nipping on my upper leg and hind end. I then showed her the reddish marks on my leg.

"Awe, Sweetie, he's just givin' ya kisses!"

The old woman gave me this crazed, goofy smile, exposing her inflamed gums and the large gap between her nicotine-stained front teeth. It was like I was speaking a foreign language, and this woman was blind! I decided it was time to make my exit and come back later when Grandma was more presentable and Dex was in a better mood. The German Shepherd followed my every step in the house. Unfortunately, Leslie's demented Grandma seemed to think it was funny. *I'm just a kid! Doesn't she know those "kisses" hurt?* Dex started to circle my legs, looking like a cunning wolf eyeing my chubby buns! Cautiously, I made my move for the door. I loved animals; however, it was often the stupid owners I didn't care for.

I decided to leave the house and come back another time. Several hours later, I saw Leslie's face, looking excitedly out the kitchen window. Cautiously, I approached, wondering, *What the heck does she want?* Leslie, seeing my hesitation, called out,

"Dang it, Moe, come on over!"

As I walked up to the screen door, I saw a big, hairy hand forcefully pull Leslie back down in her seat at the table. Curious, I peeked in and saw Leslie, now fidgeting in her seat, with spaghetti noodles hanging out of her mouth as she shouted,

"I'll be out in a..."

Suddenly there was a bang! I wasn't quite sure what happened. All I saw was a large figure by the door before it was slammed in my face. Through the little pane of glass, I saw Leslie's father. He was wearing a dirty, white, sleeveless T-shirt and jeans. He angrily glared at me. He then turned around to reseat himself at the table. So far, it seemed there was always commotion and negative energy around Leslie. Maybe we would play another day...or not!

CHAPTER 2

Japanese Dolls Meet the Carrot people

We Bender kids enjoyed having big Al in town the past month. We also loved wearing the colorful kimonos he brought home from Japan. What I wasn't too crazy about were the two-foot-tall Japanese dolls he bought for Mom. She proudly displayed them in glass cases in the living room. Strangely enough, I always felt as if they were watching my every move. Oh, yes, and watching the Twilight Zone episode where the dolls came to life made my imagination run wild! Some of the dolls had sly smiles on their faces, or so I thought.

"Mom, do you like those dolls?"

Mom seemed surprised that I'd ask such a thing.

"Yes, Moe, they are just beautiful! Don't you think so?"

Mom was constantly using window cleaner to keep the glass case spotless.

"Which one of you keeps putting finger prints on this case?"

The glass was thin, so June had to gingerly wipe for fear of it breaking. Defensively, I said,

"Mom, I wouldn't want to even touch those dolls!"

Charlee scurried out of the room when Mom mentioned the fingerprints on the glass. Charlee told me earlier that she thought they were beautiful and wanted to take them out and play with them. I knew she was the culprit.

Big Al came in the room and smiled when he saw how much pride Mom had in her souvenirs. I walked up to him and said, "Dad, do all Japanese women look like these dolls?" Big Al grinned at me, and I knew I was in for one of his lengthy explanations.

"Moe, Geisha girls are skilled professional entertainers with incredible artistic talents! They are extensively trained in singing, dancing, and playing musical instruments."

Big Al truly enjoyed sharing information about his travels to faraway places of the world. He continued, "The girls are recruited as young as three years old. The training continues until they are fifteen to twenty years old or so. The Geisha girls leave their families to live in a house that has a head woman in charge of them."

Ugh, Dad, you're killing me! I thought to myself. Big Al could never give me a simple answer. Dad then explained went on,

"It's a part of the Japanese culture, girls. Geisha girls are admired by people from all over the world!"

Dad noticed I was starting to squirm a bit and was losing interest. He didn't care, though, and continued, "Some Geishas would strictly perform in their area of expertise. Other Geishas, who weren't as experienced in the arts, would be companions to men."

Charlee then chimed in,

"You mean prostitutes, Dad!"

Whoa, What? I thought to myself. *There's that word again, prostitute!* I didn't know what it was when Charlee said it about Mary Magdalene, and I didn't know now, either. I wanted to learn, though. Big Al gasped at Charlee's comment.

"No that's a misconception Charlee!"

June said, "Charlee, do you want your mouth washed out with soap?" Charlee, being somewhat confrontational at times, said, "But Mom, it's true!" Mom, losing her patience said,

"Not one more word, Charlee! You are too big for your own britches!"

Without a word, Charlee stomped out of the room. I was looking back and forth from Mom to Dad. *Okay, the word, what is that word?* I thought, all wide-eyed. Big Al said, "I think we're about done here!" Then he and my mom quickly exited the room. *That word...that word....will I ever know that word?*

That evening I fell asleep on the couch, while watching Bonanza with the family. When I awoke, the lights were out, and everyone was in bed. I was now in the living room alone...with the *dolls*! My heart palpitated rapidly as I thought about a getaway. I envisioned these dolls escaping from their glass houses and chasing me with their pointed hair chopsticks. If that didn't kill me, then they might try to smother me with their kimonos or hit me with their tiny mandolins. Well, my adrenaline kicked in, and I was out of there faster than the speed of sound. To me, however, it seemed more like slow motion as I jumped in bed with Charlee. She rebounded a couple inches when I hit the mattress. Half dazed and confused, Charlie bellowed,

"What the heck are you running for, Looney Bird?"

Still shaken, I replied, "I'm afraid; can you make me some carrot people?"

Oh yes, carrot people. They soothed me at night, and I enjoyed watching Charlie carve the veggie characters with her teeth. How creative! I'd usually tell her whom to carve, like Ronny, the boy next door, or our brothers, Bugs Bunny, dogs, cats, and so on. The activity involved sneaking to the kitchen without being seen by the parents. Charlee looked at me like I had lost my mind,

"Do you realize it's midnight?"

"No," I replied, as I situated myself under the covers.

"I only know it's late, but it would make me feel better."

Charlie moaned, but cautiously sneaked out of the room to grab four large carrots from the refrigerator. As she entered the room, she dangled the carrots in triumph as she said, "Okay, Moe, do you want me to show you how to make carrot people?" Now, *that* sounded like a great idea! Charlie proceeded with instructions.

"Now, you have to consider what part you are making. If the person has a fat head, then you start at the big bottom end of the carrot, the part that has all the leafy stuff. If you want, keep it, so your person can have green hair." We were both now busy, gnawing away on our carrots. Crunch! Snap! Crack! Those were the sounds that filled the room.

We finished our first two characters and proceeded with the others. Charlee asked,

"What are you making now?"

I boldly declared that I was creating a friendly Geisha girl, one who was nice and had a friendly smile. Charlee rolled her eyes and said,

"Okay, whatever."

I got out of bed and demonstrated with small, slow steps how my how my Carrot Geisha would walk, with her tiny bound carrot feet. "See, her feet are the tip, and small, because they wear small shoes to make their feet little." Charlee said,

Yes, I know, but they wrap them to make them tiny. They think it looks pretty."

I was always amazed how smart Charlee was for an eleven-year-old. Enough talking about feet...guess what I'm making now?" Charlee had a sly smile on her face. I shrugged, admiring her creativity as she chiseled away like a beaver on wood. After several minutes she proudly said, "Ta-Dah!" and displayed the veggie masterpiece in her hand.

The pointed carrot tip was surely a hat...but below the belt was a projectile protrusion that looked like a bullet. Charlee suddenly started cackling like a hen, and a light bulb went on in my head. Charlee had created an anatomically correct Santa! We were now laughing so hard that we had to stifle our giggles with our hands. Then we heard Dad's booming voice,

"Shape up or ship out, you two!"

I was tired from all the laughing and forgot about the scary dolls. I actually laughed so much that my face muscles hurt! I loved Charlee's carrot people. What a fun game!

The next morning, Mom walked in the room and saw all the shaved carrots scattered on the floor and in our bed. June said,

"Charlee, were you making carrot-people again? I've told you a thousand times, no eating in bed!"

Mom usually left the discipline to my father. Heck, she'd say "You kids wait until your dad gets home," even when he was overseas. But the long months when Big Al was away forced her to take more control when we were in trouble. His temper was much scarier than Mom's, though. We had to take precautions—we knew his triggers. In his uniform, he was like General MacArthur, and we were his men. "Shape up or ship out." That's what he'd say if we started to push his buttons. That basically meant he was not super mad—but don't push him. Then there was the magic word that would evoke an immediate response for all of us to stop, now. It was "Shitbirds!" Then we knew he was really angry! What was a "shitbird," anyway? Was it something he learned in the navy? So many questions, and not enough answers.

Charlee and I had the chore of cleaning up the remains of the carrot people. I decided to keep my Carrot Geisha for a while.

"I'm naming her Oshemato,"

I told Charlee as I admired my work. Charlee laughed and said it was a goofy name. "I wouldn't keep Oshemato too long, or she'll be brown and shriveled," she added. Once we finished our work, I seized the opportunity to ask Charlie a question.

"Charlie, what's a prostitute?"

Charlie rolled her eyes and said, "You just turned six, and you don't know that?" I suddenly was embarrassed that I had asked at all. After a sigh, Charlie said, "It's when you rub your bodies together and kiss a boy for money." I must've looked as confused as I was before I asked the question. I said,

"Ewe! Why in the world would anyone kiss a boy? I wouldn't do that for a million dollars! Boys are gross!"

Okay, I was good, no further explanation needed.

That evening for dinner, we had, of all things...carrots. They were sliced into small round pieces and covered with butter. Big Al said, "Sam, elbows off the table, and T-Mac, sit up straight in your chair." Mom then asked who wanted to say our prayers before dinner. Little Alan's head perked up, and he said, "I do!" and proceeded with the prayer, "God is great, God is good, now let's eat some food!" Mom said, "No Alan, you need to say, now let us thank him for our food, Amen."

Sizing up what I had on my plate, I said, "Mom, I can't eat my carrots." Mom, somewhat perplexed, said, "What?" I then pointed to the vegetable served for the evening. "I may be eating one of Oshemato's relatives!" Mom and Dad said simultaneously, "Who the heck is Oshemato?"

"She is one of my Japanese carrot people!"

Charlee and I both looked at each other and laughed. We then, of course, ate all our carrots.

Summer came and went by all too fast, and I found myself attending my first Catholic school in Long Beach, California. It was the first time I had almost daily exposure to nuns...my future occupation. The ones I met certainly didn't smile very much, and whoa, the lengthy homework! I wondered if it was the same in public school. One day was special, though, and I brought my favorite doll for Show and Tell.

Barbie had a beautiful up-do and a full-length black velvet and white satin evening gown. It wasn't until after recess, before my presentation, that I saw the open Barbie case and a classmate holding my doll. In a sudden, loud outburst, I blurted,

"Give me my Barbie, you thitbird!"

I quickly grabbed my prized Barbie out of her hands. Yes, "thitbird"—my word of choice to represent the epitome of my first-grade anger. It's what I knew as Big Time Mad! I was also attending speech classes because of my difficulty pronouncing words beginning with "Sh." Well, needless to say, my special day went down the tubes. I was scolded by my teacher for using cuss words in class and had to bring home a paper for my mom to sign. Maybe I'm just not convent material. Surely, nuns don't *ever* call each other "shitbirds"—or "thitbirds"!

CHAPTER 3

President John F. Kennedy died November 22, 1963. I was in class when the sad news came around 1:30 p.m. All classes were canceled, and the kids walked home in silence. It was as if conversing now, at this sad time, would be a sign of disrespect. I could see the grief on my teacher's face, and then again on my parents' faces as they mourned the loss of this great man. Our thirty-fifth president was killed by an assassin's bullet as he passed the Texas Theatre in his motorcade. The replays on television were quite graphic and disturbing to me. There was talk about how a piece of bone was still attached to a flap of skin as the bullet passed through his skull. It was thought the assassin was former marine Lee Harvey Oswald. How strange it was to me that tragedy sometimes seemed to bring people together—"people" meaning my parents. June was wearing her checkered waffle-weave cotton top and slimming blue capri pants. My dad gently draped his strong arm across her shoulders. Mom briefly glanced at Dad and patted his hand in return as they sat together, glued to the news. A couple of days later, night club owner Jack Ruby killed Oswald, point blank, as he was leaving police headquarters. The twenty-four-year-old Oswald was rushed to Parkland Hospital, the same facility where John F. Kennedy was pronounced dead just forty-eight hours earlier.

My parents discussed talk of a conspiracy theory, Ruby's ties to organized crime, and how Oswald was a defector to the Soviet Union. T-Mac was in a world all his own as he pencil-sketched a werewolf and other frightening creatures on cardboard paper. T-Mac seemed unaware of the magnitude of the current events on the tube. Or maybe he was totally cognizant, and all the scary monsters on paper represented the evil in Oswald.

The turn of another year brought hopes of less trouble in class and more effort toward being "good." I truly wanted to work hard to achieve my goal of becoming a nun. Unfortunately, my mind often seemed totally unfocused in class one morning and wandered onto other subjects, like my desire to paint The Phantom of the Opera. T-Mac wasn't the only artist; he was just better at it. I was fascinated by the monster and later adored the music by Andrew Lloyd Weber in the '80s.

A loud tap on my desk by Sister Mary quickly redirected my thoughts to page 20 of our math books. That afternoon, all classes attended daily Mass. Mass, my time to daydream or sometimes sleep if no one is looking!

There was a nun in the pew behind me. She was new, mysterious, and seemed somewhat sad. Why was she here? Her garb was brown instead of black, and her habit was taller and stiff. I turned several times to look back and evaluate the situation. The students had their songbooks in hand and harmonized beautifully as they sang, "Heaven and Earth are filled with your glory, Hosanna in the highest." I was too distracted to think about singing. Why was this nun sad, and who was she? When I turned the tenth time, those sad eyes went into demon mode! Somehow the Devil took hold and burrowed upward through the depths of Hell to possess this nun, right in the middle of church! Now I could almost feel "Sister Evil" staring at me. It was as if her eyes were drilling a hole in the back of my head—ouch! Yes, and *ouch* again, when she crept up behind me and pulled me out of church by my ear. It didn't take me long to find out that Sister Agnes was the new principal. Needless to say, I was sent home with another paper for my mom to sign.

Charlie once showed me how to take a paper and trace over Mom's signature. There was a drawer with official forms that she found Mom's writing on. She signed Mom's name many times, practicing over and over again, so she could sign forms that she brought home from school.

Maybe I would do that, too! It was getting old to see the disappointment on June's face and then have a day or two of being grounded. Charlee came in while I was practicing my "official" cursive...Mrs. Albert Bender, Mrs. Albert Bender, Mrs. Albert Bender. It was after the twentieth time that it looked like a parent's signature.

"Hey, Moe" Charlee said, "Do you still want to be a nun? You know they can't get married, right?"

Puzzled, I looked up from my work.

"They can't? Why the heck not?"

Charlee laughed. "That's because nuns are married to God!"

I paused, contemplating how so many nuns could be married to one man. "Hmm. Do they see God and spend time with him?"

Charlee said, "God is everywhere, and everyone can talk to him, and he listens."

While I was in my room that evening, I took the small cross and placed it on my bedside stand and disassembled my altar. It's not that I thought being a nun wasn't a noble occupation, it's just that someday I wanted to marry someone other than God. I wanted to find someone special to spend the rest of my life with, like my mom found my father. Being divorced wasn't in our vocabulary. It's not something we ever thought of or knew happened to couples. God would still have a special place in my life, too. I continued to talk to God throughout my life. It has always comforted me to know he was listening.

People fascinated me, whether they were young, old, rich, or poor. Their personalities, strengths, and weaknesses intrigued me—and how the heck could some kids focus in class while hummingbirds were right outside the window? Did they not wonder why a hummingbird hummed, not know they flap their wings almost fifty times per second, live approximately five years, and can even fly upside down? Instead, they all stared at the teacher, listening to her monotone voice, hour after hour, like little robots. Sister Mary just didn't have anything to say that I was interested in learning. She didn't make learning fun like I would if I were in front of the class. I was more intrigued by the fact that Johnny had worn the same holey socks every day for the past week. That Janice kept picking her nose when Sister Mary turned her head—*if she doesn't cut it out, I'm going to puke!*

Then there's Natasha, who still had a slap mark imprint on her face since this morning. She would often come to school that way; however, the "hand" would gradually diminish by lunch. They all acted like they didn't see it or even care. Sometimes I would be so bored that I wanted to scream! Was anyone else tempted to climb over the chain link fence after recess? The strict regime wasn't an educational environment that helped me flourish.

I had a curious mind, but I couldn't be force fed. Even as a young child, I needed to feel, see, smell, and know *why* this was important to learn, Some kids were lucky to just sit in their chairs while absorbing all the lessons in class like little sponges. If I was interested in the topic, then I absorbed it too but if I wasn't, my brain would shut down and begin to wander.

I did realize, though, that I was blessed with a special gift of knowing things about people—a "gut feeling." Not all the time (and true, crazy Leslie caught me off guard). For instance, I had a bad feeling about one of the neighbor ladies who was friends with my Mom. We were all waiting in the car to pick her up one day, and I told Mom the woman was ugly. I'll never forget the shocked look on June's face.

"Shhhh! You shouldn't say that, Moe! Lydia probably heard you!"

Mom thought I was talking about Lydia going out in public with her curlers. That wasn't the case; I felt she was ugly on the inside, and it came across as a dark aura. A few months later, I overheard heard Mom and another girlfriend talk about Lydia flirting with my father at a neighborhood party. Right in front of my Mom! She was drunk and pulling Dad's arm, trying to get him to dance with her...slow dance. My father was too much of a gentleman to take her up on it.

Another "gifted moment" was when I was almost certain T-Mac was going to fart on Sam's pillow while he was in brushing his teeth. Just a hunch; he'd done it in the past and I figured it was about that time again.

For the life of me I wondered why anyone would risk being foolish enough to be caught by Sam. The headlocks and noogie-rubs on the head were pure torture! But I felt it in my bones...T-Mac was up to mischief!

I loved Saturdays! That morning was gorgeous with bright sun and blue skies. The only problem was, half my siblings were grounded. As I predicted the night before, T-Mac was up to no good! While Sam was brushing his teeth, he heard T-Mac's loud, squishy fart. By the time Sam ran in, T-Mac was jumping off Sam's pillow and onto the top bunk. Sam grabbed the pillow to sniff for evidence and screamed, "Uggggggh! Toxic!" Sam crinkled his nose as he inhaled the malodorous scent. What pushed him over the edge was the residual faint brown streak on his pillow! Sam's face turned crimson as he yelled,

"You had your bare asshole butt on my pillow!"

A huge fistfight ensued, and the boys wrestled right off the top of the bunk bed. Thankfully, no one was hurt—except their pride, after Big Al gave them each a whooping. T-Mac was grounded for expelling foul-smelling gases on Sam's pillow, and Sam was grounded for fighting and using curse words. Geez...See what I mean, sometimes I hate being right!

Later that day, I attempted to scout out some friends to play with in the neighborhood. Frustrated, unsuccessful, and bored, I kicked up stones and gravel in the alley as I headed home. When I glanced up, there was Leslie. Strangely, she looked a bit older to me after all these months. I'm not quite sure why. Also lingering in the alley was a brown-haired husky man, or maybe he was he a teenager, or somewhere in between.

Immediately, my internal alarm started going off, loud and clear. My heart started pounding as I looked closer at this eerie, stocky male. First of all, he was on a red bike that was way too small for him. He had small dark narrow set eyes and this lecherous smirk on his unshaven face. He was circling around Leslie like a hungry vulture.

The evil grin on his face mad me shudder! I was now fully aware that the hair on the back of my neck was raised. I looked side to side while plotting my escape!

I thought to myself...run home now! He then reached for his groin area as he pulled off to the side of the road behind a large trash bin. This guy was wearing a stained undershirt, with his chubby abdomen hanging over his jeans. He suddenly flagged me over. Oh no! I have to pass him in order to get to our alley gate! Leslie casually walked toward the man, who was now unzipping his pants.

"I'm not afraid to talk to him," she said looking back at me. Frantically, I yelled,

"Leslie, *no*! Don't go!"

Both retreated behind the trash bin for what seemed like an hour. I wanted to run, yet I froze. Frightened for Leslie's safety, I screamed,

"Charlee! Sam! T-Mac! Help!"

That's when Leslie suddenly popped out from behind the can.

"All he wants you to do is touch it."

I immediately thought of what Charlee told me and wondered if Leslie was now a prostitute. Leslie was calm and said it as if nothing horrible just happened, as if she were speaking of touching the fuzz on a peach. Frantic now, I turned to run and heard the man say in a very low voice,

"Don't tell, or I will come to find you both. I know where you live."

His voice was not that of a boy or teen but of a grown man! It was the voice of evil!

I turned round now, running the opposite direction up the alley. Yes, it was the long way—but today it was the safe way home. I was able to avoid passing the pervert and didn't allow him to see where I lived.

I sprinted into the house past my siblings, who were gathered around the television. Their eyes left the program, and in unison Charlee, Sam, and T-Mac stood up and followed me to the bedroom.

"Hey, what's going on…where is the fire?" said Charlee. Sam asked, "Did Leslie kill another ladybug?" I grabbed my rosary and hesitantly started to reveal what I just experienced.

"No, she didn't, but there was a weirdo in our alley, and Leslie was with him!"

I further explained what I just witnessed and told my siblings that the strange man knew where we lived and told me not to tell. Sam and T-Mac went to retrieve their holsters and pseudo cowboy guns.

"Don't worry we'll shoot him if he comes near the house!" Both of them were yelling

"Pow! Bang! Bang!"

The boys were now firing wildly at the imaginary intruder.

"Hmmm," said Charlie, "Don't you think we should tell Mom?"

My eyes widened at the suggestion. "That man said he knows where we live! We can't tell!" That night was the first of many nightmares about the man on the bike. I was more certain than ever not to tell or else he would come and find me.

The next morning Mom and Dad took us to Seal Beach for the afternoon. It seemed to take my mind away from the chubby pervert. It was a gorgeous, sunny, blustery day, so windy that you had to keep your mouth closed or you'd crunch on the little grains of sand. Sam and T-Mac were so excited that they opened the car door before Big Al was in park.

"Last one to the beach is a rotten egg!"

Charlee didn't care to participate in the run, as she had to watch three-year-old Alan.

"Hey, you had a head start, no fair!"

I yelled, tripping over my big beach towel. I decided to throw it down and ran with my hands up in the air, inhaling the salty breeze. The blue

Pacific Ocean was cold! T-Mac and Sam didn't care and started to find a wave to ride on into the shore. Charlee, Alan, and I started working on a sandcastle with our pink plastic shovel and bucket.

It kept us busy for hours! Sam and T-Mac were exhausted, fighting the surf so we decided to bury each other under the warm sand. Charlee wrote "Rest in Peace" with her finger on top of Sam's pseudo beach grave.

Sam calmly closed his eyes, saying,

"I feel pretty good for a dead man!"

I too was enjoying the warmth of the sun on the beach. I slowly poked my toes out of the grains of sand as the waves rushed over my body. T-Mac took the opportunity to whisper to little Alan. My little brother Alan always did what the boys told him to, even if that meant getting in trouble. Alan went to grab a handful of wet sand and proceeded to throw it in my face

"Ugh! Alan, I hate you! You little Thitbird!"

June opened her eyes enough to scold me,

"Moe, are you cussing? I'm sure I can find soap somewhere to wash your mouth out!"

My little brother ran to the safety of Mom's towel and clung to her arm. The annoyingly innocent look on his face made me sick! June reach over to pat Alan on his head.

I decided to chase after the instigator of it all—T-Mac. I was still wiping sand from my face as I sprinted after him. Dang, he was just too fast! I looked back at Alan and held up my fist. That was my nonverbal warning to my younger brother.

Nodding, I gave him the evil eye, like *you can run but you can't hide forever!* Alan giggled and leaned closer to Mom.

"Save me, Mom!"

Mom pointed a finger at me before she rolled over on her towel. It was now *her* non-verbal warning—*behave*!

I resumed my chase while swinging my fist in windmill fashion. I was hoping at least one punch would catch T-Mac on his fat, sassy head. No such luck. Why couldn't I have been an only child? Ugh! My primary thought was how annoying it was to have brothers like mine. Yes, even Sam, because he was laughing, too.

Once home from the beach, I looked in the mirror and smiled at my rose-colored cheeks. I loved the sunshine, but unfortunately, prolonged exposure meant even more freckles on my nose.

My rosy face was nice, but more brown freckles were not! My eyelids were heavy, and I felt too sleepy to worry about the spots on my nose.

I thought all the sun and activity on the beach would give me a sound night's sleep. Unfortunately, no such luck! Instead, I had another horrible nightmare, where the weird man in the alley broke into our house. We were all sleeping, and he entered through a window with a long steak knife. This time he had an accomplice. It was Leslie! In my nightmare, Leslie came after me like she went after the ladybugs.

The next day, Charlee finally had enough of my bad dreams and told Mom. When June heard the story firsthand from me, she called Leslie's Father. A couple of police officers came to my school later that Monday to ask me questions. Mom, Dad, and I saw Leslie and her father early that evening at the police station. We had to sit to view photos of men and were instructed to tell the officers if any looked like the man in the alley. The carefree days of kids roaming the city unattended and taking rides to school from strangers on rainy days were now gone.

The police told Mom that a predator was on the loose, and some of the girls were not as lucky as Leslie and I. What happened to the other girls was now in the newspaper, and people were afraid. I only heard bits and pieces of the officers' comments about the recent incidents in our town—words like "tragic," "psychotic," and "murderer." The teachers at school and also my parents taught us to always listen to adults. These were the early '60s, when it actually was okay to talk to strangers. We were expected to be nice and talk to everyone. I now realized that I needed to trust my gut when it came to people in general. Yes, it was an eye-opening experience to find that bad people existed, not only in movies but in real life. There were evil people who lurked in alleys or parks, waiting for their next prey. I guess they don't have a particular "look." They could seem as pleasant as the boy next door. A more harsh reality is that it's not always a stranger but may be someone you know and think you can trust.

After my parents and I came home from the police station, I never saw Leslie ever again. Not even around the neighborhood or at school. There was a certain odd behavior among my parents every time I'd bring up Leslie's name. I often wondered what happened to her but figured I'd never know.

The next morning we were all seated at the table, eating breakfast. Charlee momentarily stopped chewing her toast as she heard thunder outside. Sam quickly scooted to the window to pull back the curtain. His eyes grew big as saucers as the dark clouds rolled in.

"Wow! Mom, looks like a big storm! Can you take us to school?"

June shook her head as she lit her cigarette. She had just finished making the last of our sandwiches for lunch. Oh, how she relished the thought of having four the kids in school! She continued to shake her head "no" while inhaling her cigarette. She closed her eyes, as if it were a form of stress release, then slowly exhaled.

"A little rain never killed anyone! Now get on out the door before you're late!"

Sam made an exasperated sigh as he grumbled under his breath. The next audible crack of lightening made him once again protest walking to school.

"Ralph's mom said our school was almost a mile away. She takes Ralph to school, even on nice days!"

June flipped her cigarette hand up in the air as she nonchalantly replied, "Well, I'm not Ralph's mom."

I honestly never recalled Mom taking us to school before, so was not sure why Sam asked. She previously relied on other moms picking us up like stray cats. Not this time, though. The cold droplets of rain started to slowly trickle from above. I opened my mouth to catch a few on my tongue. Then I quickly shielded my face as it started to pour! The four of us kids huddled close together and used our books as umbrellas.

Kids were now told NOT to accept rides with strangers, and no one offered. Not after what was in the paper. So today we walked as the rain poured down upon our heads and saturated the clothes on our backs. Charlee, Sam, T-Mac, and I headed towards school in silence. The intensity of the lightning was now almost palpable. Without saying a word, I anxiously reached up to grasp onto my sisters' hand. Charlee reassuringly smiled, then looked up at the angry sky above. It was then that I realized our world would somehow never be the same.

CHAPTER 4

Three years passed since Leslie's family suddenly moved from the area. It was now 1965, yet my mind lingered to when Leslie was molested by the man on the bike. How our parents were with us at the police station going through multiple mug shots trying to identify the pervert. The angry scowl on Leslie's father's face as he hovered over Leslie yelling, "Is that him? Don't you remember how he looked?" Her father was dressed in a grungy T-shirt, went on and on.

"Damn it child! He could have murdered you like he did the rest of the girls! Instead of running from him you walk up to him! Arrrrgh! Wait till I get you home!" That's when an officer intervened,

"Mr. Ward, please calm down!"

Mr. Ward grabbed his daughter's arm and stormed out of the police station. That was the last time I saw Leslie but not the last time I saw "him". Yes, the dark haired man on the red bike who molested Leslie. I'd manage to catch a glimpse of him riding by our house every few months. Just as I peered out the window, his dark evil eyes met mine and he smiled. That creepy type of eerie grin that sends chills up the back of your neck. Just when my nightmares would subside, "he" would come back again and again. He knows Leslie and I told! It's my warning that I'm next if I do it again.

That evening we were all seated at the dinner table, gobbling our platefuls of spaghetti. Big Al cleared his throat before he proudly stated he had news for all of us. He proceeded to inform us that we would be moving to Missouri. In unison, we all yelled, "Missouri?!" My mom's head shot up and she looked totally stunned by Big Al's comment. It was as if she heard it for the first time. After all the yelling, I realized it *was* the first my mom had heard about moving half way across the country!

"The movers will be here on Monday." His voice was very hard and final. There was definitely no changing his mind. "But Al, it's already Friday!" June's voice broke as she said these last words.

This was hard for me to digest. I looked at my siblings and saw similar conflicting emotions on their faces. In California, I had my friends, the beach and finally a great teacher that I loved. What I didn't like about California was the growing fear plaguing me about the man on the bike. Having a glimpse of any adult male on a bike now haunted me. A move sounded good to me. I will have to find out more about this place in the Midwest. When I told one of the neighbor boys we were moving to Missouri, he said, "Missouri? There's nothing but cows and hillbillies there. It's just country!" I responded, "Really? Hmmm, now Missouri does sounds like not many people live there." I then raced home and asked, "Dad, are we moving to the country? Does Missouri have indoor bathrooms?" Big Al wasn't listening; he was too busy being scolded by June.

"Daaad, will we have to walk *outside* to the bathroom?"

I wasn't so sure about this new place we were moving to in the Midwest. After all, our neighbor told me it was true! There were banjo-playing hillbillies and mountain cabins in Missouri. I, asked repeatedly,

"Why Missouri, Dad? Why not Wisconsin? So we could live by Grandpa and Grandma?"

Big Al just whisked right by me. He had bigger things to think about now, like my mom's temper. June was busy packing; however, she hadn't been too happy with the news of moving half way across the United States. In the room, Mom was slamming suitcases shut as a way to vent her anger. June yelled,

"You didn't even consult me about this, Al!"

Big Al threw his hands up and replied sarcastically,

"Hey, you're the one who complained about wanting me out of the navy! I'm out now, so be happy. Look at this move as an adventure!"

Big Al gave us some money to run to the dime store to pick out new comics and coloring books to occupy our time on the trip. It was his way to get us out of the house so they could continue arguing without little ears listening in. It was fun to pick out the large assortment of new crayons with a built-in sharpener. I also bought a few *Little LuLu* comic books. T-Mac purchased a sketchpad to draw on, Sam chose several Westerns, and Charlee selected any reading material on the Beatles. Later that day, the moving truck came and went. We packed up enough clothes for a week, and the rest were shipped to St. Louis. The 1959 four-door Mercury station wagon was loaded from floor to ceiling with blankets, pillows, comic books, snacks, and boxes of cigarettes.

Our new, wonderful city would be the Gateway to the West. As the station wagon pulled out of driveway and onto the street, an angry dark haired man suddenly pedaled out from behind a bush. He was racing frantically to catch up while his mouth gaped open as if he were yelling something fowl. I gasped loudly throwing my hands up to cover my face. My siblings looked at me as if I lost my mind. I never shared the horror of his random visits the past few years. I slowly withdrew my hands from my eyes to look out the window. "He" was gone, gone forever. The burden of fear was now lifted off my shoulders. I was now free, free to leave this nightmare behind and be a kid again. St. Louis here we come!

My siblings and I were packed in the station wagon like sardines in a can. We made due though and passed time playing, the color game, "I see something red, or blue or green. After two hours, we exhausted every shade of color, read our comic books and ate the last two bags of candy. That's when Sam and T-Mac played their own game of; Who Can Pass the Deadliest Gas. When I think about the past and growing up with my brothers, I think of gas. Yes, you heard it right, the act of farting and passing malodorous wind! To them, the louder, the smellier, the better! One brother would occasionally let a "SBD"—the worst, silent but deadly!

We would all blame it on each other, and Dad would finally settle it by saying,

"It was *me,* okay? Is everyone satisfied?"

That made us crack up even more, because I don't believe I had *ever* heard my father fart. No, Big Al was pretty strict when it came to manners.

In our cramped quarters in the car, we created a little corner to call our own. T-Mac was a gifted artist, who drew perfect Disney characters even at age five. He created this little book of cartoon characters, where each page had a slightly different pose. When you'd flip the pages, it actually showed them moving! As annoying as T-Mac was, I thought he was a creative genius.

I was steadfastly working on drawing a scary Phantom, from *Phantom of the Opera*. His face was almost done; however, I erased, redrew, and re-erased his mouth several times. It was my goal to draw a realistic, intense, scary mouth on my tortured Phantom.

"Ugh! I just can't draw a monster mouth on him! T-Mac, will you draw it for me? I want to be afraid when I see it. So make my picture *real* scary, okay?"

T-Mac was being unusually accommodating and quickly replied, "Sure!" He took my white construction paper and appeared to be hard at work on our now combined masterpiece.

It felt good to gaze out the window as we crossed the Arizona desert.

"Mom, I remembered the difference between a sandy hot 'desert' and a yummy 'dessert.' You have two s's in a yummy dessert, because you want more of it!" I smiled as I looked up, but there was no response from Mom. She was too engaged in each word of her juicy gothic romance novel. On the cover was a tall, handsome, muscular, scantily clad man, embracing a beautiful blond woman with torn clothes. I wondered if Mom ever wished Big Al looked like the man on the cover.

"Dad, Mom, are we almost there yet?"

"No, we have another couple days," said Big Al. I crawled over the middle seat and peered over the front to check out the gas gauge.

"Dad, what if we run out of gas? The arrow's almost on E!"

Big Al shook his head and sighed.

"Don't worry, the tank is half full...plenty of gas to get us to the next town."

I was still worried about this vast desert full of brown sand, cactus and rattlesnakes!

"Dad, you passed, you passed the sign, and the sign said *no* passing. You weren't supposed to pass that sign!" Big Al was getting tired and wanted silence.

"Please sit back, in the very back seat where you belong!"

Charlee chimed in, "Duh, it meant you weren't supposed to pass any cars in that lane!"

I crawled over the middle seat and slid into the back, where T-Mac was finishing up "the mouth." T-Mac raised his eyebrows and had this smug look on his face. *Hmmm*, I thought, *he must be real proud of himself.*

"Are you done?" I asked enthusiastically.

T-Mac handed over the Phantom, art side down. T-Mac was known for his sense of humor and was a real conniver at times, like now. He knew it was my objective to have a grisly oral shape on the picture. When I turned it over, I was shocked to see the wide-open, joker-like smile with perfect dental work on my Phantom!

"Oh, I hate you! You made my monster *happy*!"

T-Mac grabbed my picture and handed it off to Charlee, Sam, and even little Alan to get a laugh. Oh, yes, they were all rolling around in the back seat.

That picture was supposed to be my seriously horrifying recreation of Phantom. Charlie continued to pass Erik, the fictional Phantom character's name, up to the front seat.

"Hey, Mom, look at this...hilariously scary, huh!"

Oh, great, now the whole car was cracking up at my expense. T-Mac was now pressing it up on the back window for a trucker to see. In my rage, I grabbed it and tore it up. I pinched T-Mac in the back, and he farted in my face. Big Al growled, "Am I going to have to pull this car over?" That's all it took to calm us all down as we drove past canyons, mountains, and mesas down I-40 East.

It must have been somewhere outside Flagstaff, Arizona, that we stopped at an old roadside motel. We were all anxious to stretch our legs and to sleep in a real bed rather than the backseat of a car. Big Al announced that we must have driven almost five hundred miles! The man at the counter seemed ancient; he was missing some teeth and a lot of hair. He wasn't too old to notice my mom, though; he winked when we all walked in the motel. *Creepy*, I thought, *only Big Al should be winking at my mom*. All of us were anxious to check out the pool, which we discovered was a big hole with no water. That took the wind out of our sails as we wondered what else we could do in this small town. There was a commercial laundry across the street, so June gathered up our dirty clothes to do a batch of clothes.

There hadn't been enough time to wash everything before we left, and we had over a thousand miles before we arrived in St. Louis. The four of us Bender kids were trying to avoid the gaps in the cracked sidewalk as we scurried to the local diner. I yelled,

"Mom, Sam just broke your back when he stepped on a crack!"

Sam then pushed me onto the blades of grass growing between the cement.

"There ya go," Sam said. "Guess you broke Dad's back now!"

It turned into a mass push attack as we walked behind the parents. Then we noticed Big Al turning his head, and in unison we walked like little toy soldiers.

After dinner, we stopped by the laundry to take our clothes out of the dryer. The whole place was empty—and so were the dryers our clothes had been in. We had nothing but the clothes on our backs to wear to St. Louis! Mom washed our socks in the sink and hung them out to dry on the shower rod. It's amazing how dirty your clothes get when you travel in the car. My T-shirt had ketchup from lunch, chocolate smudges, and also pencil marks from my sketching the Phantom. Mom instructed us to be more careful; she didn't want us to look like vagabonds when we stopped at restaurants.

In New Mexico, we pulled into a truck stop that had a variety of souvenirs. T-Mac was playing with this miniature toilet that said; "Good-bye, cruel world," when you raised the seat. Sam looked around the aisle and called us over to see a pretty topless hula dancer doll. You turned a bar on her back, and her hips would move from side to side. They snickered, as they knew they'd get in trouble if Big Al saw us.

I decided to do the hula dance in the aisle.

"See, I can do that!"

Sam and T-Mac pulled their T-shirts out at the chest, as if they had big breasts like the hula dancer. They laughed while wiggling their hips. When we saw Mom, Dad, Alan, and Charlee at the soda fountain counter, we scrambled to place our order. I sat on the tall stool and noticed the man behind the bar had a badge that read "Ask Me My Name." So I did–

"Hey, what's your name?"

The man gave me a broad grin,

"Puddin Tane, ask me again and I'll tell you the same."

The four of us kids looked at each other, then all shouted,

"What's your name! What's your name!"

Once again he repeated,

"Puddin Tane, ask me again and I'll tell you the same."

The line was growing longer now, and Big Al told us to

"zip it"—meaning, of course, all four of our pie holes.

June was now scurrying us all out the door. I suddenly said,

"Wait Mom, we need to pay for this!"

June looked surprised as I pulled the Hula girl out of my pocket.

"Moe, where did you get that?"

I meekly pointed to the store,

June, firmly yelled,

"Put it back right now! Then get your butt in this car!"

I hesitated,

"But, but... I want to name her "Karina" and go to Hawaii someday!"

Big Al suddenly turned, lowered his brows and looked angry, very angry! With that, I instantly sprinted into the store and put "Karina" back on the shelf.

CHAPTER 5

All of us Bender kids were fast asleep when Big Al pulled up to our new home on Mullford Road. It was a small, three-bedroom ranch with one bathroom. It was just temporary, until Dad and Mom had a chance to know the area. The house didn't have an avocado tree or an orange tree, or many flowers for that matter. I figured that would be my project until I made a few friends in the area. The neighbor next door had meat on the grill that emitted an unusual odor. We did know that beer was one of the ingredients, as we witnessed him pouring it on the meat. The neighbor and several other men were sitting on the lawn chairs in the front yard, barefoot, wearing white T-shirts and jeans. My dad would only wear a T-shirt under his dress shirt and would never walk around in the front yard without shoes. You see, Grandma and Grandpa Bender were from England and raised Big Al to be a bit more formal. I'm not quite sure what happened to us along the way.

Big Al thought it was a polite gesture to walk over and introduce his family to our neighbors. A few of the men already had their meat on a plate, with sauce all over their fingers and dripping on their dirty toes. It seemed like they enjoyed the flavor, because I could hear them smacking as they chewed. I whispered to my brothers, "Are they hillbillies?" Sam gave me a "Shhh!" Big Al walked up, and as he said,

"I'm Albert, this is my wife June, and my children—"

The neighbor suddenly blurted out, "Awe, shit, ya bunch of little assholes!" The kids suddenly burst through while playing chase and knocked over several lawn chairs. He then apologized, "Oh, sorry, the young'uns are getting rowdy! I'm Daryl Wyatt, and these are my brothers, Joe, Homer,

Harold, and Bud." The brothers each had between four and six children, who were all swarming around the house like bees in a hive.

We excused ourselves to start unpacking what was in the car. Our furniture would be arriving tomorrow, so we brought home some fast food. We ate dinner that night at our picnic table in our new backyard. I'm not quite sure who it came from, but there was an audible "smack" from one of us kids at the table. Big Al looked up, like he was going to erupt with anger. It was the first but not the last time that my Father said,

"Quit eating like a Missourian!"

That phrase was developed, of course, after he witnessed Daryl, Harold, Homer, and Bud's vigorous "smackathon" at the BBQ. Dad was a good man, but quite intolerant of ill manners at the table. Big Al Bender's rules for dinner dining: elbows off the table, don't reach over your plate or anyone else's, don't shovel food into your mouth, sit straight, no fighting, no talking with your mouth full, and...geez, did I forget anything? Oh, yes, and now: no eating like a Missourian!

Of course, we all knew everyone from Missouri didn't eat that way! It was just our first experience with hearing so much noise while food was being chewed. Our neighbor and his brothers ate with passion, as if it would be their last meal. To our amusement, Big Al would continue to use that phrase whenever we chewed our meals with the same gusto. What tickled us is that it went on year after year. One day when I was accused of eating like one, I told Big Al proudly, "We *are* Missourians, Dad! We've been here for years!" Then I gulped as I saw the dark look on his face. I knew he was not appreciating the humor in my response.

The Wyatt's had four children, and one of their daughters was just a year younger than I. The Wyatt's were actually a nice family, and we eventually all became good friends. Their dad was loud, with a hearty laugh that echoed around the neighborhood. He threw big parties and played loud music when he grilled on the pit. Mrs. Wyatt was okay with the whole neighborhood playing in her house, and she didn't have many rules. Needless to say, I preferred to play over at their place.

Mom hadn't been herself since we moved to Missouri. She decided at that time not to renew her driver's license. I'm not sure she realized, though, that was a step toward *losing* her independence. She blamed it on the "crazy drivers," but in reality it was a revolt against moving in the first place.

June loved California and never wanted to leave the West Coast. June felt she had the entire responsibility of raising us kids while Big Al was overseas. My Dad alone made the decision to move. Not sure if June will ever forgive him for that! June felt that now Big Al alone be responsible for carting all over too!. Charlee helped later, once she had her driver's license.

One afternoon, June started pulling out cans from the shelves as I passed through the kitchen. My mom called me back in.

"Moe...Moe?"

"Yes Mom." I secretly sighed and rolled my eyes, because I knew I was the chosen one.

"Moe, can you run up to the store for some chili beans and a carton of cigarettes?"

Oh, no, *not* cigarettes! Many parents in the 1960s and '70s smoked. I must admit that even then, I despised cigarettes! Now I was rolling not only my eyes but also my head while sighing at the same time. I hated the way cigarettes smelled and how they made me cough.

"Mom, do I have to buy cigarettes? I wish you and Dad would quit smoking."

June was growing irritated at my defiant behavior and yelled,

"Don't give me any lip, young lady! Here is the money. Oh, and don't forget three cans of chili beans. Hurry now!"

I stuffed the rolled-up dollars deep into my pocket. It was a beautiful sunny afternoon with clear blue skies. The temperature was cool enough for me to run up there without perspiring too much. I always played these strange mind games to increase my endurance. Today's game was that I had to run the entire way unless I saw a cat. Yes, weird huh! No, I didn't see a cat, so I ran the entire half mile without stopping!

I strolled quickly down the aisle, looking for chili beans. Beans, beans, beans—dang, so many types of beans! White beans, baked beans, black beans, lima beans...oh yes, chili beans! I scooped up three cans and headed for the counter. I timidly asked for a carton of Winston Cigarettes. Once out the door, I played another crazy mind game. This time I had to keep running until I saw a friend. I tucked the grocery bag under my arm and dashed down the street. Where in tarnation are my friends? I dug my fingers into my side as it started to ache. I slowed down but didn't stop until I set foot on our front lawn.

"Here, Mom, cigs and chili beans."

June thanked me while rummaging through the bag. She grabbed the cigarettes then let out a loud frustrated sigh as she picked up a can.

"Ugh! These aren't the beans I use for chili! Take them back and get red kidney beans.

That's what I've always used!"

I felt like saying, *you should just go up there and get the right beans yourself!*

I didn't; however, my face was surely as red as the beans she wanted.

"What? I have to go back to the store?"

June put the cans back in the bag and handed them to me.

"Yes and pronto!"

Oh, I ran again, even faster than the first time. My anger-fueled energy propelled me faster than any other trip to the store. Once back through the door I began my search of the right beans for our chili. I thought to myself, Okay, red beans...red beans, where are you? Then I saw the cans labeled "Light Red Kidney Beans." I went up to the counter for the exchange and out the door. No mind games this time. I just wanted to be home.

"Here are your beans, Mom."

I put the cans on the counter and went to my room. It was then I heard another loud sigh, almost an "Argh," come from the kitchen. June opened my door and handed me the bag.

"You need to go back to the store! We use *dark* red kidney beans, not light!"

In my head I was thinking how my mother was absolutely mad! Who the heck cares if the beans are chili, light red or dark? I'm sure they all taste great!

"But Mom, my legs are tired! Can't someone else go?"

She put her hands on her hips while shaking her head. At this moment June had an ugly scowl on her face. Pointing to the door, she yelled,

"You are the one who made the mistake! Now hurry up, before dinner is late!"

I walked down the street, thinking how lucky my friends were to have mothers who drove. A lingering cogitation on my third trip to the store was how my mom was different. My siblings and I grew to love being in St. Louis. June, however, grew more resentful of how little control she had in such a big decision among couples. What June hadn't lost control over, though, was us kids. I soon learned that Mom also loved to play mind games, and unfortunately it wasn't always fun.

Big Al came home from work that night to take me to softball practice. No matter how tired Big Al was after working a full day, he would take time to take me to softball or teach me the game. We would take our gloves and go into the backyard. I'd practice throwing, bunting, or hitting, and he would give me advice. I was left-handed and soon found that batting left-handed was unacceptable to my new coach. This was a struggle for me, as I could hardly hit anything batting right-handed.

My new softball coach was Mr. Harding. His philosophy was "Just win!" That meant the same girls that played on his team for the past few years played three-quarters of the game. That meant *if* I was lucky, I'd get to play maybe a couple of innings. Coach Harding was a thick, gruff man who became irritated if anyone asked too many questions—"Just play the game!" I was left-handed, but in practice, he would only allow me to bat right-handed. So naturally, I looked like a clumsy fool trying to swing. It was just too foreign for me to hit that way. Mom and Dad were frustrated, coming to games week after week where I only played one inning. They saw us kids play in the field and knew I could hit—*if* I batted left-handed.

One evening, before our last game, Dad went up to the coach and said,

"Look, your way isn't working. When my daughter goes up to bat, she'll do so as a lefty."

Coach Harding didn't say a word. Dad walked up to me to tell me the news and a couple pointers as I went to the plate.

What was important to Big Al wasn't winning but for every child to be given a chance. To do that, they had to have a coach who truly cared that each player be given that opportunity.

The butterflies in my stomach were ready to fly up my esophagus or explode out of my gut! My whole family was watching, and the pressure was on to make contact. I would have been happy to hit a single, as long as I didn't strike out. I wanted to contribute to the team and also make my family proud, especially Dad. I carefully swung the bat to warm up then placed my feet on the opposite side of the bag. You could hear a pin drop and I briefly saw Coach Harding smirk at me—*O ye of little faith*. He wanted me to fail, to show my dad *he* knew what was best for me.

Dear God, be with me, I thought to myself. Then I watched the pitcher wind up and release the fast pitch softball. I watched that ball come toward me as if in slow motion, then "Pop" and it soared to right field. I was so happy that my crazy long legs were going a mile a minute. I stopped at third base.

No, it didn't drive in the winning run for the game, nor did we win that night, but I did. Hearing my family cheer louder than I ever heard before was my prize.

By the end of the summer of 1965, Sam and T-Mac excelled in baseball and were looking forward to football tryouts. That Monday, Charlie, Sam, T-Mac, and I were once again the new kids, but this time we registered at the local public school. It was like a breath of fresh air, and I welcomed the experience. The girls in my class were quite inquisitive about the new person from California. At recess that afternoon, while playing Red Rover, I met my first real friend. Her nickname was Tigger, from Winnie the Pooh. Tigger, was actually Ann Johansen. She had a warm, friendly face and a smile that went from ear to ear. She whispered to the girl on the left and they called,

"Red Rover, Red Rover, send Winnie right over!"

I looked around, wondering who that was. Tigger called out,

"I don't know your name, but you can be Winnie!"

Little did I know then that the friendship between Winnie and Tigger would last a lifetime.

The field at the end of the block became our means of networking with the neighborhood kids. Every weekend we'd have a variety of sports events, where we needed warm bodies to play. It didn't matter if someone wasn't an athlete, or was short, fat, young, or old. We just wanted to play! 12 year old Sam and 10 year old T-Mac were new to the area but soon became popular. T-Mac was known for his speed and weird sense of humor. Now Sam, too, was well liked for his macho, no-nonsense approach to sports. He was a born leader. If there was a newcomer to the neighborhood, Sam and T-Mac held an initiation, where the newcomer would have to wrestle with their sister. Yes, that was me. It was their way of evaluating strength for team placement. As a wrestler, I was stronger than the average girl, yet weaker than the strongest boy.

Our first two years in our new town flew by. Between 1965 and 1967, we built fond memories of playing sports in the field until the dark and the street lights came on. Little Alan would chase fireflies under the stars while the neighborhood kids gathered under an old oak tree telling scary stories or tall tales. It was Big Al's sudden shrill whistle that alerted to end our play and come running home. All four of us older Bender kids breathed a sigh of relief and confidence, knowing we were here to stay. We soon realized that not everyone from Missouri was a hillbilly, with an outhouse in the backyard. For the first time, we felt connected to this town.

Our roots would continue to grow deep here in the Midwest as we developed many close friendships and continue to be involved in community sports teams and school activities. This city had beautiful Forest Park and one of the only free zoos in the country! My favorite animals were the chimpanzees and gorillas. St. Louis was a great sports town, too, with the St. Louis Cardinals football and baseball teams. Oh yes, back then our football team was still the Cardinals; it wasn't the Rams until much later. Back then, we kids frequently took the bus downtown to the stadium for a night of baseball, hot dogs, and lots of popcorn. Yes, I'd say we were now truly proud to say Missouri was our home.

CHAPTER 6

I turned twelve the summer of 1969. Richard Nixon was our president. There were massive demonstrations that eventually led to Nixon withdrawing some of the troops. Charlee, now seventeen years old, wanted to be a part of protesting the U.S. involvement in the Vietnam War. In her bell bottoms and tie-dyed T-shirt, she hung peace signs up in our room. Some people said Charlee was a contradiction. I think she was just ahead of her time. She did not believe in the war. She said it was not a winnable war, but she always supported our troops. She said our soldiers should not be vilified, because they were only following orders and going where our government sent them.

There was another battle besides Vietnam that we were all concerned about. It was Big Al's battle with his health. Dad worked six days a week and each day turned around and got back into the car to take all five of us to our numerous after-school activities. Big Al and Charlee were both taking turns taxiing us kids back and forth until eight or nine o'clock at night. It was at the beginning of one week when he developed a cough and fever that lasted another week. It was on a Thursday that all of us packed into the station wagon to pick up some groceries. When we were in the parking lot, returning to the car, Big Al said,

"Oh, geez, he overpaid me by fifty cents."

All of us looked at each other, like *so what?* I said,

"That's okay, Dad; just keep it!"

He grumbled back, "No, I'm not going to *keep* it, it's not my money! Keeping this money is just like stealing!" We all turned around and back into the store. We could tell that Dad was unusually grumpy and didn't say a word the whole way home. While we were in the car, June said,

"Al, you didn't have to bark at the kids like that."

His reply was,

"Don't you know I'm not feeling good?"

What? We had never seen Big Al sick before, ever!

When we arrived home, we kids took out the groceries from the back, and Dad walked into the house. He was so weak that he almost collapsed in the hallway. June, Charlee, and Sam helped Dad back in the car. Mom sat in the backseat with my father while Charlee drove to the doctor's office at the military base. June said in a confused voice, "When did you start to feel worse, Al? I thought your case of the flu was better."

"My toes became numb a couple days ago, and early today the numbness moved up my legs, and now both legs are weak from toes to thighs."

Al then rested his head on the seat and closed his eyes. June's face was red with anger. She was now upset at Al's failure to disclose these symptoms earlier. June was tempted to give him a piece of her mind, but just then Charlee pulled up in front of the office.

The nurses rushed Big Al to the back in a wheelchair so he could be evaluated by Dr. Stone. My dad described in detail what symptoms he had been experiencing over the last week. The weakness occurred after a short bout with the flu. The doctor gave Al a thorough examination and grew more concerned. He looked at his nurse and said, "Call the emergency room and tell them I'm on my way!"

Dr. Stone quickly called my mom back, while Charlie and Sam sat in the waiting room. "Your husband is quite ill and needs to be admitted to the hospital as soon as possible. I believe he may have a rare disease called Guillain-Barré. It sometimes occurs after an infection, when the body's immune system attacks the nerves. I'm not sure, though, and we will need to wait until all the tests are in."

It was the physician at the base who actually rushed Big Al into the car and drove him to the hospital. The doctor told Mom that Dad would be in the ER for quite some time, and they should just go home for the night.

"Geez, what's taking so long?"

I said, alternately pacing the living room and looking out the window. Alan was unusually calm as he sat in front of the television. Fifteen-year-old

Sam and thirteen-year-old T-Mac were quiet too...too quiet! I hadn't seen them for the last hour. Hmmm...I decided to look down the hall, and their door was closed. The only time their door was shut was when they were in trouble. I peeped in and saw the two sipping out of two milk jugs filled with a purple liquid. Being inquisitive, I asked,

Hey, what the heck is that? Kool-Aid?"

Both boys started giggling like five-year-olds. Sam said,

"It's my first batch of homemade wine! We made it two months ago and hid it in the closet!"

T-Mac piped up, "Yeah, Mr. Wyatt had a book in the garage on how to make wine *and* beer! We're going to try that next!" Sam continued,

"It's easy, all you do is take grape juice, sugar, and yeast and boil it. I emptied a milk jug and put a balloon on the top. Yum, it's good; wanna taste?"

Sam and T-Mac stood up and started walking wobbly and singing, "How dry I am, how dry I'll be, if I don't find the bathroom key!" They both laughed and laughed. I put my hands on my hips.

"Are you two drunk or just acting like it? You are fakers!"

I reached for the jug and took a sip.

"Awe, that's just juice!"

Suddenly, car lights pulled up in the driveway, and we put the questionable home brew away.

"Mom, Charlee, where's Dad?"

June sadly replied,

"Your dad is sick and needs to be admitted to the hospital." Charlee, wide eyed, added,

"Yeah, the doctor said he has Gilligan's Disease!"

June laughed.

"No, it's called Guillain-Barré."

Charlee continued, "Dad might need a respirator! You know a machine to help him breathe!"

June quickly interjected, "Charlee, don't frighten the kids! The doctor did say that most patients with this disease have a full recovery. Let's pray and hope Dad is one of them."

Two weeks passed, and Dad was still in the hospital. Mom had not been back to visit Dad in the hospital. I found that to be strange, very strange. The hospital was quite a ways from our house, though, probably a good forty-five-minute ride. She managed to have frequent updates from the doctors and friends who went to see Dad. Mom would say she didn't have a ride, or that she had to take care of all of us. We were old enough to take care of ourselves, though, at least long enough so she could visit Dad. I often wondered if he was lonely—or was he just too sick to even care?

Mom had given up her license the day we moved to Missouri and never drove again. My dad never questioned Mom's decision to stop driving and accepted it. I don't think he ever complained. I felt sorry that my dad had to be in the hospital without any of the family at his bedside. I wanted to be there, but they said we were too young.

The living room was filled with flowers and looked more like a funeral parlor. I don't believe Mom shared the seriousness of Dad's syndrome with us kids. The neurologist informed her that Guillain-Barré attacks the peripheral nervous system. The weakness that ensues frequently starts in the lower extremities and can work its way up to the fingers, arms, and the entire upper body. The symptoms can increase in intensity until the patient can no longer walk. If the respiratory muscles are also affected, then this syndrome can be life-threatening.

Sam and T-Mac took every opportunity during Dad's absence to continue making wine. Sam leisurely walked up to his wine concoction and took a sip.

"Hmmm, it was written in the instructions that it may take up to six weeks to ferment."

T-Mac was on the bunk, looking at a *National Geographic* magazine. He had found a whole assortment of old magazines at the neighbor's house.

"Whoa, Sam, look at these!"

He meant the large breasts on the topless tribal woman. Charlee poked her head in and sneered.

"That's supposed to be an educational magazine, you perverts!"

Charlee had a passion for the Democratic Party. All she thought about was stopping the war, government, and law. She would make a great lawyer someday. She had an amazing talent at presenting Mom and Dad with a good argument as to why she should be allowed to stay out later, date older boys, not be grounded, and so on. When Charlee truly believed in something, she would clamp down like a pit bull and fight to the end. The end was in making her point, loud and clear.

It was a couple weeks later that Big Al was finally released from the hospital. He had been admitted for more than a month. The doctor said it could be several months, even up to a year, before he fully regained his strength. Mom helped Dad out of the car and draped her arm around his waist to stabilize him. I gasped when I saw how frail and thin Big Al was after his discharge.

Dad was one of those who needed assistance from a ventilator, but thank God he started responding to medical treatment. That evening, Big Al was sitting in his big recliner and seemed to be staring off in to space. I patted his hand. "Hey, Dad, how are you feeling?"

He sighed and nodded his head. "Much better! I'm on the road to recovery. Slow but sure... Your Grandpa Bender told me I would be okay." I scrunched up my nose and replied,

"What? Grandpa Bender is dead!"

Big Al, who looked really small right now, chuckled. "Yes, he is, but he came to me one night. He sat right on the foot of my bed."

I put my hands over my mouth.

"Oh, my gosh! Were you afraid?"

Dad smiled and said, "No, it was a comfort to see him. He appeared to me while I was on the respirator, when I felt so defeated by this illness. I was feeling like I'd never be weaned off that breathing machine and my life would be a living hell."

I wanted to know more.

"What did he look like, and what did he say?"

"Well," Dad said, "he was still wearing his old hound's-tooth newsboy cap and button-up work shirt. Your Grandpa Bender illuminated that corner of the room. With his deep English accent, he said

'Albert, hang in there and be strong, for this illness will soon be behind you.'"

Dad raised his shoulders and went on, "That's all he said, and then Grandpa Bender was gone."

Mom entered the room as Dad finished telling me the story.

"Oh, Al, are you talking about Grandpa Bender again? You probably had too much medication!"

Defensively, Big Al replied, "It was the *very* next day that I was off that damn respirator. There must be something to it, June! He was my ray of hope, my guardian angel, and he gave me the will to get through my hospital ordeal." Big Al looked skyward and added, "Thank you, Pop."

CHAPTER 7

The first true friend I made when we moved to Missouri was Ann, and unfortunately, her family moved to Black Jack, Missouri. It wasn't like relocating out of state, but it was ten miles away. It meant Ann went to another junior high. We wouldn't be back in school together again until we went to Haywood High. My second partner in crime also was a close friend to Ann; her name was Marie Murphy. She was an amazing athlete and had beautiful, wavy, dark brown hair and eyes. Marie and I met when we were on opposing softball teams. Oh, geez, could that girl pitch—and fast! Thank goodness her dad, Coach Ralph Murphy, recruited me on his team the following year. It was better to play on Marie's team than against her.

Ann invited Marie, me, and one of the other girls in the neighborhood to stay overnight at her new house in Black Jack. We thought it would be a splendid idea to walk and have her meet us halfway. We stopped over at Janelle's house around 11:00 a.m. Janelle was another friend from school who was joining us on the walk and sleepover at Ann's. She asked us if we wanted to have an early lunch before we left on our long journey. Janelle's mom was cooking hamburger for spaghetti.

We said in unison,

"Sounds great!"

We walked into the kitchen. We assumed Janelle had already asked her mom. "Hello, Mrs. Gurley. Thanks for having us for lunch!" Mrs. Gurley looked up and said, "Oh?" Then she gave Janelle a cool, annoyed glare. In an even voice, she said, "You didn't ask me, but go ahead and set a couple extra plates." Janelle covered her mouth and whispered.

"That's okay, she hates me."

Mrs. Gurley sat by herself at the bar across the table and didn't say a word the whole time. Janelle said,

"Okay, helpee-selfee, come and get it!"

As I walked up to the stove, I scooped up a pile of noodles and went for the sauce. In the big black pot was simmering hamburger and grease.

"Umm, Janelle, is there any red sauce?"

She looked up and said, "Yer looking at it!" It was hamburger, with seasoning, onions, and olive oil. It was actually fantastic over noodles! The big carbo-packed meal was helpful in in supplying extra energy for our ten-mile power-walk.

The three of us girls carried pillow sacks, which contained our pj's and a few snacks. We passed time discussing possible activities for the evening. Ann's house was always fun! Especially when her mom would take us on convertible rides in the country. Mrs. Johansen was a make-up artist who gave us cosmetic tips and samples to try on.

I looked up to see the Jamestown Mall. That meant we were only three miles from Ann's house. "Ugh, my feet hurt!" I kicked off my tennis shoe to see a red, fluid-filled blister on my toe. Putting the shoe back on would be pure torture. I decided to walk barefoot on the grass for a while.

"My gosh! There's a cemetery almost right in her backyard! She didn't tell us that!" We looked up and finally saw twelve-year-old Ann coming toward us, wearing blue jeans and a Winnie the Pooh T-shirt. She still loved them after all these years! We screamed at her playfully, "Whatever happened to *half way*? You walked one block of the ten miles!" Janelle piped in, "Is that fair? No it is not, but life is not fair either!" Janelle was likeable but had a strange way about her. Suddenly, I excitedly said,

"Oh, oh, now how many people are dead in that cemetery, Ann?"

Ann cast her eyes from left to right as if she were counting.

"I'm not sure; maybe two hundred?"

I laughed and slapped her on the back. "No, *all* of them are dead! Hahaha, it's a sick little joke that my dad taught me." Janelle and Marie said,

"Yuk, yuk, yuk, see we are laughing!"

We walked the rest of the way to Ann's house.

Ann's house was only a short walk to a lake, which was ideal for skating in the winter and swimming in the summer. A stately old oak tree had a large tire swing next to the water. We just had to remember to leap way out to avoid the rocky shore. Her neighborhood seemed to have it all, with a large shopping mall nearby, scenic country roads...and now we could add "cemetery" to the list.

One thing girls can do at a pajama party is eat, and Ann's mom always made sure we had an abundance of food. Great party food, too, like candy and pizza. (At the Bender house, we had to ration our portion of cookies, chips, and other snacks. If we ate a whole bag of anything yummy, then we not only had to deal with Mom and Dad but also with Sam. He was like the Junk Food Mafia Boss. He had a cut of everything. That evening a couple more of Ann's new friends from the neighborhood came by to join us to stay overnight. Ann cheerfully yelled, "Hey, Willie and Lynn!" Then she excitedly pulled them both through the doorway to meet us. Willie and Lynn were beautiful, feisty Irish sisters with shiny, dark brown hair, fair skin, and the brightest green eyes! Willie's real name was Elizabeth, but she was called "Willie" because her last name was Wilkerson.

Willie brought each of us a tube of white bubble gum–flavored lipstick, which I ended up wearing all the time. I liked the sisters immediately and was happy Ann had fun friends at her new home in Black Jack. Willie entertained us for a while, twirling and tossing her baton, which occasionally clunked her on the head.

Afterward, we took turns making a few innocent prank calls to cute boys at our school. Thank goodness that was before caller ID! The six of us then decided to play Ouija board game. Ann dimmed the lights and said excitedly, "This is real! You can actually have ghosts talk to you on this board! My one friend Kate won't play it anymore, because she said evil can enter into your life!"

Lynn reluctantly shook her head.

"I'm not so sure I want to stir up any ghosts tonight!"

Willie then gave her sister a push, saying,

"You big fraidy-cat!"

I personally was amused by this intriguing game. All of us placed our hands on the planchette, the device that moves across the letters on the board. Ann chimed in among the excited chatter,

"Okay, settle down, girls! Let's ask it a question!

Okay, who is here in the room with us tonight?" She repeated, "Who is here with us tonight...

What is your name?" Nothing happened at for a long while. Then, slowly, the device started moving and stopped on:

"L." Then to "E"..."S"..."L"..."I"....the movement almost stopped, then "E."

We all looked up. Marie had an inquisitive gaze with a raised eyebrow as she scanned the room in search of a guilty face.

"Don't look at me, I didn't move it!"

Ann defensively replied. Janelle, seemed like she was in a trance, asked,

"Leslie? Who knows a Leslie here?"

We all thought a few minutes and shrugged. Ann, the leader of the Ouija board, anxiously continued to ask our ghost questions.

"Hmmm, how old are you, Leslie, and how did you die?"

Once again we carefully placed our hands on the device. This time it went swiftly to the number 6, then to a variety of letters, which we pieced together as..."He found me." Then, as if I were struck by lightning, my head shot up as I reflected way back. Leslie!

Leslie was my neighbor in California! When my family left California, she was still alive. For the life of me, I could no longer even remember her last name! Marie asked, "Now why would she follow you all the way from California to Missouri? It must be another Leslie." Janelle then said, "Those that are a part of the spirit world can travel anywhere to deliver a message." *No*, I thought to myself, *Marie is right; it's not the same Leslie*. Ann then stood to put the game away and brought out a basketful of candy bars.

It was now close to midnight, and we were still energized from the assortment of chocolate and caffeine drinks. At the typical pajama party, we usually stayed up the whole night and slept at our own homes the next day. Ann stood up from the table and said, "Is anyone up for a game of Truth or Dare?"

You could hear the rustling of leaves blow up onto the patio door and the light howling of the wind. In our game, we picked a truth or a dare out of the hat. We would then make up the questions to answer or what the dare would be. Janelle picked a truth.

Marie thought momentarily and asked Janelle, "How many times have you kissed a boy?" Janelle was cute with a narrow birdlike nose, small brown beady eyes, and a huge wild side!

"Oh, easy," she said, "That'll be one! It was a friend's older brother. I tried to give him a French kiss but he pushed me away!" We started rolling on the floor, cackling like a bunch of old hens. I was laughing but I wasn't quite sure what a French kiss was!

It was now my turn to pick. I carefully put my hand in the hat, hoping for a truth card. I blurted out my frustration with the draw.

"Oh, darn it, Dare!"

Ann turned to Marie and smiled. They whispered for a moment and said,

"We dare you to run through the cemetery."

Ugh, out of all dares to have, I get the cemetery run.

"Can I streak instead?"

All three heads shook no. "Okay, I'll do this, but only if someone walks part way with me." Willie, Lynn, and Marie were my rocks that night. They offered to walk to the cemetery gates and wait for me. Ann and Janelle followed along to make sure I actually followed through with it. We had heard Ann's parents retire to bed just minutes before, so we knew we could probably sneak out without being heard. Ann, Marie, Janelle, Willie, Lynn, and I each slowly grabbed our jackets and walked into the black of night. Our only guiding light was a three-quarter moon that illuminated a small walkway past the gate.

At the cemetery entrance, the old weeping willow's tresses were swaying in the wind. The branches and tendrils seemed to be reaching for me, as if to pull me in. I was so nervous that the butterflies in my stomach were making me sick.

"Sorry, girls, the dare's over, not going to happen!"

My five friends were all fired up for the scary dare. They reluctantly settled for one that I'd agree to conquer. Ann and Janelle whispered. Then they revealed the revised dare.

"Moe, how about you walk to the largest tombstone under the oak tree, close your eyes, and count to fifty. Then you can run back, that's all; how about it?"

"You all will stay here?"

I asked. They agreed. The gravel under my feet shot up behind me as I raced into the dark. A swirling mist gradually formed and seemed to dance above the tallest stone monument. My breathing was so fast that I could almost hear myself wheezing. Once at the base of the grand granite tombstone, I closed my eyes and started counting, 1, 2, 3, 4, 5,6...continuing on to 50 in record-breaking speed.

When I was at 49, I felt a small tap on my shoulder and opened my eyes. It was then I heard a distinct whisper in my ear:

"Leslie Ward, Ward was my last name."

Then I screamed, "Fifty!" No, I did not hear that! No, it was not her! A suddenly circular swirling of leaves blew before me, and I felt a cold, bone-chilling wind that made me shiver. I quickly scrambled to my feet while wiping away leaves that blew in my face. There was a hazy mist that seemed to follow my every move! I thought, *Darn,! I can't out run this, this...whatever it is!*

They took one look at my face and laughed.

"What in the world spooked you?" I ran passed my friends and motioned for them to follow me.

"I'll tell you at the house, now let's get outta here!"

The rest of the evening I sat by the fireplace with my circle of friends. They all had attentive ears and eyes as I shared the story of Leslie Ward and what happened to her in 1963. We all wondered if she were actually dead, and if that was her spirit with us earlier that night. Just after I finished my story, I felt someone gently stroke the back of my hair. I turned...but no one was there.

We all took a break to fill up on more candy, cookies, and whatever else was in the kitchen. Mrs. Johansen was such a good sport to allow us to eat the family out of house and home. We all were attempting to twirl Willie's baton. Lynn and Willie were fighting over it until Marie settled it by picking it up when they dropped the baton. It was now almost 5:00 a.m., and Willie was still going strong.

Marie and I showed up at practice at 8:00 a.m. without having slept at all. We were so drowsy that we could hardly keep our eyes open. It was a bad idea to stay up late when practice was scheduled so early on weekends. I had momentarily closed my dry, weary eyes to sneak in a few winks when—"bonk!"—a softball hit me on the top of my head. Mr. Murphy was a wonderful coach, and so patient with our foolishness. He laughed and yelled, "Serves you right! Remember, no partying the night before practice!"

By the next year, 1970, Big Al did regain full strength following his diagnosis of Guillain-Barré. The family was getting back into a normal routine and also welcomed the new addition of my fifth sibling, a beautiful, bouncing baby girl named Abby. I loved Abby dearly but must say that babysitting didn't come naturally to me. I looked at it like a ball and chain that kept me housebound. Now, I did help Ann babysit her two younger sisters, Dee and Bailey, who were seven and eight years old. That is, when her older brother was working. Ann was always responsible, making sure the kids had their baths, brushed their teeth, and were fed. One memory still makes me chuckle.

I recall how Ann and I made "Breakfast for Dinner." It was a favorite for the girls; after all, everyone loves pancakes! The kitchen looked like a restaurant, with our homemade menus, folded napkins, and a candle in the middle of the table. We even had dandelion salad as the first course! Dee and Bailey gleefully ran to the table. Ann asked each to review the menu and place their order. Now unlike a restaurant, Ann and I were charging for our services *before* the meal! That was also news to our "patrons," Dee and Bailey. Dee yelled, "But we don't have any money, and we're hungry!"

Both scrambled from the table in search of any coins or unopened candy for trade. Yes, I know it was mean. But I was still a kid, and sometimes kids do mean things. Don't worry, the girls scraped up enough coins for their food and enjoyed every bite. We also received a little scolding from Ann's mom for charging her sisters for their food.

CHAPTER 8

It was 1972. Ann, Marie, and I were in our sophomore year at Haywood High School. The sacred school "seal" was a large medallion located on the floor of the school's main entrance.

Upper class students liked to hang out there. They'd carefully watch for unsuspecting sophomores to step on the school seal. Each new sophomore was expected to get down on his or her hands and knees to kiss it. Thankfully, we managed to escape that humiliation. I imagine that was due to Sam and T-Mac being my siblings. They were popular studs in their junior and senior classes.

Sam was on the varsity football team and T-Mac was quarterback on junior varsity. Both boys were easygoing and welcomed us to sit at their "jock table" at lunch. We, of course, felt honored, hoping they would also remember to invite us to the wild parties! My brothers had grown into quite a handsome duo, with their sandy blonde hair and athletics physiques. Some of the cheerleaders in the upper class became friends with me. I often wondered if it was because of Sam and T-Mac. Whatever the case, I enjoyed the acceptance and started off the tenth grade feeling confident that this would be a good year.

My new project was to get rid of my baby fat and get into shape. I made the cheerleading team for my sophomore year. However, I was one of the larger cheerleaders. I decided to join my brothers whenever they went to the track. Over several weeks we developed a great camaraderie as running partners. Our goal was to increase our mileage and speed each week and maybe run a marathon someday. It wasn't long before we asked Big Al to drive us nine miles and drop us off at the old St. Charles Bridge. We thought it would be fun to run all the way home through the winding country roads. Big Al had a big smile on his face as he sped away in our green station wagon.

"See you around dinner time!"

Haha, Dad! It was funny, as it was only 9:00 a.m. It was our first real long-distance run, and our goal was to not stop to walk, pee, or for any reason.

Now, back in the '70s you didn't hear much about women's sports bras. Most of the baby fat I had at the time was in my chest! It must've been around the five-mile mark when my old bra just couldn't take the stress of the rebounding fatty flesh. Suddenly...snap! The strap broke. "Darn!" Sam and T-Mac were in the lead as I groped to find the cotton strap. Geez, there was absolutely nothing to tie it to, as the plastic bracket also broke.

Sam turned and yelled,

"Moe, hurry up, you're slowing down!"

Needless to say, with the other lone strap carrying twice the load, it broke too. I create my own support by running with my upper forearms pressed close to my sides and forward to restrain some of the motion. The three of us finally made it home in about an hour and a half.

Wow! There's no doubt I was proud of myself and was thankful to have brothers who believed in me. They always gave me supportive words of encouragement. Even though in the beginning, the mere act of running was downright painful! Running eventually became my therapy and my passion. It's a sport that I continue to love to this day.

This was the first year I had to juggle a sixteen- to twenty-hour–a-week job, along with cheerleading and school. It sometimes made me feel overwhelmed. However, I had no choice if I wanted to save up for a car or college money. It seemed like Mom just wasn't the same since we moved. In fact, she seemed worse now that she had to cope with all us teenagers. Heck, I'm sure having five teenagers in one small house was no picnic! What made all the emotions worse was the early menopause. June seemed to be in a constant cloud of tension, and everyone tried hard not to upset her. When Mom wasn't happy, she made sure no one else was, either.

I tried to keep busy with outside work and sports so I wouldn't have to experience the icy atmosphere at home. Big Al now worked long hours and watched little Abby in the evenings. June considered that her tmie to play bingo, her way to release stress. The one thing that always seemed to bring us all together was our school sports activities. One Saturday our varsity football team was playing one of our huge rivals. Sam was a great team player who never failed to praise and encourage other players. I respected him for it. Marie was one of the editors and student writers of the high school newspaper. She was an amazing writer and covered the school sports; she personally wrote several articles about Sam and T-Mac.

It was the fourth quarter, and we were trailing 13–14 in the last few seconds of the game. Sam was in the perfect strategic position to catch the ball. In the meantime, Sam was knocked unconscious by the Riverbend Warriors' -two hundred and fifty pound defensive tackle. His helmet slammed against the tackles, and his head snapped and rebounded hard off the ground a couple times. Haywood scored the winning touchdown; however, Sam was still lying on the ground, unconscious. The coaches and trainer ran to evaluate the seriousness of Sam's injury. "Sam! Sam! Are you okay?" Sam wearily opened his eyes and said,

"Dad, what's for dinner?"

Leave it to a Bender to still manage to talk about food first with a concussion.

"This is Coach Jason, Sam, and you will be going on a little trip to the hospital."

The ambulance pulled up, and the EMTs loaded Sam onto the gurney. Mom was a wreck; it was the most emotion I'd seen from her in months. Sam had a thorough evaluation and was kept overnight for observation. The very next day he was discharged and driven home by Big Al. One thing was certain, he would not be playing football for several weeks. This was torture for Sam, but he was at least able to dress out in uniform and sit on the bench during games. Sam was bummed out and threw his jacket down as he and Dad walked in the door.

"Did you hear?" Sam said to Mom. "I can't play at our next game!"

T-Mac walked up to Sam with a silly grin and gave his head a light push. "You can't afford to lose anymore marbles!" Sam retorted, "Eh, those are fighting words, boy! Lucky I have doctor's orders not to kick your ass!"

Over the years, T-Mac developed amazing artistic talents. He attended art school in addition to classes at Haywood. There were several beautiful oil paintings hanging in our living room. T-Mac's artistic passion though was drawing these strange weirdo cartoons. He was also an incredibly gifted athlete who was as fast as lightning. The coaches were excited about recruiting T-Mac for football, track, and wresting. In his last year, though, something was brewing in his life that made him retreat behind canvas. Maybe it was the tension at home, or maybe he wanted to focus more on art or dating than sports. The quick-witted brother I knew was usually always ready for a joke and would do anything to make someone laugh! These days he was more quiet, intense and content to be by himself. Who knows, maybe T-Mac was just following his own dreams rather than everyone else's.

Three to four nights a week, I'd work the evening shift at the old folks' home. I was fond of my senior citizens who resided at the Crystal Park Nursing Home. My favorite little feisty gal was Mrs. Swanson, but I called her Mrs. Swanny. The ninety-five-year-old was a Southern belle, raised in Georgia, not far from the Suwannee River. She was always singing the darn song, over and over again. When I walked in the room one day, Mrs. Swanson was leaning over to one side in her wheelchair and had a horrible case of bedhead.

"Hey! Mrs. Swanny!"

I noted her tousled hair and the smashed oatmeal on her gown. I asked her, "Didn't anyone give you a bath or brush your hair today?"

She piped up with the usual, "No, baby girl, I was just hoping you would come and make me look pretty.

I'm all wrinkled like an old Bull dog!"

I replied,

"Swanny, I *love* Bulldogs! I happen to think they are cute!"

She rolled her eyes.

"Nothin' cute 'bout this old gal, though."

That made me smile, especially since I always brought my Mom's samples of Avon and Mary Kay products. I dug deep into my pockets for the tiny tubes of lipstick.

"Mrs. Swanny, I'm going to get you all gussied up for old Mr. Brown next door!" Swanny giggled as she tried to make herself upright in the wheelchair.

"Baby girl, if you hurry up and do your magic, maybe he'll ask me out after dinner! Mr. Brown just may decide to move his bed into my room!"

Swanny looked at me and winked. My eyes opened wide.

"Mrs. Swanny!

Heck, I don't even know if that's allowed here! It briefly crossed my mind to wonder if people that age still "do it." Mrs. Swanny realized she embarrassed me and was laughing so hard that I thought she would choke. I, too, laughed so hard I thought I would pee my pants.

I quickly took out a basin and filled it with warm water for Swanny's bed bath. I then worked my magic with her make-up and hair, using all of my Mary Kay samples. When I was finished, I gave her the mirror, and Mrs. Swanson gazed at her reflection. She slowly looked up at me. It was then that I saw the glistening tears on her cheeks.

"You make me feel young again, Moe...thank you."

I smiled and wheeled Mrs. Swanson to Mr. Brown's table. The true magic that night was seeing the exchange of romantic glances between two people in their mid nineties and the realization that the beauty of love can last a lifetime.

CHAPTER 9

Word of Mrs. Swanny's new-look and boyfriend spread like wildfire! Every time I worked, it seemed like there was a flood of make-up application request. Mr. Brown and Swanny, were now an "item" at the nursing home. No doubt some of the women were down right envious! Even at ninety-five years of age, Mr. Brown was considered a real *catch* ! He had a great sense of humor and a head-full of curly grey hair. Unfortunately, the stats weren't in a senior women's favor at this home. There were four women for every male! Swanny, was one of the lucky ones who found her soul-mate late in life. It was obvious to everyone that what Swanny and Mr. Brown had was truly special.

This morning, Mrs. Swanny was already up in her wheel chair wearing a pink floral dress. She turned and smiled at me when I walked in the room. I smiled back when I saw she was now applying her own make-up.

"Moe, notice my lipstick and blush match my pretty pink dress?" With pride I answered,

"Yes I did. You look so beautiful!" My sweet senior friend picked up a small hand held mirror as she continued...

"Oh and can you work your make-up magic on Mrs. Booker in room -thirty? That Old Coot's says she an Autumn (color analysis) and I swear she's a winter! AND...Mrs. Booker has more wrinkles than a bulldog! Do you have any moisture cream samples? At that moment, Mr. Brown passed her room in his wheelchair. He stopped just long enough to blow her a kiss. Mrs. Swanny winked back then giggled like a teenager. I was witnessing Senior-flirtation! I wasn't use to seeing adults do that...just kids. It kind of made me blush!

Before I left that evening, I made my make-up rounds. I past Mrs. Swanny's room and heard her cough like there was no tomorrow. The night shift nurse was in giving her medications and taking her vital signs. Unfortunately, Swanny's coughing episodes were the first of many to come.

I had to take off last next weekend at the nursing home. There was rarely a day of rest for me and always something scheduled, whether it was work, family or school functions. It was my Sunday for the 7:00 a.m. to 3:00 p.m. shift at the nursing home. I slowly opened the door to room thirty-nine. I was looking forward to seeing Swanny's smiling face. Instead, the room was dark, and I heard moaning, the deep sound of pain. When I turned on the light, I noted Mrs. Swanson's condition deteriorated while I was away. She continued to moan with her eyes closed with a frightening grimace on her face. Her body looked so small in the huge hospital bed.

"Swanny,"

I said softly as I went to hold her hand. My heart was pounding with worry.

"Swanny?"

Mrs. Swanson, unaware of my presence, continued with an inarticulate sound and then whispered,

"I hurt so bad."

I started to pat her hand to comfort her. I knew Mrs. Swanson had lung cancer. She had been so stubborn and feisty that I never imagined the day she would die from it. She was a fighter and did one hell of a job concealing her agony.

"Swanny, do you want me to call your family?" She now heard my voice and slowly turned.

"There's no one but me."

Swanny then opened her eyes and moaned. In a weak voice she said,

"The children, I love to hear them sing."

I perked up listening for voices. There was nothing, not a sound and no children in sight.

"I'll be right back, Swanny. I'm letting the nurses know I'll be staying with you."

I always had this fear of dying alone, and I didn't want Swanny to be alone, either. The registered nurse informed me Mrs. Swanson had gone downhill a couple days ago. Unfortunately, the large doses of morphine were not touching the depth of her pain.

"The poor old woman, all she does is scream in agony!" the nurse said. "I'll call the doctor to see what else we can do."

On the way back to Mrs. Swanson's room, Mr. Brown poked his head in the door and asked if he could see her. I wheeled Mr. Brown up close. He tenderly put his hand in hers. I gently combed her hair, knowing that even in pain, she would want to look pretty for Mr. Brown.

Her rhythmic, guttural groans continued, over and over again.

I decided to empty the small amount of urine in Mrs. Swanson's catheter bag. As I knelt down, the air was suddenly so still you could hear a pin drop. No more moaning! Apprehensively, I stood and saw Swanny was now looking at Mr. Brown. Her brown eyes were more opaque and she had a serene smile on her face.

He said,

"Moe, she's with Jesus now."

It happened so quickly that I was stunned. I was never with anyone at the moment of death. I could see that Mrs. Swanny was now in peace. That intense grimace on her face from all the pain was gone. Mr. Brown held one hand, and I held the other. Mrs. Swanson knew that two people who truly cared for her were with her in her final moments. I was glad my dear friend didn't die alone.

Big Al picked me up from work that evening. Seeing the sad look on my face, Big Al asked,

"Did you have a bad day at work?"

I gave a deep sigh.

"Yes, big time bad. Remember my favorite patient, Swanny?"

Big Al nodded replying, "Oh, yes."

"Well, she died today. Dang, I'm going to miss her! The next time I work, I'll have this big empty hollow feeling when I look into room thirty-nine."

Big Al gave me a pat and reminded me not to forget about all the other lonely or ailing patients. We drove home in silence as I reflected on how my life was enriched by knowing such a special lady. She was one that had a gentle old exterior, yet still able to release the light, energy, and wisdom of her youth.

I loved hearing what her life was like in the late 1800s. The day she first met her husband, who was a young ranch hand on her parents' farm. She knew it was love at first sight but played hard to get until the day he stole a kiss behind the stack of hay in the barn. Her husband unfortunately died at age thirty-seven, and there wasn't anyone else in her life until she met Mr. Brown.

Big Al broke the silence and said,

"Well, I was going to make you wait until you got home, but you need some cheering up now! Charlee brought home an English bulldog pup from the rescue!"

Immediately, I cheered up.

"What? This is the best news ever!"

When we pulled up, Charlee was waiting outside with the pup, which she called Maggie Moo Bender.

Little Maggie looked just like a fawn-and-white jersey cow, grazing on the outdoors plants.

The Wyatts' beagle from next door came running up to Maggie. The beagle started sniffing the new pups rear-end. I started laughing and said,

"That's the doggie handshake!"

Charlee said, "Can you believe this wrinkly cutie-pie was in a rescue?" Maggie was almost five months old. She had been returned by the first owners for her destructive behavior. I remember Swanny referring herself as a wrinkled old bulldog. I responded how I absolutely loved Bulldogs and thought they were cute! It was then that I looked up to the sky,

"Swanny, was this your gift?"

Charlee, confused, asked,

"What the heck are you talking about, goofball?"

I kissed Maggie Moo and said, "Never mind, long story."

Alan was thirteen now and had a way of being eternally annoying to me—and probably to Maggie, too. June was also getting perturbed

"Alan, I said to keep Maggie in the kitchen!"

Of course, that required Alan to obey a directive. Unfortunately, Alan always said okay but would do whatever he wanted to do. He continued to chase Maggie out into the living room where she promptly pooped. Alan, swiftly ran out of the house to avoid a scolding from June.

"Alan! Where did he go? I smell crap! Moe, can you pick that up for me?"

I was now holding my breath and cursing my little brother's mere existence.

"Ugh! Mom, you should have stopped having kids after me!"

My stomach was churning when I saw the sight.

"Oh geez, I think I see little worms in this mushy pile!"

I started gagging as I took newspaper to swipe it up and carry it to the trash.

June laughed as she saw the look on my face. "You work in a nursing home and should be used to BMs." I rolled my eyes and replied,

"Yes, but it doesn't have worms, and I usually wear gloves!"

Maggie was so darn cute that she was worth all the trouble. I'd do anything so we could continue to keep her in the family.

Later that evening, the kids gathered in the family room to watch television. Alan was lying on his abdomen on the shag carpet. He was watching television trying to stir up some trouble. He had his chin propped up with one palm, while holding a carrot in the other hand. He always had problems sitting still and seemed to be in constant motion. I sat behind Alan with my knees crossed, Indian style. Thump, thump, thump, he rhythmically kept hitting my legs with his foot.

"Knock it off!"

I yelled while reaching to pinch his foot. He unfortunately was much too fast. Thump! Thump! Thump! I was all red-faced now and warned him,

"You do it one more time and—"

Thump! Alan now kicked me harder. I jumped onto my feet then slapped him on the back of the head. Alan must have been in the process of swallowing the carrot while yelling at the same time. That's when he started to choke!

I was horrified when I saw the look on his face. I heard of people choking to death and knew this was serious! He was not faking.

"Alan! I'm sorry, Alan! Dad! Alan's choking!"

All the other siblings were surrounded Alan. We all weren't quite sure what to do! Big Al and Mom came running in the room. There wasn't time for an exchange of words. Big Al picked Alan up in such a way, with his arms wrapped under his diaphragm. In an instant, the carrot ejected from his mouth and onto the carpet.

Alan was coughing over and over again, but thank goodness he was now able to breathe! I was gently patting his back, saying,

"Are you okay, Alan? Are you okay?"

He nodded and, amazingly, didn't show one bit of anger toward me. Alan and I were both relieved. No doubt, Alan could really get on my nerves, but I never meant to hurt him.

Big Al and June were confused. They asked sternly,

"Hey, what went on in here, anyway? What happened?"

Alan replied,

"I just choked on my carrot."

He then gave me a sideways glance. No one in the room told the parents anything different. I was now full of guilt, not wanting to make eye contact with anyone. I learned a huge lesson that day. No one could possibly punish me or make me feel any worse than I felt at that moment. I whispered to Alan,

"I'm sorry."

Unfortunately, that day wasn't the end of our fighting. Needless to say, I sure waited on him hand and foot for the next several weeks.

CHAPTER 10

That Thursday there were black clouds were forming in the early evening sky. The droplets of rain seemed unusually large as they began to pelt the window of the intramural bus. . I felt totally physically exhausted and brain dead at the same time. I momentarily closed my eyes as I waited for the other students to board. My warm breath formed a fog on the window. In a dream-like state as I whimsically stroked my finger over the film to clear my view. Suddenly, I bolted upright and pressed my face on the glass! A heavy set man with a hooded raincoat peddled up on a red vintage bike. His face! I couldn't see his face! His hood was cloaked over his eyes. It was almost in slow motion that he inched his profile to face me. I was wide-eyed and my heart was pounding so hard it made my chest ache. A bolt of lighting shook the bus while illuminating the stormy sky. A gust of wind blew his hood back to expose a thick wiry blonde fro and a man too young to be "him." Thank God, It was not he same man who molested Leslie many years ago. I shook my head chuckling; "Sheesh, What's wrong with me?"

Mom was busy making dinner for all of us. She smiled when I walked in the room.

"Moe, how was school?"

The first thing T-Mac, Sam, Charlee and I did when we came home was raid the refrigerator. I momentarily ceased chugging my chocolate milk to answer June's question.

"Um, it was schoolish,"

June chuckled. "What in the world does 'schoolish' mean?"

I sighed and sat down at the table.

"Mom, it means just a lot of hard work, and I didn't have time to be social!"

At that time in my life, school was my social playing field, where I planned my weekend activities, flirted with the junior or senior boys, and participated in cheerleading.

Big Al came into the kitchen and gave his words of wisdom.

"You better focus more energy on your homework rather than boys. If you want to go to college, you have to make the grades. Making Cs and Bs, just isn't good enough."

"Oh, yeah, Dad, I have chemistry homework. Can you help me?"

What I actually meant was could the former chemistry major do it for me?

Big Al was getting tougher on me to learn the material myself. Big Al was thorough though. In a serious monotone voice, he went over each question with college-level detail. We reviewed the material over and over again. It was like repeatedly throwing a rubber ball at my head. The information was bouncing right off and **not** into my brain.

"Dad, you're killing me!"

That evening after the parents went to sleep, I snuck little wrinkly Maggie into my bed. Charlee and I now had twin beds that were joined by a solid wood nightstand.

"Look, Charlee, I put a red light in the lamp! Doesn't it look pretty?"

The switch illuminated red across the four walls. Charlee howled with laughter.

"Sheesh! You'll have the neighborhood thinkin' we have a whorehouse!"

I looked at Charlee as if she had two heads.

"What? What do you mean? I just thought it would go nicely with our red and yellow floral bedspreads."

Charlee laughed,

"Haven't you ever heard of a red-light district?"

She then rummaged through some old albums.

"Oh, and I have the perfect theme song on my record. It's was sung by a group called The Animals!

The House of the Rising Sun! Oh! Oh, good, here it is!"

The House of the Rising Sun was a brothel in New Orleans, run by a Madam. It was around the 1860s, and the funny thing is that the house was on St. Louis street! Okay, sing with me Sister!" Charlee started to shimmy her shoulders as she sang the lyrics of the song.

There is a house in New Orleans,
They call the rising sun.
And it's been the ruin of many a poor boy
And God, I know I'm one.

I danced as the music played and strummed the air as if I had an electric guitar. Maggie the bulldog jumped off the bed and started humping my leg. I yelled,

"Hey, get off me, horny dog!"

Charlee and I both started laughing. She explained,

"Maggie's not horny, just a dominant little bulldog. Our bullie is trying to tell you she's the boss and she did *not* like your funky dancing!"

June opened the door and scolded us for having Maggie out of the kitchen.

"And turn off that music; some of us are trying to sleep!"

June took a second look at the red light as she left the room. I heard her chuckle as she shook her head.

I looked at my sister in the next twin bed,

"Maybe I'll replace that red with a black light—cool, huh! Charlee, how is it that you know so much about prostitutes and whore houses?"

Charlee pulled the covers up over her shoulders, turned, and said,

"Hmm, well, to tell you the truth, it's a strange curiosity. I wonder why women resorted to selling their bodies and souls to men. I've come to realize that maybe they were victims of sexual abuse, or were desperate single mothers trying to feed their family. Maybe they were just trying to support a drug habit. I don't know, probably a variety of reasons. Mainly I feel for sorry for them. Maybe when I'm a lawyer, I can help them get their lives back together."

I looked at my sister with admiration. She was always on a mission to help the less fortunate.

"That's cool, Sis!" I said. "I know you will make one fine lawyer someday!"

Charlee gave me a concerned smiled and said,

"Moe, you do know I'll be moving out soon, right?"

I nodded my head sadly and replied,

"Yeah, you're twenty-one years old, and I figured it would be soon."

Charlee finished her degree in political science and was accepted into law school at Saint Louis University. In the meantime, she planned on moving downtown to be closer to school. I left the room and came back in with a handful of carrots. Laughing, I said,

"Hey, Charlee, who is going to make me carrot people when you leave?"

She chuckled, "Wow, I haven't made you carrot people in ages! I might be a bit rusty, but I'll see what I can do!"

The next morning I ran up to my younger sister Abby, was now three years old, and asked, "Do you want to see the animals at the shelter?"

Mom overheard. "Don't even go there thinking another dog is an option! One puppy who isn't housebroken is *enough*!"

I grabbed Abby's little hand and said,

"Cool down Mom! Abby and I enjoy petting the animals. They don't have anyone to love them!"

Abby was pulling on my arm, saying,

"Let's go, let's go!"

We walked hand in hand past the corner lot. There were Sam, T-Mac, several neighbor boys, and little Alan in football formation on the field. Like I mentioned before, all neighbor kids were allowed to play the daily field sport. We didn't care how tall, heavy, or short you were. We just wanted enough bodies to form teams.

We used to call Alan "Little Monkey-Man." He had these long arms, legs, and fingers, just like a chimp.

Sam said, "I don't want you acting like a whiner if you're tackled, Alan!"

Alan spat on the ground sarcastically replying,

"They're not gonna catch me you pudge-muffin."

Sam burst out laughing then pounded on his chest.

"I'm one hundred percent pure muscle! Maybe someday you will be as strong and handsome as moi!"

The teams were divided up, and the football game resumed. Alan was literally climbing up the back of the tight end like a monkey, wrapping his primate-like arms around his head. The stocky player struggled to see as he sprinted with Alan's hands covering his eyes. Suddenly he tripped and fell hard, really hard, on top of Alan.

That's when everyone heard a loud *pop*! It was like a shotgun on a quiet night. Alan let out a bloodcurdling scream as he held his lower leg. The game ended, and the entire team carried him home.

My mom took one look at Alan's leg and knew it was fractured. She was furiously yelling at Sam and T-Mac as they loaded my brother into the station wagon. My dad gave an angry glare as he shook his head from side to side.

"You two should know better! He's younger and half your weight!" I'll have words with you two boys when we get home!"

Sam and T-Mac had a look of fear in their eyes. All of us jammed ourselves in the car to accompany Alan to the hospital.

An orthopedic surgeon was called to the emergency room to treat Alan. He told my parents Alan had a non-displaced tibial fracture. Alan was proud of the large plaster cast that was applied to his right leg. It was like his badge of courage for playing football with the older boys.

The surgeon walked out of the room after ordering a shot for Alan's pain. He instructed my parents to expect a minimum of eight weeks before Alan's cast was removed. A slender, blond nurse walked in the room with the injection and some crutches. Alan yelled,

"Are you giving me a shot in the *butt*?"

She sweetly replied, "In your hip, dear. It's for your pain."

"Dang, why can't I take a pill? I don't want you to see my butt!" Alan replied, turning a dark shade of crimson. Big Al left the room, and the nurse, whose name was Kathy, calmly put her hand on Alan's shoulder. She explained that his pain would be relieved more quickly with an injection than a pill.

Alan surrendered and said,

"Ohhhhhh, alright."

He slowly rolled over, exposing his peach-colored bum.

T-Mac and Sam were snickering at their brother's embarrassment. Sam sarcastically said,

"Try not to fart in her face!"

June yelled angrily,

"Sam Bender!" You and T-Mac, get out of the room, now! Go wait behind the curtain or in the waiting room! I don't want to hear another word!"

Before long, Alan giggled as he gave his nurse a goofy Demerol induced grin.

"Whoa, Nurse Kathy, you're so pretty! Do you ever go for younger men?"

The English nurse smiled at my fresh little brother. She then proceeded to give my parents discharge instructions and paused to say,

"He's a charming lil chap isn't he?"

On the drive home, Alan had his leg propped up on his brother's lap. T-Mac leaned over to whisper to Sam. He planned to draw a cartoon babe with big boobs on Alan's cast. Mom raised her voice without turning her head,

"I heard that, T-Mac! I better not see any cartoon porn on that plaster, or you'll be history!"

The next morning Alan was feeling better as long as he had his pain medication. He was in for several weeks of recovery and counted signatures when he didn't have visitors. He was already unbearably cocky and spoiled from everyone waiting on him hand and foot.

It was obvious he felt like a rugged stud as the neighborhood girls flocked to sign his cast. The older boys came to tell him what a good defensive game he played. Alan was little but absolutely fearless! That was both good and bad. I worried the accolades only encouraged more reckless behavior.

CHAPTER 11

I was looking forward to spending the night at Ann's house. The same crew of girls would be there, Ann, Marie, Janelle, Willie, Lynn, and me. Unfortunately, I had to work that day, and my dad dropped me off at Ann's house sometime after 8:00 p.m.

"Whoa! What a day!"

I said as I plopped my overnight case on the bed. "My poor dad and Charlee drive the five of us all over the place! I can't wait until I drive... seven more months until I'm sweet sixteen!"

Ann was combing her long blonde tresses.

"Only four months for me, but I've been practicing!"

she said with a sly smile. We all looked at each other and asked what she meant.

"Well, when my parents go to sleep, I take out the car and drive around the neighborhood."

Our mouths were wide open with surprise that sweet Ann would be so gutsy—or stupid, whichever. "Want to take out the convertible out tonight?" Ann asked.

There was only one answer for that question..."Heck, yeah!"

It must've been around 12:30 a.m., when Ann's parents *finally* fell asleep, we started our plan. Ann went to get the keys and got behind the wheel and put the car in neutral. Marie, Janelle, and I pushed it down the driveway and to then to the street. The car rolled a bit before Ann turned the car on. *Vrrrooom!* Ann was like an old pro, driving all over Black Jack and even by our house in Florissant! It was just after two in the morning when the tire blew and became flat as a pancake.

"Oh that's just great!" I said "We're right in front of the cemetery!"

Ann started to panic and said,

"Moe, Marie, can you two run to the house and get my brother? He surely knows how to change a tire. Just cut through the cemetery, it's faster!"

My heart was now beating faster, and I felt this impending doom. Yes, getting into *big* trouble was a very real possibility, and the thought of going into the cemetery made my skin crawl. Janelle said,

"Oooh, are you afraid of ghosts?"

I sneered at Janelle and didn't bother to answer. Marie, who can be as tough as nails, said,

"C'mon, Moe! Let's run like the wind!"

It was another cold, blustery autumn morning, with wisps of snow falling delicately falling to the ground. Marie ran with her mouth open, trying to catch the cool flakes on her tongue. The cemetery gate creaked loudly when its rusty hinges were forced to move on this icy morning. I was looking down, trying to zip up my coat, when my slipper came off my foot. Yes, I was wearing slippers, cotton pajamas, and a coat. The slippers were my mom's new leopard prints, which I brought because they matched my tiger-striped pj's.

I thought about not going back to retrieve the slipper at all; however, knew I would be in deep shit if I didn't. Marie was no longer in sight, and here I was in a cemetery, looking for my furry foot mitt. I thought to myself, *why me?* To my surprise, when I looked to the left, I saw my slipper was propped up under a light post. "Geez, that's weird!" I said out loud. Almost as if someone wanted me to find it. As I knelt to put it on my foot, I looked up to see an illuminated figure of a little girl. In her tiny voice, she softly said my name:

"Moe..."

My mouth opened wide, and I screamed,

"What?"

I was clumsily stumbling to my feet as her voice softly echoed through the air.

"You were my only friend.... "

Despite the fear, I stopped and turned to see Leslie, reaching out with one hand. Lord knows I'm not quite sure how, but my fear dissipated as I walked forward to touch her hand with mine. I suddenly felt heat generate throughout my body as the warmth in Leslie's smile touched my heart.

"Leslie, what happened to you?"

It was then that her illuminated presence broke into a million pieces that looked like stars. The glittering fragments swirled then dimmed as they blew away into the cold autumn night.

"Hey slowpoke, are you coming?"

I could see Marie, who was on the other side of the gate, now back up by the car with Ann's brother. The sound shook me back into reality; I grabbed my slipper and went back to the car and waited as Joe changed the tire. We drove the car back home, and not a word was ever mentioned about the car or tire. Apparently, Ann's older brother told their parents he found another nail in the tire and went ahead and changed it for them. They were grateful. Whew, we were so lucky! We might not be so lucky the next time, though, and we never drove the car again, until we were of legal age.

My mom was sitting at the table reading the paper and drinking her coffee when I walked into the house. I was reflecting on my strange paranormal experience last night and decided to inquire if she knew anything about Leslie.

"Mom, remember my friend Leslie in California?"

June looked puzzled when I asked, then sighed deeply and replied,

"Wow, what made you think about her after all these years?"

When I thought of retelling people my experience, I truly thought they would think I had lost my mind! "Um...I just had a strange dream about Leslie, and wondered what ever happened to her. We never saw her after we left the police station."

June shook her head and said,

"Oh, yes, I do know what happened to her, but I never wanted to share the dreadful information with you kids. Heck, you were having nightmares every night, going through that whole ordeal!"

When I heard that, I immediately sat down across the table from her. In my most serious voice, I pleaded, "Mom, I'm fifteen years old now; please tell me all about it!"

Shaking her head, she proceeded to tell me what happened to six-year-old Leslie Ward.

"Her Father was furious when he left the police station after hearing Leslie was sexually abused by the perverted offender. He felt Leslie was responsible! Can you imagine that, the poor girl was only six years old!" My ears were glued to every word. June continued, "Anyway according to the newspaper, he beat the living daylights out of her, while the family watched, and then locked her outside. He was quoted as saying it was to teach her a lesson! What an absolute psycho!"

June took another sip of coffee and inhaled deeply on her cigarette before she proceeded.

"The theory is that the predator was stalking the house after the incident. When Leslie's father threw her outside in the dark, it made the child an easier to target...poor girl!" June shook her head. "She was found raped and murdered behind the trash can in the ally. Her damn father didn't even bother to look for her until the next day!"

My stomach turned as I heard the details. "Mom, how did the stalker kill her?"

June paused a moment as her eyes filled with sadness.

"He strangled her, just like he did the other four girls in the area. That's what made the decision to move away easier for your dad."

I leaned forward and asked urgently, "Mom, did they catch him? Arrest him for what he did?" She gently patted my hand, "No, dear, they never found him."

I decided to share Leslie's story and cemetery incident with Charlee. She had turned on the black light in our small bedside lamp. Maggie the bulldog was also sprawled on the bed. Her teeth looked so white, but all the doggie drool spots were now clearly visible on my bedspread. Charlee pointed at them. "Eww, gross!" she sneered. "Maggie is *not* sleeping in my bed! Okay, now finish telling me your *little* ghost story."

I felt rather insulted, as if she wouldn't believe what I was about to say. Then Alan, T-Mac, and Sam walked into the small room. Sam asked, "Hey what are you guys up to?"

Charlee chuckled. "Moe is telling me 'bout seeing Leslie's ghost in the cemetery." I snapped at her,

"It's true!"

Charlie waved the boys into our ten-by-ten room.

"Come on in and shut the door behind you."

Alan pointed to the rug. "Ewe, there's also a dingle berry on the carpet! I'm not sitting on the floor!"

I retorted to Alan, "Those are the sacrifices you make when you have animals! Anywaaaaay, do you want to hear about Leslie or not?"

I then started retelling my story, though I was unsure if it was a good idea, with all the sarcastic knuckleheads in the room. I momentarily looked up to gather my thoughts about that particular night in the cemetery.

"No kidding, I had huge goose bumps when I saw Leslie in front of me. Heck, I didn't even know she died! Then she said I was her only friend... isn't that sad? I was the only friend she had in her short life, and I was afraid of her!" I stopped and placed the palm of my hand on my chin, pondering the complexity of it all.

Charlee sat up to face all of us, "Leslie wasn't evil, just misunderstood. Poor kid was surrounded by such anger that was unfortunately all she knew. Unfortunately it's might also be what she would have become if she lived long enough. Poor helpless child, she never had a chance!"

Sam rolled his eyes and piped up, "Interesting story Moe, quite an imagination you have! Maybe you should stay away from my homemade wine in the closet!"

Alan started to giggle while adding his two-cents.

"Maybe Moe was smoking some Mary Jane, ya know, pot!"

Alan, the little monkey-man, rolled around laughing on the floor. I wrinkled my nose and said, "Huh? Alan, what do *you* know about pot?" Then I stood up and said,

"All of you boys...out of my room! This is why I never tell you anything!"

T-Mac had listened quietly while he was in the room. He hadn't been himself for many months. He had been more withdrawn, not the funny, feisty wise guy. His artistic talents had been soaring. He produced some amazing oil paintings and original comics with hilarious characters. Yes, T-Mac was funny on paper, but he seemed more intense about life.

That next Saturday, T-Mac, who was a phenomenal light weight wrestler, never showed up for the meet. The coach saw me in the hall and waved me over.

"Where in the world is your brother? He never showed up today. Is he sick? Please, can you call him and remind him that we have a game?"

When I left the house that morning, T-Mac had looked like he was gathering his gear to prepare for the meet. I fumbled in my purse to find coins for the pay phone. I ran back inside the school to call home. After a few rings, T-Mac answered the phone. I was huffing and puffing after running the entire way back to the auditorium.

"T-Mac! Where the heck are you? Coach wants you here ASAP!"

There was silence at the other end. I again yelled,

"T-Mac! What is going on with you?"

Silence...then he casually replied,

"I'm not going."

Frantic for explanations and very confused, I asked,

"Do you mean you're not coming to this meet, or *any* of them?"

T-Mac simply said, "I quit."

He then hung up the phone. I yelled, "Darn it!" as I tried to fumble through my pocket to find more change. Again, I put coins in the machine. This time my mom answered the phone.

"Yes?"

She said casually as if she expected my call. The words were spilling out of my mouth at an amazing speed. "Mom, something is wrong with T-Mac! He didn't show up for the game today and said he quit! Mom, Mom, do you hear me?"

June, sounding so cool and calm, replied,

"Maybe he just doesn't feel well. Don't worry. He will be okay."

Click, she hung up. I thought, *Oh my! What am I going to tell the coaches?*

The old T-Mac was ever so cocky and excelled in academics, arts, and sports. He was one of the rare gifted people with so many talents. This was now the beginning of an artist recluse who never played organized sports, ever again. T-Mac fought his growing desire to create phenomenal art on canvas or any medium he could splash color on. He no longer wanted to be the athlete but the artist. It was his calling.

Girls became more intrigued though with T-Mac's mysterious, elusive nature. Friends of my brother knew he was one of a kind. I personally felt T-Mac was destined for greatness, for fame and fortune. It was all within his reach, yet at that moment he didn't want to grasp any of it. T-Mac, would find greatness however, it wouldn't be for many decades and after many hardships.

Several years ago, June discovered Bingo. It became her passion and she played several evenings a week. No doubt that having so many teenagers under one roof was chaotic. Bingo offered June a temporary escape and an opportunity to have fun with friends.

Big Al was a busy man who worked six days a week and shuffled us kids to our after school events in the evening. I don't ever remember hearing him complain. Charlee since moved out to apartments closer to St. Louis University. She had a brief marriage and became pregnant with her first child. It wouldn't be easy completing law school as a single parent. Charlee was determined though to contribute to society and make this world a better place. Sam had been accepted into FIU on a baseball scholarship and would soon be leaving, too. Alan and a couple other thirteen-year-old friends were now casually experimenting with marijuana and alcohol. I found out they were getting it from a seventeen-year-old high school dropout on the next block. Sheesh, too many changes—what next?

The youngest and most innocent of the Bender family was precious Abby. She was a little now 4 -year-old gem who loved to sing. She would use her little fist as her microphone as she'd dance, swirling round and round to her imaginary audience. I thought to myself how I wanted to be that carefree again.

Yes, raise my hands up and swirl round and round, singing at the top of my lungs, not in the least concerned as to who heard or saw me or that I'd look insane.

That Friday night, Marie, Willie, Lynn, and I went to the drive-in to see *Young Frankenstein*. Of course, Marie and I sneaked into the truck, and I guess Ann looked innocent, because they didn't check it at the gate. I believe we were always more interested in checking out the guys at the theatre than the movie. After the first flick played, the intermission music started playing with the dancing popcorn: "Let's all go to the lobby, Let's all go to the lobby, Let's all go to the lobby and have ourselves a treat!" That was my cue to stretch my legs, go to the bathroom, scope out the boys, and of course to eat! I opened the car door and asked, "Is anyone hungry?" All five of us scrambled toward the lobby and were too busy talking to look exactly where we were headed. As we scurried along in the general direction of the lobby, we unfortunately walked right in the middle of a brawl! When I turned my head, *bam*! I instantly saw stars and fell backward off my feet. My hand immediately went to my nose to catch the blood which now flowed from my nostrils.

My friends were all helping me up, and the boy who punched me actually stopped fighting to apologize. I gasped again when I saw my crooked nose in the bathroom mirror.

"Dang! My nose is broken!"

My mom rarely took us to the doctor, so I knew there was only one thing for me to do. I instantly raised my hand and swiftly shifted my nose in the opposite direction. There was an audible *crack*! The girls all said,

"Ugh!"

My nose was no longer resting on my left cheek, but the bump on the middle remained. We then all went to the lobby for a treat and an ice to pack for my nose. My poor nose from that day forward was never the same, but it is what it is. To my surprise, no one at home noticed a change in the alignment of my nose. Charlee however spent many a night telling me to rollover and quit snoring!

It was 1975, and my high school years came to a close. Ann, Marie, and I maintained a cohesive bond as that of the Three Amigos. I considered myself lucky to have found two people who would share not only high school but a lifetime of memories. No doubt we would attend each other's weddings, possibly have children around the same time, and grow old together, discussing our aches, pains, and doctors' appointments. It's a rare gift to have experienced that loyalty, trust, and devotion. After graduation, we wrote in each other's yearbooks LYLAS, which translated into "Love ya like a Sis." Over the years, we've witnessed the worst and the best in each other.

In working through our tears, and senseless arguments, we were able to grow as friends and individuals. It's my hope that everyone at some point in their lives can call at least one special person their true friend.

My plans for the following fall were to start nursing school at a diploma program at one of the hospitals in downtown St. Louis. One of my nursing aide cohorts at the nursing home was going to Hawaii to stay with friends of her family, and she asked me to go with her! My parents were contributing only five hundred dollars for our education, so I was in turmoil, wondering how in the heck I would pay for both Hawaii and nursing school. Maybe I would sell my Chevette to pay for both. My red Chevette was my pride and joy! I had saved up for three years for my hefty down payment. Geez, I was anxious to be an adult, travel, and experience life! I had two more weeks to let Marcy know if I would be going with her to the land of Hawaii Five-O, Honolulu.

My cousin Bonnie from Chicago was coming to visit for a few days with her family. Over the years, we had stopped to stay with them on the way to the grandparents' house in Wisconsin. They were a good-looking Irish family. My tall, handsome uncle was a former college linebacker. He had this strong square jaw and muscular frame. I'm sure he was quite intimidating to face on a football field! Aunt Jenny had the class and looks of Grace Kelly. I was proud of them and was anxious for Marie to meet some of the McKinleys.

The cousin I was closest to was fifteen-year-old Bonnie. I always adored her sweet nature, but sometimes I felt like my siblings and I would corrupt her! Not really, however, Bonnie always seemed so angelic in nature. Her shiny black hair flowed past her shoulders, and her clear, light green eyes were a beautiful contrast to her porcelain skin. She was so humble and oblivious to her beauty.

I asked Marie to stop by and meet my aunt, uncle and cousins. The McKinley cousins were fifteen-year-old Bonnie, ten-year-old Collette, and eight-year-old Jack. All had dark hair and brilliant Irish green eyes. Unlike the Irish, they were quiet, much more so than the rowdy Benders!

When Marie stopped by, we asked Bonnie to show us some cheers she learned in her cheerleading camp. Then the three of us took a walk to show her our junior high and onward to the Five & Dime for some candy. On our return we shut ourselves in the room to play records. I've always adored music and had a new make-up game for us to play.

"Hey, do you know songs that begin with your name?"

Marie and Bonnie thought for a moment. "Hmm," Marie said,

"My grandmother used to sing me an old Vaudeville song by Irving Berlin called 'Marie from Sunny Italy'! Dang, I don't remember the words."

There was silence as we all tried to recall famous songs that have our names in the title.

I finally piped up,

"Nothing comes to mind with my name, but I know one with yours!"

I said as I pointed to my cousin. "It's 'My Bonnie Lies Over The Ocean'!

Bonnie perked up and said, "Yes, of course! I know that song well! Bonnie blushed, giggled, and said, "I'm embarrassed to sing in front of people!"

I reassured my cousin,

"Well, look at Maggie's adorable wrinkly face and pretend you're singing to her.

Believe it or not, animals love music!"

Bonnie moved over to Maggie, who was sprawled belly-up on the bed with her pink jowls flapped upside down. Gently she patted Maggie as she sang the most beautiful rendition of My Bonnie, with a slight hint of a Scottish accent.

My Bonnie lies over the ocean,
My Bonnie lies over the sea,
My Bonnie lies over the ocean,
Oh bring back my Bonnie to me.
Bring back, bring back,
Oh bring back my Bonnie to me, to me,
Bring back, bring back,
Oh bring back my Bonnie to me.

Last night as I lay on my pillow,
Last night as I lay on my bed;
Last night as I lay on my pillow,
I dreamt that my Bonnie was dead.

Bring back, bring back,
Oh bring back my Bonnie to me, to me,
Bring back, bring back,
Oh bring back my Bonnie to me.

Bonnie surely must've practice this song before! Marie and I turned to one another, surprised.

"Wow, I would buy that version!"

I looked at my friend and agreed.

"Me too, but I never realized the lyrics were...*I dreamt Bonnie* was *dead*!?"

My cousin laughed softly and said,

"Well, I believe that's a traditional Scottish version, but there are different lyrics with the ending. Oh yes, like, as the winds brought back my Bonnie to me, or something like that."

I nodded my head,

"Yes, a more comforting thought!"

I had an interest in songs and their meanings and wanted to share an interesting tidbit with them. "Hey, did you know that the nursery rhythm 'Ring around the Rosie' is about the Black Death, otherwise known as the bubonic plague? Yes, now listen to this." I recited the nursery rhyme:

Ring around the rosie, pocket full of posies,
Ashes, ashes, we all fall down!

Marie said,

"Wow, cool, I never knew it was in reference to the plague!"

We all sat Indian-style on the floor of my room.

I continued, "Well, my dad told me the bubonic plague killed entire families and villages—millions of people! Not sure how many, but millions! Now, 'Ring around the Rosie' refers to one of the first signs of the plague, which was a red rash. Posies were an herb. Folks thought it protected them from the plague. Hmm, now the ashes have two meanings: the sound of a violent sneeze when you had the disease and cremation when you died from it. Yep, they would throw the bodies onto a cart and haul them away to be cremated! Horrible, isn't it?

"How did they catch the plague?" Bonnie scooted closer within our circle.

I responded with what my Father previously told me,

"It's caused by fleas carried by rats. Oh, that reminds me, I saw a couple on Maggie. Anyway, there was a *huge* fire in 1660 that killed most of the rats."

Marie said, "Cool, I didn't know that little bit of trivia, but I'll think about it every time I hear 'Ring around the Rosie'!" We all stood up to stretch our legs and head toward the kitchen for some snacks.

My parents, aunt, and uncle settled in to play cards that evening. All of us kids got together to play Monopoly, the Dating Game, and several others we had in our closet. We always enjoyed seeing our relatives. Such a shame we didn't live closer! Maybe that would change when I graduated from nursing school.

Unfortunately, the next day, my aunt and uncle were getting ready to head back to Chicago. Bonnie gave me a hug and told me that I should come on up to the Windy City someday. We all lined up on the front porch to watch them pull out of the driveway. Bonnie and her siblings had their foreheads, noses and cheeks pressed up against the back window. We laughed at their funny faces and waved at their departing station wagon.

The "Bonnie Song" was stuck in my head. It happens all the time when I hear a particular tune. Like the previous week, when I hummed "Smoke on the Water" all day! Now it was "Bring back, bring back, bring back Bonnie to me." I'm sure we have all had those contagious tunes playing over and over in our heads. I would hum the tune, and later catch Charlee, T-Mac, and Alan humming too! They would say,

"I haven't heard this song since elementary school; why am I humming it?"

It was funny how my subliminal message was stuck in their subconscious minds.

A few hours later, T-Mac started whistling, "Bring back, bring back, bring back my Bonnie to me." He caught me laughing and yelled, "I don't even *like* that song! Why am I whistling that darn song?"

CHAPTER 13

Having six kids was a double-edged sword to June. We drove her absolutely mad most of the time. She seemed to enjoy getting us out of the house for the day or leaving by herself to play bingo. When we'd talk about moving out someday, though, June thought of all the reasons we shouldn't. She found it quite difficult to allow us to spread our wings and soar as independent adults. Whew, Mom really threw a fit when I told her that I was indeed going to Hawaii.

"You don't even know these people in Honolulu, and you're staying at their house? Great! They could be criminals! What do you know about them?"

My friend Marcy and I had worked together for three years at the nursing home. I had a gut feeling that this trip would be one heck of a learning experience! The plan was to stay a month and a half, returning just before school started in September. Marcy's dad was a successful business man who was married to a Hawaiian woman. We would be staying with Marcy's stepmother's sister. Strangely, her name was Karina! She and her husband, Haku Kinimaku, offered for us to stay at their home in Oahu. It was Marcy's second trip to Hawaii and the first time I was ever on a plane!

The morning of our departure, I had the worst cramps in the world and felt bloated. Oh, wonderful! I popped a couple aspirin for my discomfort and struggled to button my now very snug jeans. How in the world do you pack for a month in one suitcase? I believe I threw in everything I owned, which necessitated sitting on the suitcase for the lock to buckle. We were supposed to be at the airport by 7:30 a.m., and it was almost 8:00 before Marcy and her dad pulled up in the Cadillac. It felt good to buy a one-way ticket to Hawaii, and I frequently had thoughts that I'd love it there and never come back.

At the airport, I whispered to Marcy that I was on my period and felt like a bloated blimp!

"Oh?" said Marie. She then rummaged through her purse and pulled out a small pill.

"This will help your bloating!"

Looking back, it was really stupid not to even inquire what I just put in my mouth! The boarding and my excitement for the trip began! Marcy was, of course, kind enough to give me the window seat, as it was my first time any aircraft. Smiling broadly, I said,

"Hey, Marcy, I'm asking the stewardess for wings!"

Marcy and I sat next to two large grumpy women who weren't interested in becoming friends with us. They wanted to be left alone to read their books in peace. We were, up, up, and away when I saw the St. Louis Arch.

"Oh, my gosh, there's the gateway to the West! Can you believe I've never even been up it?"

Marcy briefly glanced and said, "You go up six hundred thirty feet in a small capsule to the top. Pretty scary if you're claustrophobic!" I was the one now pressing my face on the window to see all the sites from a thousand feet up.

It wasn't long before I started to squirm in my seat. It wasn't because of the inactivity but because I had to pee like a race horse! My bladder felt absolutely overloaded, and the full sensation made me start to panic!

"Whoa, Marie, I've got to pee now, please move. Oh, and ma'ams," I said to the two women closest to the aisle seat, "could you excuse me?"

Oh geez, their knees were tightly wedged into the back of the seat. They both turned to give me a scowl. It was their nonverbal way to let me know they didn't appreciate being inconvenienced, not one bit! I was jumping up and down with my legs tightly crossed, waiting and waiting for the women let me out of the seat. I thought, *Dang, they move like freakin' tortoises!*

If there were awards for speed in running from seat 14F to the bathroom, then surely records would have been broken that day! Once on the safety of the toilet, I peed like possibly no woman had ever peed before. It sounded like the Hoover dam burst! Then...

Knock! Knock!

"Ugh!" I yelled. "Please just a minute!"

When I finally made my exit, there were several people lined up waiting for the restroom.

Much to my absolute dismay, it was only twenty more minutes before the horrible sensation came back! I had to pee like a race horse—again! The women sitting closest to the aisle were now more vocal about having to move for me. I felt like slapping their faces as I squeezed by, but instead just said,

"Thank You."

Now, the third incident occurred only thirty minutes later.

"Sheesh, Marie! What the heck did you give me?"

Marie nonchalantly replied,

"Oh, it was one of my Mom's water pills, called Lasix."

Lasix, of course, was a potent prescription water pill. The ladies were now asking the stewardess if there were other available seats. By the time we were flying over the Pacific, my mouth felt like the Sahara Desert. I was between a rock and a hard place. If I drank too much, then the cycle started all over again.

The stewardess walked by, handing out packages of nuts. As I opened the little bag, I looked up and told Marcy,

"You do know that peanut breath and farts are the worst, right?"

She raised her eyebrows and replied,

"Oh really?"

We both laughed at the thought of methane gas and nut breath filling the plane. I turned my head and quickly fell asleep. It certainly felt so soothing to close my dry eyes for a while. I'm not sure how long I slept before an absolutely wretched odor filled my nasal passages!

" Marcy! Do you smell those peanut farts?"

I quickly added, "Breathe through your mouth, breathe through your mouth quickly, it helps!" Marcy grimaced as we both looked around to see others sniffing the polluted air. You could almost hear sniff, sniff, sniff! I elbowed Marcy.

"For Pete's sake! Why is it that when something, smells good, like a rose, people inhale once, and when something smells bad, people tend to sniff not once or twice but over and over again? Now seriously, a psychologist should research that topic someday!"

Hmm. I silently wondered if the second sniff was to decipher what the heck that poor soul ate (or if the second sniff would be as bad as the first) and the third sniff was to see if it was all clear. I reflected on the time my friend Ann told me that Maggie had "Frito feet." I asked her what the heck she was talking about—sweet Maggie smelled like a puppy! Everybody loves puppy scent! It's equivalent to that new car smell or a cuddly baby. So I'm not quite sure why, but I had Marie, Big Al, Charlee, T-Mac, Sam, and even Alan smell Maggie's paws. Most smelled her paws more than once! Everyone in the olfactory survey agreed hands down that my precious bulldog had Frito feet. Heck, we had a few more hours before we landed in Hawaii, so I had plenty of time to ponder crazy thoughts. I suddenly laughed out loud. Marcy woke up and turned.

"What's so funny?"

I chuckled again and told her I was wondering why my dog's feet smelled like Fritos. "

It was only five minutes later when Marcy fell back to sleep. My mind was racing with excitement and unfortunately no one available to listen. My travel companion started to snore so I gave her a light elbow in her shoulder. She snorted while attempting to open her heavy lids. It was enough to stop the snore cycle. Marcy had more of a calm, subdued personality; some referred to her as aloof. She had a large frame but was pretty, with her shoulder-length, jet-black hair, porcelain skin, and blue eyes. She was raised in a household where she had maids, was pampered, and got a bright, shiny new car at the age of sixteen. In our household, we kids were the maids. Big Al was an executive with a good income; however, he also had six mouths to feed.

The only time we got new clothes was at Christmas or Easter. All of us kids had to work for any of the extras, including cars, clothes, weekend spending money, or our education. Unfortunately, Charlee and I weren't able to share our clothes. Charlee was a curvy, petite little gal at five feet two with size 5 shoes. I was several inches taller and wore big size 9 shoes. Once when I was eleven, I felt like it was time for a bra. I tried on one of Charlee's; however, it was way too big. I took a sewing needle, inverted Charlee's new bra, and sewed the size C into an A cup. Quickly, I grew tired of all the sewing. I decided to put the combo A & C cup bra, back in Charlee's drawer. The funny part was seeing her try it on several days later.

Booby flesh was spilling over the altered bra. Let me tell you, it's not a good idea to get Charlee mad! And oh, was she mad!

My flood of random thoughts ended abruptly when I saw Oahu from the window. Marcy! I exclaimed suddenly, I can see the airport! We are finally getting ready to land! When the jets tires touched down on the air-strip, I wanted to cheer! The faces of the other passengers were filled with a relief that the flight was finally over. This was the first time in my life that I felt like an adult in this exotic far away land. Who knows, I just may love it here and never go back.

When Marcy and I disembarked from the plane, we saw a beautiful Polynesian woman with hip-length black hair, holding two floral leis. Next to her were her two children, two-year-old Chiquita and ten-year-old Kala. All three had ear-to-ear smiles on their faces when they recognized Marcy. Karina said,

"Aloha! Welcome to Hawaii!"

She then gave us both a warm hug as she placed the leis around our necks. I was waiting for someone to wake me up from this dream. After all, it had always been my dream to come to this beautiful island someday—and now my dream had come true! Karina was absolutely stunning in her bright royal blue sarong wrap. She said,

"You two are coming at an exciting time! The King Kamehameha celebration is this weekend! There will be a spectacular parade that will pass the Punchbowl, which isn't far from our house."

Karina shared a little about her adorable children and herself. She worked full time at a bank; however, she earned college money by hula dancing at her husband's restaurant. Haku still managed the Polynesian restaurant where they had met eleven years ago. Ten-year-old Kala was holding my hand during our ride in the car. The precocious young child looked up at me and said,

"You are a pretty Haole!"

Karina said sharply, "Kala, mind your manners, her name is Moe!"

I laughed. "What in the world is a Haole?"

Kala, giggling now, replied,

"It means you are a whitey...you are white and from the mainland! You also have hair the color of honey; can I touch it?"

Kala gingerly reached up and patted my hair from my roots and all the way down. Hands down, Kala reminded me of a young Polynesian version of Charlee. Charlee didn't have a verbal "edit button," and I don't believe Kala did, either. I enjoyed her, though, and looked forward to getting to know the Kinimaku family.

"Girls, there's the Polynesian Cultural Center! You can see an authentic Hawaiian Luau there." Karina was pointing to every site she thought we'd be interested in visiting during our stay. "You know, Hawaii is really a melting pot of cultures, not only Hawaiians but also people from Japan, China, the Philippines, and mixes like me! I am of Hawaiian and Philippine heritage. You must be starving, so we are going to meet Haku at his restaurant. He has a wonderful meal planned for us."

The restaurant was amazing, and I loved all the tropical plants, thatched roof over the outdoor tables, and the fragrant air on this exotic island. I tasted luscious food like mahi-mahi, huli huli chicken, purple Hawaiian sweet potatoes, a plate of bright colored fruits, and haupia, which is a stiff, coconut-flavored pudding. That was little Chiquita's favorite! This was all such a new, exciting experience that I wanted to take every incredible sight, scent, taste, and sound and store it deep in my memory bank. Marcy seemed amused; however, she was more subdued about showing her emotions.

Karina said, "It's late now, and we should head home so you two can unpack, where we can all talk and get to know each other a little better. Of course, if you're not too tired later, feel free to take the car out!"

My eyes opened wide and I thought, *Did I just die and go to heaven? Who wants to sleep at all?* Big Al would *never* let just anyone drive his car—not even us kids, unless it was an emergency. I was ready to party and experience the night life in Honolulu!

Karina and Haku had a large three-bedroom condo on Magellan Street, which was below the Punchbowl National Cemetery. Karina pointed upward and said, The Punchbowl was built as a memorial to honor all those in the armed services who sacrificed their lives during the war."

We finally pulled in the garage and headed up to our new home away from home.

Haku and Karina seemed like an unlikely couple. She was beautiful, tall, and slender, the most warm, gracious woman I had ever met. Haku, on the other hand, was short and round and had a tough, businesslike exterior. They had separated for a year and just recently moved back in together. Karina told us that she and Haku did not celebrate Chiquita's milestone first birthday due to the separation. Now that the couple had mended their marriage, they planned a grand celebration for Chiquita's second birthday. It would be held at one of the hotels in Waikiki. It was a couple weeks off, and it would be an event where I would don my one and only dress.

That evening Marcy and I toured Waikiki and the surrounding areas—unfortunately, after we drove the wrong way several times! It was before the days of navigation systems, where one would write down directions or read a map. That was a fantastic idea; however, it was difficult to read directions at night. We eventually found our way and parked near a spot that looked like it was thriving with music and activity. Marcy and I seated ourselves at a tall table by the bar and ordered a pitcher of sangria. It was strange to be of legal age and able to order drinks. What was more foreign was having a variety of male suitors come to our table!

Marcy had been rather quiet, so it was nice to see her hang loose and dance. We danced and danced until our feet hurt, and then we ventured off to yet another nightclub. While we were walking down the beach, a wide-eyed man who looked like an old surfer rushed up. He took my hand and said,

"You, your birthday is in July, am I right?"

Stunned, I replied, "Yes, how did you know?"

He closed his eyes and replied,

"It is the sixteenth, and you are meant to live by the water, but it won't be on Oahu. You should come and have a reading. I need to tell you more about your future."

Marcy said,

"Not now, Buster!"

I exclaimed, "Wow, how did he know that?" Marcy threw his card down and dragged me past the old psychic surfer. *Dang*, I thought, *why did she throw that card away*? I wanted to see what else he had to say about the years to come.

The following day, Marcy and I had planned a day at the beach, and that night all of us were going to Karina's parents' house. She was from a large family with three sisters, two brothers, and numerous aunts and uncles! It was my routine in the Midwest to run a few miles first thing in the morning, and I needed even more exercise with all this amazing tropical food! It was only At 6:00 a.m., everyone else was still asleep. As I started to tie my tennis shoes, Kala came out of her room. She had this big, openmouthed grin when she saw I was getting ready to jog.

"Hey, I'll go with you, Moe! Wait, let me get my shoes!"

I figured I could go a few blocks with Kala, then drop her off and go for a longer run.

"Hey, you better wake your mom and ask her first."

Karina was coming out of her room, wearing a long floral robe, and heard the last part of the conversation.

"You sure you don't mind, Moe? She does run periodically with my brother and Haku."

"Oh don't worry! No problem!" I said. "Kala can show me around the neighborhood."

Karina informed me, "You are lucky that June tends to be one of our drier months here in Honolulu. There may be a light misting around nine, though." Kala was ready in no time, and we headed out the door and down the elevator. Kala had big brown eyes and long black hair like her mother. She was also quite tall, which made her look much older than her age. Kala started off sprinting, and I had to remind her that we were not racing.

"Hey, we need to pace ourselves, so we can run longer!"

In every fresh breath of moist air, I could smell the lovely scent of the fragipani sea breeze. We were surrounded by a variety of flowering shrubs, birds-of-paradise, and hibiscus plants. I felt so free and so adult, being so far away from my family in the Midwest. I told Kala that a nice pace was where you could talk and run at the same time without getting winded.

"Kala, I just love it here on this picturesque island!"

As I finished my sentence, I noted Kala held one nostril, turned her head to the side, and blew mucus from her nose.

"Oh, my GOSH! Kala, what are you doing? That's GROSS!"

Kala started laughing.

"Haole, that's the Samoan nose blow! My uncle taught me that and does it when he races!"

I shook my head and said,

"Kala, all Samoans do *not* blow their noses like that! Next time I'm bringing you some Kleenex!"

When we turned the corner, heading back home toward the condo, Kala swatted me on the rear as she ran past me. "I'm winning!" she yelled as she waved her arms over her head. Kala went back home, and I continued to explore this scenic island by foot.

It was 7:30 a.m. when I returned, and Marcy was still snoring away. Haku left for work, and Karina was preparing breakfast, which consisted of tropical fruits, rice, and poi porridge. Poi is a bland side dish, somewhat like the equivalent of Southern grits. Kala was thumping her spoon on the porridge.

"Please, I need more sugar, milk, and taste! She then said, "Mom" (pointing to the sleeping guest on the couch), "Marcy has a personality like poi—boring!"

Karina shushed her daughter.

"Do you want her to hear you? That wasn't nice!"

Chiquita, Karina, and I all giggled at Kala's brutal honesty. When I was finished with breakfast, I started collecting my plates and others that were empty on the table. Karina warmly informed me that no one should leave the table until everyone finished their meal.

"Oh, I am so sorry, just a habit!"

I was looking forward to enjoying a leisurely meal and more time with my new family.

"Karina, I just didn't want you to think I was lazy and didn't want to pick up after myself."

Karina smiled and said, "Oh, I know, and I want you to also relax and have fun on your vacation." She was the most incredible hostess and had taken off a week to entertain us. I was a poor nursing student-to-be and didn't have a lot of spending money. I felt like helping around the house or offering to babysit as a way to pay her back for all she's done for us. By 11:00 a.m., Marcy was still sleeping, so I decided to wake her up.

"Marcy! It's time for sun and fun! Let's go!"

She slowly rolled over, "Okay, okay, give me a half hour!" I knew if I let her go back to sleep, we would still be here at noon. "No way, the boat is leaving now, right, Karina?" She replied firmly, "Most definitely! If you want time to go to Waikiki, then we need to leave by eleven thirty."

Karina was an amazing tour guide. She drove us past Kapiolani Park, her work place, and the International Marketplace.

"We'll go there later and shop for jewelry and food. And practically any Hawaiian souvenir is sold at the marketplace!"

We then arrived at the beach, and Karina had barely put the car in park before I jumped out. "Look! There's Diamond Head! It's one of the most famous volcanoes in the world!"

Kala said, "It used to be named Laeahi by ancient Hawaiians!" Karina then chimed in, saying,

"Yes, that means brow of tuna, and it resembles one if you look at the shape! It was many years later that it was renamed Diamond Head."

My mind wasn't absorbing the information; it was on overdrive at the reality of being on Waikiki beach! It wasn't long before our towels were on the warm sand, and we were basking in the sun. I said, "I'm in paradise! Geez, I want to come here every day!" Karina, Kala, and Chiquita were busy building a sand castle. It wasn't long before Marcy was complaining about being hot. I started to panic and worried Marcy might want to go home and nap.

"No, Marcy, it's seventy-six degrees; how could you be hot? Here, sit under the umbrella and absorb the beauty of Waikiki!" Marcy slowly flipped over on her towel, and I sighed, feeling relieved that we had more time. Marcy and I were now belly down, when we heard Kala say,

"Mom, look! The Haoles are burning their Okole [butt]!"

Marcy and I looked at each other and laughed. Marcy then said,

"That girl cracks me up! Oh, and Kala, I heard you say I was boring like poi this morning!"

Kala covered her mouth and raised her eyebrows. She then picked up her bucket of water from the great Pacific and poured it on our backs. She said,

"Do you feel better? I'm trying to make your red go away!"

No doubt the sun's rays turned us both into lobsters. Back then we were not aware of the increase incidence of skin cancer with overexposure, and unfortunately we encouraged more rays with the use of baby oil for tanning.

It wasn't long before we packed up our towels and headed for the International Marketplace. There was a diverse selection of souvenirs, and I was anxious to pick out a slice of Hawaii to send to Mom and Dad. The pace in Honolulu in general was more relaxed, with so many friendly locals. *I want to be one of them,* I thought—a local. We went home to get ready to meet Karina's family that evening. Haku came home with additional food to take to the relatives. He was always pleasant but seemed preoccupied with work and home responsibilities. While we were in the car, Karina took the opportunity to tell us about monuments, the best surf sites, and great places to go for nightlife.

"Oh, Moe and Marcy, you will have to try out that place" (a bar) "since it's popular with the University of Hawaii students!"

We drove along the highway for several miles and exited onto a long, winding mountain road.

Karina said, "If you look to the right, you'll see a couple feral pigs, and chances are you'll see some goats too!" I chuckled and said, "Geez, we are in the country!" It wasn't long before we pulled up to a small, older ranch home with a variety of palms and floral bushes lining the front yard. To my amazement, a flood of people came out the front door to welcome us.

"Aloha! Aloha!"

This little house was filled with so many people who truly cared and loved one another.

The Grandma, Grandpa, aunts, uncles, cousins, great aunts...a truly educational experience of what an extended family should be. Karina's mother walked up to Marcy and me to give us a hug and said, "In Hawaii, we cherish not only our blood relatives but also our adopted ones. Like you and Marcy!"

It reminded me of the large McKinley family in Wisconsin and made me miss them too.

How sad that we Benders only saw our extended family every year or two—maybe. How lucky we would be if we could all see each other more often! I reflected on how exposure to my new warm, friendly Polynesian family would forever have a positive influence on my life. I would never forget all their kindness and was impressed with the strength and bond of their extended family.

The kids were all outside doing the limbo and playing with hula hoops. Karina's mother told her to show us a traditional hula dance for us. She danced with such grace and poise. Karina slowly moved her arms so that each movement told a story with rainbows and palms trees. She made it look so easy. When she finished, she tried to teach Marcy and me, which made everyone laugh when we clumsily wiggled our hips. We became the comedy entertainment for the family party! Karina's father was a former bartender at one of the top restaurants in Waikiki. He asked,

"Have you ever had a Blue Hawaii or a Chi Chi?"

Throughout the evening, Marcy and I sampled several tropical drinks. My taste buds have never experienced such amazing flavors! At around 10:00 p.m., the families started leaving one by one. We were the last to leave, and it was when Marcy and I tried to stand up that we realized we were drunk! Karina took us arm in arm and walked us to the car. We slept during the long ride, and Kala gingerly patted my hair the whole way home.

The next couple of weekends flew by with a whirlwind of activities that included the King Kamehameha celebration. Karina, Marcy, the kids, and I stood on the curb to watch the beautiful assortment of floats parade along Ala Moana and on to somewhere around Queen Kapioloani Park. The next Saturday night we attended a real luau and dinner show at the Polynesian Cultural Center. At almost every tourist attraction, Karina refused to let us pay our own way. She surely must be growing weary of visitors occupying her living room and her life! As for Haku, he wasn't home very much and seemed to work all the time. The good thing was, Haku was always available for important family functions, which made Karina & the kids happy.

That Monday, Marcy wanted to stay home, as she was so sunburned. I asked Karina if it was all right if I took Kala for a day at the beach. She was surprised and replied,

"Oh, yes, but are you sure? Kala will love it—but you know how she can be!"

Karina was in a hurry to leave for work so she could also drop Chiquita off at the sitters. As for Kala, she was thrilled she would be spending the day with her favorite Haole! Kala and I boarded the bus and headed for a day at Waikiki beach. When we came to a particular stop, Kala insisted we get off.

"Come on, Moe, there are sites to see at this stop! Come on, check it out!"

I looked out the window in search of the blue ocean...nope, not there yet. I wasn't impressed but needed to make a decision fast.

"Okay, I guess it won't hurt to walk around."

Kala took my hand, and when we got off the bus, the only thing I could see was a seedy strip joint, several women at the corner, and hole–in-the-wall bars. My anxiety was mounting, and I said,

"Kala, where are we?"

She looked at me with this sly smile and said,

"It's the Red Light District!"

I pulled her hand and started to run after the bus, but it didn't stop. Shaking my head in disbelief, I exclaimed, "Kala, I'm responsible for you, and we shouldn't be here! It's dangerous! Heck, I didn't even think there was a red light district in Oahu! How did you know that, anyway?"

Kala replied, "My uncle told me when he drove past here one day. Don't worry! We can catch the bus down the street."

My whole body was shaking as I looked around and realized we were in the midst of some undesirable characters.

"Kala, please do not *ever* do that again! If I tell your mom we are going to the beach, then that is where we will go. No other stops, okay?" I did believe Kala might give me a heart attack.

Thank God, a bus came before long, and we made it safely to Waikiki. Kala and I took a walk first to pick out the perfect spot to sunbathe. As we sat down, a little piece of paper blew on my towel. It was a business card. "Oh, this is weird!" Kala sat up and asked, "What do you mean?" As I read the name, I realized it was the same psychic that guessed my birth date, when I was out with Marcy.

"Kala, a few days back, this psychic ran up to me and guessed my birth day, July 16! He said I needed to come for a reading. Marcy threw his card down, and now here it blows up on my towel! It's crazy huh? I wonder what he wanted to tell me?"

Kala looked at it and said, "Guess you'll never know!"

We both sunned ourselves, and I closed my eyes. The sun rays, sound of the waves, and salty sea breeze felt magnificent! *It won't be long before I'll be heading back home—or maybe I'll stay?* I'm not sure how much time passed when I heard a *click, click, click*. When I opened my eyes, several Japanese tourists were taking my picture, standing directly over me with their cameras! The small group was fully clothed with shoes on at the beach. I got up and said,

"Excuse me!"

They said something to me in their language, but of course I didn't understand a word of it. Kala and I got up to move to another location. Marcy sure missed one heck of a day!

That was Chiquita's second birthday, which would be celebrated at the Sheraton Waikiki. Karina was expecting around two hundred guests, so we had to leave early to help set up for the event. The birthday girl had her long black hair wound up in a little braided bun, all decorated with flowers. She definitely was all smiles, knowing this day was special, a day to honor her belated milestone birthday. I felt that it was also a celebration of Karina and Haku being together again as man and wife. They had spent the last fifteen years together, and I could tell they were committed to making union last a lifetime.

Unfortunately, it took us all longer to get ready than we thought, so people were already starting to arrive at Chiquita's party. One of the many aunts rushed up and said,

"Hau oli la hanau, Chiquita!" That's Hawaiian for "Happy birthday!"

This all truly amazed me, as I was a middle-class girl from the Midwest. Our big treat was to select what we wanted for dinner on our birthday. My family rarely ate out at restaurants, so Mom would make our special meal. I usually would choose hamburgers, ravioli, or June's amazing pizza. The Benders then sat down to dinner, after which we had cake and the opening of gifts. It was nice and very special to me; it was what I was used to. Never in my life had I seen such an extravagant birthday celebration for a two-year-old child! When you think how relatively short our lives are, though, it would be nice to share them more with all the people we love.

The large banquet hall was filled with song and a hula birthday dance for Chiquita. Marcy and I were introduced by Chiquita's mother as her adopted grandchildren from the Mainland. There were people at the party from all walks of life, including an actor who had played a few parts on *Hawaii Five-O*, which was one of my favorite shows. Marcy and I both asked a million questions about his life as an actor. He seemed quite unaffected about any fame he had with his role. My feet were starting to hurt, so I went to the bar and grabbed myself a drink. I scanned the tables and started to observe those in the room. It seemed that most of the women were so open with their emotions. The kids knew just were they stood with the parents. They were lovingly firm and direct, and would quickly redirect if someone was out of line. Yet, they were the first to give praise and hugs. In evaluating my time in Hawaii, what I would hold dear for years to come was the human interaction of this loving, large, extended family. I realize that all Polynesian families are not the same, but I was blessed to be a part of this one.

Marcy was making her way to the table now, and Kala was right behind her. Kala said,

"I am putting a flower behind your right ear. This will let all the single boys know you are single!"

Kala pointed to her mother, who had a flower behind her left ear. "You see, left means taken, and right means available!."

By the end of the evening, Karina's younger brother's friend Eric expressed that he wanted to take me out on a date. He was a former football player and recent graduate from the University of Hawaii. Karina was busy telling me all about him as we prepared to leave the hotel. "Oh, he is a great guy and a gentleman!" The thought of going on a blind date with no one there made me nervous.

"Karina, doesn't he have a friend for Marcy? How about you and Haku, can you come too?"

Later, I was getting ready for my blind date with Eric and must say I had some ambivalent feelings. "Hey, Karina, Marcy, does this look okay?" I pointed to my deep turquoise sundress and sandals. Kala went to grab a comb to brush the back of my waist-length blonde hair, then continued to smooth it with her little hand.

"Oh, yes, the color makes your eyes look like the ocean. Good choice!"

The doorbell rang, and when Karina opened the door, there stood the tallest man I had ever seen in my life! Eric had brown hair, brown eyes, and an athletic build. He was of mixed Polynesian and German heritage. He had erect posture with clean cut hair, wearing Khaki slacks and a Hawaiian shirt. He was somewhat handsome in a rugged way; however, there was no immediate chemistry. This Eric seemed like the type who was used to girls flocking to him and not vice versa.

What I did like, though, was his kind, broad smile and white teeth. Karina graciously performed the formal introductions. She then added,

"I'm sure you two will have a great time! Enjoy yourselves!"

As she scooted us out the door, I noticed Marcy and Kala had sly grins on their faces when I turned to say good-bye. Hmm, so far my date seemed comfortable, with his big arm at my waist, guiding me to the car. We went to dinner that evening at a wonderful restaurant on Waikiki Beach. Amazingly, the conversation just flowed between us. Eric sat across from me, and talked about playing football at the University, his family, his last serious relationship, and so on. I had two glasses of Sangria wine, while Eric had a few beers. I truly enjoyed the company but still felt no romantic connection. It had been so long since I had a crush on anyone—maybe in tenth grade? *Am I just picky, in search of my pseudo-man?* Of course, pseudo means false—the man so perfect that he doesn't exist. I'm not even sure if I even knew what man or type was most perfect for me. My grandma always said, "You will know it when you see him." She said she didn't know what love was until the very moment she met my grandfather, when she almost said out loud, "This is the man I'm going to marry!" Was Eric my pseudo-man? No...no, he was not, but there would be plenty of time to find him.

After dinner, Eric and I decided to walk on the beach, and he suddenly stopped and looked at me. I cringed and thought, *Oh-oh, first kiss time*. Yep, I was right, but no stars or fireworks. Eric said, "Hey, there's this absolutely incredible place called The Fern. It's the most romantic place in Honolulu!" I thought to myself that it was getting late, but thought it would be nice to see the most romantic spot on this beautiful island. We were in the car and seemed to be going away from Waikiki beach.

"How far is this place, Eric?"

"Oh it's just around the corner!" he said as he gave me a sly grin. After several turns, his Corvette stopped in front of a nicely manicured home that had ferns planted everywhere. I started to feel uncomfortable and not happy that Eric was deceptive about taking me to his "Love Shack"! I squirmed as I said,

"Hey, Eric, I had a great time, but I'm ready to go home."

Thank goodness, he was a gentleman and took me home—but not without trying to talk me into coming in for "just a drink or two."

Karina was a bit disappointed that Eric and I didn't have a love connection but continued to think of other eligible men in the area. That week continued to be busy as I contemplated staying in Hawaii permanently. Marcy and I went to Queens Hospital to apply for jobs and to the University of Hawaii for a tour. Unfortunately, the out-of-state tuition made it impossible to afford, but it was still nice to dream. It was a possibility if I worked really hard and considered a local junior college. Marcy slept in late almost every day, sometimes until noon or later. So Kala became my little friend and jogging buddy. Oh, yes, she still would do the Samoan nose blow now and then, just to see me gag, which she found hysterical. She'd say, "Haole, you get the funniest look on your face when I do that!" Then Kala would mock me and act like she was gagging too. She always managed to make me laugh.

One afternoon, Marcy wanted to buy souvenirs for her mom and sister. She asked if I wanted to go to the International Marketplace and shop for a while.

"Oh, yes! I'd love to!"

A cab dropped us off, as Karina had left earlier with the kids. We walked to several shops and then passed one with a small sign, "Psychic." Its neon "Open" sign was lit. I pulled Marcy's arm and said, "Hey this is the same address of the guy who gave us a business card!" She stomped and said, "Oh, Moe, that guy was crazy!" Too late, I was already in the door as the man was finishing a reading. Marcy said, "Okay, but I'm only staying for five minutes, then I'm outta here!" The tan, long-haired psychic smiled. "Oh, you came back. Good!"

The cost was more than I had, so I asked if he could give me a discount by doing a very short reading. We sat at the table as Marcy listened in on the other side of the drape. The psychic took both of my hands in his while closing his eyes for several minutes before he spoke. The room was so quiet, you could hear a pin drop.

"You have many guardian angels looking after you. In the past, they have saved you from evil intentions and pushed you far away from it. Not all will be as lucky." As he said that, I assumed he was possibly referring to Leslie. He continued,

"You are meant to eventually live where it's warm year round, where you can feel the gentle sea breeze, close to coastal waters, but it's not in

Hawaii. You are meant to go home to finish your education. If you stay here, you will not. There will be too many obstacles." In your last four decades, I see a bridge. There are two. One is the tallest bridge I've ever seen! The other is a calm serene place where you will retire. Chenango... Chenango Bridge.

"Wow, that's amazing!" I said. "Do you have time to tell me anything else?" He squeezed my hands for a moment.

"Listen to your guardian angels. Life won't be easy; however, they will be there to help and show you the way." The older man then released my hands, and we both stood up.

"Thank you so much, that was very interesting!" I said.

He gave my shoulder a firm pat. "There is one last thing I will tell you... Sometimes, with prolonged anger and negativity, family members can be their own worst enemies. Eventually, it reaches a point when the family unit self-destructs and the members become strangers to one another. Take what you've learned here and start your long mission to stop the cycle. It's not too late."

Marcy poked her head through the curtain with an impressed look on her face.

"Man, that was deep! What can you tell me?"

Just as she finished her sentence, a couple walked in for their scheduled reading. He chuckled and said, "This one is for free! Do more, listen more, and take less!" The man escorted the other clients back and turned, saying, "Thanks for stopping by girls! Good luck!" Marcy grumbled the entire way out the door.

"What the hell did he mean by that? Awe, he's a quack!"

The following day I called my mom, and she informed me that our phone was ringing off the hook! As I was in need of additional funds for school, I was trying to sell my new Chevette and purchase an old used car. My mom had placed an ad in the local paper—with a typo. It was listed as a new Corvette (super-cool, expensive car) for the price of a new Chevette (basic starter car that's *not* as cool). There's quite a price difference in price. Those reading the ad thought it was quite a steal! June was frustrated and asked, "When are you coming home so you can handle this yourself? Do you realize school starts in another month?"

I thought, *Oh, and I miss you too, Mom!* Slowly I answered, "Hmm, I was thinking about it and will be home soon. I'll let you know, so you can pick me up from the airport."

Yes, that was the moment I decided it was time to move on and head back home. I had to go, after all. There was my wrinkly bulldog Maggie, my lifelong friends, and the need to prepare for my future as a registered nurse. That night, I had a long conversation with Karina and Marcy. What an amazing person Karina was; she had me camp out at her house for a month and still wanted me to stay. The hospital also called Marcy and me to schedule interviews.

"Think about it Moe, okay? But if you decide to go home, you can always come back when you graduate!"

So far, Marcy still planned to stay; however, Karina would be discussing new rules for her. First, she would need to find a job; second, no more sleeping until noon or even later; and third, she would need to pitch in with household duties.

That Friday morning, all the girls piled in the car to take me to the airport. Kala looked sad and held my hand the entire way. I was trying so hard not to cry at the thought of leaving this wonderful family. I truly learned so much from them and couldn't wait to share my experiences with Ann and Marie. We exchanged hugs and some tears. When I turned to start boarding, Kala handed me a letter. "Wait and read it on the plane, okay?"

Once I found my window seat, I opened up the envelope, and the note written in pencil read:

Aloha Moe,

You are my pretty Haole sister from the Mainland. I will never forget you and hope you don't forget me either. I had so much fun going to the beach with you, making sand castles, listening to your stories about St. Louis, and going running with you. Last night I had a dream about the next time you come to see me. In my dream, you were a grownup and a real nurse. You made me want to become one too. Maybe I will. So remember your family here, and Aloha, until we meet again.

P.S. Aloha means both hello and good-bye. Oh, and P.S., if you are running and don't have Kleenex, remember the Samoan nose blow!

Your sister, Kala

Once again, Kala made me laugh, but I felt sad, too, at the thought of leaving my little friend. I held onto her letter while gazing out the window at the island below. Sadly, that day was the last time I ever saw my Polynesian family.

We continued to exchange letters for three years. Then one day Karina told me that Haku was getting transferred, and they were moving away to the Big Island of Hawaii. They never knew how much their love, kindness, compassion, and zest for life still influenced my life almost three decades later. *No, Kala, I will never forget you...ever.*

On my flight home, I sat next to a well-dressed Asian man. For more than an hour, he didn't even look at me or say a word. Then, slowly, we broke into conversation about our families, which lasted the entire trip across the Pacific. He was a retired research scientist who also resided in the Midwest. He was the father of four adult children, all with successful careers. Mr. Chen had the look of intelligence, but sadness was reflected in his eyes.

"I was goal oriented and too immersed in my career. Unfortunately, that meant I had little time for my children. My wife was the one who attended their recitals, their games, their conferences. It didn't seem important at the time, as I knew we could all catch up when I retired. Now I'm retired, and it's my wife they ask to talk to when they call. It's my wife they come to visit. They never really have much to say to me. Now I have all time in the world, yet I am a stranger to my own children."

Long after we said our good-byes, Mr. Chen's words stayed with me—that he thought "later" he would make up time with his children. Yes, later, when he had more time for his children. As a young lady, I learned a valuable lesson on that trip home: one may never have a second chance at forming special bonds with loved ones.

CHAPTER 15

When I walked in the door after my long trip across the Pacific, June said,

"It's about time!"

That meant, I was in Hawaii way too long and needed now to prepare for nursing school. Due to insufficient funds, I practically gave my new car away to Sam to have some money for tuition. There was not enough left over for a decent car, but enough for a used grey Jeep. It looked so sporty without the canvas top, and because the sun was shining, I left it off. I'm not sure if I was given instructions as how to put it back on before I left. I was back to working full time at the nursing home and picked up any extra shifts that were available. I had this overwhelming fear that I wouldn't be able to make enough money for my first semester or boarding at the dorm. The school was located in downtown St. Louis, in a high-crime area. The projects were just a few blocks down from the hospital, and the state mental institution was across the street.

On the day of my registration, I was running late and decided there wasn't enough time to put the top back on. The clouds were moving in fast, though, as I headed toward the highway. A lightning bold lit up the sky, and black clouds now loomed so low I could almost touch them!

It was then I knew I had to turn off to an old boyfriend's home to see if he could help me put the canvas top on the Jeep. The wind was blowing fiercely, and it started to rain as I ran up to his door. No one was home except his mother. I was amazed that Mrs. Cunningham offered to help me tackle the project. Let me tell you, it was not easy. The wind would blow off the canvas, just as we started to button up the sides. We were persistent, though, and managed to tuck, pull, and snap the sides to secure the canvas. Or at least so I thought! While I was driving down the highway, the top bowed and popped repeatedly, and I expected it to blow right off! Thank goodness, it somehow stayed attached.

The nursing school was on the west side of the hospital, which was located on the corner of Lafayette and Fourteenth. This old majestic Georgian revival structure was so rich in history that going to school here seemed like an exciting adventure! The hospital was initially built in the mid-1880s to serve the cholera-infested city. The hospital site was built over an old, abandoned cemetery, which was creepy, yet also fascinating.. Unfortunately, the city remained segregated back then and only accepted white patients. African American physicians also had difficulty getting staff privileges at the city's only public hospital that served the poor. A second large city hospital was built several miles away in the north side of St. Louis in 1937, the Homer G. Phillips Hospital (1880–1931). It was named after a prominent local attorney who fought for a public hospital that would serve the area's indigent black population. Unfortunately, Homer G. Phillips passed on before he was able to see this amazing hospital that was built in his name. As a middle-class girl from a predominately white suburb, this was my voyage into an incredible and culturally diverse learning experience.

I parked my old Jeep in the doctors' parking lot, as it was closest to the building.

"Ma'am! Ma'am!"

I turned and looked to see a security guard approaching my car. He said, "You can't park there! It's for doctors only!"

Awe, darn! I thought. *Caught!*

"Sir, I'm looking for the nursing school. I'm a new student. Can I still park in the employee lot, just for today?"

He smiled and said, "No problem, just for today, okay, missy?"

A light bulb went on in my head, and I turned around to face the guard.

"Oh Sir! Can you help me with the canvas top on my Jeep? The wind almost blew it off!"

The guard came closer to examine how the top was applied and laughed out loud. "Sheesh, it looks like my grandmother could've done a better job! Missy, come on over so I can give you a quick lesson!" After my lesson and re-parking my Jeep, there were now only minutes left to spare. Thank God, the rain stopped just in time as I ran to register.

The building's interior was amazing, with pillars, a stately fireplace, and marble floors in the beautiful parlor. It smelled and looked ancient, though, like the old nurse behind the desk in a stiff white cap and uniform. She almost looked like a statue. In a monotone voice, she introduced herself as the resident nurse of the dormitory. *Hmmm,* I thought to myself, *she probably runs a tight ship, which means no wild parties.* In looking about the room, there were several men in our program who were in their mid-twenties to late thirties. It wasn't as common to see men in nursing programs in the seventies. I noticed a tall girl with long brown hair that fell to her hips. She seemed shy, but had a nice face.

"Hi! I'm Moe Bender! Are you registering for the freshman class?"

She turned and smiled at me. "Yes, I am. Nice to meet you, Moe! I'm Candy Venetti."

We exchanged stories about how we ended up at City Hospital's program. I told her that one of my favorite nurses, named Juanita, had attended City's program many years ago. I thought she was the most skilled and compassionate nurse that I ever had the honor of working with at the Nursing home."Juanita was my mentor and actually arranged my first tour here last spring!" I told her.

Candy looked at me and said, "I'm pleasantly surprised that you're so friendly! You seemed like the stuck-up type at first! No offense, but glad I'm wrong." To tell you the truth, I've always appreciated honesty (yes, even brutal honesty) more than when someone sugarcoats how they really feel. The ones who say what people want to hear rather than what they feel. Of course, I'm not referring to" brutally mean," but when a person innocently shares how they feel, one on one. I replied, "No problem, Candy! Hey, after the testing, let's check out the dorms!"

Almost two hours had gone by before we filled out our forms, paid for tuition and books, took our math/pharmacology exam, and had a short intro to our professors. Then Candy and I met up to explore the dormitory. The building had the dorms upstairs on the second and third floors, and there were two kitchens on each floor, with standard shower and toilet facilities. Our rooms had one twin bed, an old-fashioned radiator for heat, no air conditioning, one dresser, and a sink. My room was, unfortunately, on the other side of the hall from my new friend, Candy. The classrooms and offices were on the first floor, and the library and additional classrooms were on the ground floor. There was also a creepy, long, winding underground tunnel, with holes in the walls and peeling paint, from the dorms to the hospital. The woman giving us the tour pointed out that the tunnel would also lead us right to the hospital cafeteria. That was where we would eat our meals for the next three years! Little did I know then how tired I would become of turkey tetra-terrible, watery scrambled eggs, and some of the other routine foods in the cafeteria!

It was a beautiful day, so I decided to take the canvas doors off my Jeep on my way home. Yes, call me naive and not used to being in areas where crime rates were much higher than the burbs. It wasn't long until, at a stoplight, a carload of guys and girls threw a can of soda at the car. I felt some of the sugary caramel spray before it bounced off the door and into the street. It was then that I learned not to take my frickin' doors off when driving downtown!

I spent the weekend with my family before my program started. I will be immersed in nursing school for the next three years with little time off during the summer. . Charlee was coming home, planning to go to a bingo hall in Granite City with Mom and her friend Berdie. I never caught the bingo bug, especially as it meant also being subjected a smoke-filled hall. That was pure torture to me! Marie would be going away and starting her nursing program in Cape Girardeau, so I was hopeful we would have time to see each other before she left. As for Ann, she was now engaged to be married and managing a banquet hall.

The weekends were her busiest time, and there was little chance we would see one another. I went over to Marie's before she left Sunday morning and brought a care package filled with goodies and a poem that I wrote for my dear friend Marie.

The longtime dream of graduation is past,
For the many years of high school ended all too fast.

Remember sitting through those cold football games?
Cheering, yelling, leaping, while trying to keep sane.

Remember how hard it was to keep your mind sound?
When after our North Victory, I swung you to the ground.
Remember all the friends we met that school brought about?
Each a lasting memory to share without a doubt!
Remember all the parties we said were such a blast?
Getting home at 1:30 a.m. explaining, "Dad, your watch is too fast!"
Remember the fun our obnoxious trio had?
Three faces of innocence saying, we're really not that bad!
But I'll remember Marie how you're one friend close in heart.
A bright future lies ahead and this is only just a start!

From your Sis Moe 1975!

Marie and I reminisced about all the memories, and then I gave her a hug good-bye so she could continue packing. I had only been home a short time when Charlee and my mom returned from playing bingo. Their faces were as white as ghosts when they walked in the door! I said,

"Hey, what happened? Lose all your money?"

Charlee shook her head, saying,

"You would not believe what we just went through!"

Mom then added, "Our guardian angels were with us. That's for sure!" She went on to explain that while driving home from the bingo hall, they came to a railroad crossing. Berdie, Charlee, and my mom heard the dinging of an oncoming train yet the guard rail was still up. The women all looked to the left and Berdie, who was driving thought she could still make it across. The small compact vehicle was on the track, when they suddenly looked to the right. That was when Mom saw the grill of the train in her window. It just seemed to pop out of nowhere! Instinctively, Berdie pushed the accelerator and the car cleared that track, then stalled.

"Whew", close call!" said Berdie

Charlee then started to hyperventilate as she looked up to see yet another train on the track they stalled on! What they hadn't realized was there wasn't just one track but ***multiple*** tracks at the crossing. That is when all three realized they were only seconds away from being hit by another locomotive! All three of the women prepared for impact. Berdie instinctively pressed the gas. June claimed for many decades later that the little compact vehicle actually flew off the track! Berdie and Charlee,... one by one, opened their eyes. In that split second, it was as if someone or something stopped time and ever so gently placed them in the arms of safety. Their car now faced the line of cars waiting for the rail to rise. People in the other cars were casually conversing as if nothing happened. No one got out of their car to comfort the hysterical women or seemed to wonder why they were on the other side of the crossing guard rail with the trains? Life went on as usual, as if they never saw a car miraculously escape being hit by two trains.

"Wow, how absolutely frightened you must've been! If you won anything at bingo tonight, then you should donate it to the church!" June, who wasn't known for her generosity, looked at me like I was crazy. After a pause, she said,

"I will certainly say a few extra prayers!"

That Sunday, Abby and I walked up to the shelter to pet all the homeless or runaway pets. There were many times that I wished we could bring them all home with us. Oh yes, I could clearly imagine...

"Hi Mom! Here we are with your new canine kids! Bourbon the mixed breed, Brandy the setter, Bubba the hound dog, Tango the shepherd, and all the others!" In my vision, all I could see was June, waving her arms while surrounded by all the slobbery kisses. It was just a dream, a funny one.

These precious dogs and cats were all so happy to have some attention, someone to pet and talk to them, even if it was only for a little while. Abby prayed they would all find homes; however, the reality was more than half would be put to sleep by Friday. I couldn't think about that, though, or I'd surely cry. What was important to us was that we somehow made them feel loved their last few days on Earth.

My bulldog Maggie was now five years old. She's so sweet that there was no shortage of hugs. I looked at her and felt sadness as I headed back to school.

"Be good, my little Mag-Pie, and no pooping in the house!"

Charlee was headed back to St. Louis University; I followed her in my Jeep, as we were both headed downtown. I pulled up at the same time another student pulled in with her car. She, too, was unloading her belongings and heading up to the dorm. Penny was a second-year student and worked at the hospital. She said, "I've been working since my freshman year. The hospital actually pays the students quite well to work in the hospital. It's convenient to finish classes and then walk through the tunnel to the hospital!"

That very next day, I applied for a job on my lunch hour. The program went from 7:00 a.m. to 3:30 p.m., Monday through Friday. I worked from 4:00 p.m. to 11:30 p.m. or midnight three or four days a week and some weekends. I would then study from midnight to 3:00 a.m., and then wake up at 6:00 a.m. Over the first few weeks, Candy and I were able to meet several dynamic women in the program. All except two were on the same floor at the dorm. We formed a study group that met on a regular basis and before each test. In the group, we had twenty-eight-year-old Sandy, a vibrant, barely five-foot-tall blonde, who lived with two medical students at a nearby condo. Then there was Muriel, sometimes outspoken, who was married, living in a trailer in Illinois; then five-foot-nine, attractive, sweet-natured Candy; then flirtatious, three–times-divorced, black-haired Deanna. She most certainly had hardcore street smarts about life. Last but not least, there was me, Moe Bender.

I was newly independent and still so very naïve. My sandy brown hair was bleached very light and my skin was quite dark, after spending a month in Hawaii. The combination of personalities made our little study group enjoyable. Once we were in the parlor, flipping through the chapters until we were at "The 12 Cranial Nerves." "Ugh," I said, "how are we going to remember all of these? Let's see, maybe if we do some kind of mnemonic to remember the nerves." The girls were rattling off the twelve cranial nerves:

Olfactory, Optic, Oculmotor, Trochlear, trigeminal, Abducens, facial, Auditory (now vestiulococlear), Glossopharyngeal, Vagus, Spinal Accesory, Hypoglossal.

"Okay, girls, we have O,O,O,T,T,A,F,A,G,V,S,H...What can we do with that? Let's think!"

One by one, we put it all together and this is what we came up with—*Oh, Oh, Ohhhh, To Touch A Face And Gluteal Verrrry Special Ha!* That was followed by *our* laughter. Yes, it was absolutely silly, yet effective! We remembered our cranial nerves and their functions for the test.

The next morning we headed for the cafeteria for our pancake breakfast. Most of the girls had cash and kept their rooms stocked with junk food. I, on the other hand, didn't have extra money for snack food. By the time breakfast came around, I was starved!

As we walked down the underground tunnel, Candy said, "Geez, Moe, I don't know how you can walk down this dim, eerie tunnel at night after work! I'm uncomfortable in the daytime with all the noise. Have you heard it? Footsteps! Yes, I always hear footsteps behind me, and no one is there!"

"Hmm, you know, I *do* hear noises!" I told her. "Yes, a creaking and an echo, as if someone is calling me. I turn long enough to see plaster fall from the walls. You know I heard this hospital was built on an old cemetery!"

Candy's mouth dropped, "No way! Are you kidding me?"

I laughed at her expression. "Nope, I am not kidding you, and *yes,* it does freak me out to walk back to the dorm at night. That's why I run! I run so fast my side hurts."

I don't believe many hospitals existed in this day and age that had wards. They were basically long, wide halls with beds on each side. There were around thirty beds that day, maybe more or less, depending on the census. The patients frequently developed a cohesive camaraderie and looked out for one another. If someone at the very back of the ward needed something, then a message would travel up to the desk one by one. Patient at the end would say, "Hey, I need to go real bad, can ya tell the nurse?"

That patient would holler to the next, and the communication flowed patient by patient toward the front of the ward. This time it stopped in the middle, when someone with a booming voice just yelled, "Hey, Blondie! Vern needs a bucket, or he's gonna piss in bed!"

We would see things at City Hospital that were not usually seen at others in the area. City Hospital floors 1 and 2 had indigent patients, who unfortunately couldn't afford routine vaccinations. It was on one rotation to Homer G. Phillips that I saw my first case of tetanus, which is more commonly called lockjaw. This man was only in his early thirties and was experiencing severe and progressive muscle spasms, with rigidity to the point where his back was arched high up off the stretcher. He also had the classic "lock jaw," where the nerve toxin affects the muscles of the jaw and, in his case, muscles used to breath. The nerve toxin is found in the soil and can enter the system via a wound. This patient's condition became very critical, and he was moved to the ICU for close observation. The next day while on the ward, a patient in the back had a violent tonic-clonic seizure. His extreme spasms vigorously shook the whole bed. During the seizure, the patient bit his tongue, causing profuse bleeding from his mouth. There were so many patients and so few nurses. Unfortunately, it wasn't possible to keep an eye on everyone at all times. We were thankful to have any alerts from the eyes of concerned ward mates.

I had to work after clinical that day and was totally exhausted. A couple of staff nurses had called in, so we were the additional help. We were kept so busy throughout the day, none of us had a chance to eat lunch or drink water. If we did attempt to hydrate ourselves, we might not have a chance to go to the bathroom.

I believe many nurses develop that camel bladder as a result of not allowing themselves to pee and holding it for as long as humanly possible. So I walked back to the dorm, changed, finally went to the bathroom, and then back to work the 3p- 11 p.m shift. I stuffed my pockets with crackers then drank what might be my last drink of water until I came home. This was my third seventeen-hour day, and it was taking its toll on me. I was pale, losing weight, and dehydrated; however, this is what I had to do.

I was assigned several patients on the left side of the ward, and there was only one other student nurse on the right side. The darn nursing instructor was constantly breathing down my back, making sure every corner of the bed was mitered perfectly (military style). The professor also monitored my every move, and we were taught how to deliver safe, quality nursing care. But in the evenings when I worked, I was on my own. I prayed for God to guide me, to somehow assist me through the night without making any mistakes, when at times there wasn't anyone to ask for help. Staffing in the facility was horrendous, so the administration was thankful for medical students and nursing students to help cover shifts.

My new patient had cellulitis from injecting heroin into her arms, legs, toes, or anywhere there was a vein. Drug addicts would frequently reuse and even share their needles and develop an infection—often a serious one. The resident on duty needed some blood drawn on her, which ended up being mission impossible! Emma, the patient said,

"No way you're gonna find a vein, honey! The only one who *can* is me!"

I looked up from scanning her arm for anything that looked or felt like a vessel.

"Emma, I'm sorry, but you can't draw your own blood. You're in a hospital, and that's not something your doctor would allow."

I attempted without success, then asked the medical student, who asked the intern and finally a resident physician.

He made another unsuccessful stab. Emma looked at the handsome doctor.

"You're cute, baby, but I'm not gonna allow you to keep sticking me like that. I ain't no pin cushion!

Now give me that needle!"

The resident now feeling defeated, said,

"Okay, let's see what you can do!"

Emma went directly to one that she knew would give her some blood. Before she stuck herself, I gave the area a quick swipe with an alcohol swab. "Bingo!" Emma was really proud of herself.

"Maybe I should be wearing that white coat and teaching you young doctors!"

Believe it or not, after 10:00 p.m., it started to slow down as the patients went to sleep. Emma was lying there awake, so I took the opportunity to get to know her better. I sat there and listened as she told me her story.

"Oh, I've just been through so much in my thirty-eight years; I'm tired, so tired. You know, I've been on the streets since my momma's boyfriend kicked me out. I was only thirteen years old! The only way I could eat was standing on corners, waiting for the next John. Some of those assholes were so rough that I needed drugs to deal with it. I have five kids, who are all in foster homes—or who knows where! I have no one, no one."

I felt so touched and sad at the harsh reality that she wasn't the only one living a life like that. "Emma, you've had one tough life and must be a strong woman to have gotten this far. I'd like to assist you somehow." I thought for a moment and went on, "I'll ask your physician if we can call social services for you. It's a start; maybe they can help you find a place to stay, rehab, counseling, whatever it takes to get you off the streets."

I suddenly heard a high-pitched screech: "Nurrrrrrrrse, nurrrrrrse!"

It was the senile elderly woman with uncontrolled diabetes and hypertension. She was massively incontinent and needed cleaning up and the linens changed on her bed. "Emma, I better go for now. I'll give social services a call. Hang in there, okay?" I gave her a hug before I finished my shift.

It was 12:30 a.m. when I closed the metal bars in the antiquated elevator to head for the tunnel. "Cling, Clang!" It always started off with a big jolt as it proceeded to move to the ground floor. Unfortunately, there was not one other student who was heading back late from the evening shift. For some strange reason, the tunnel seemed darker than usual and ever so quiet. I could hear my own steps and started counting them. Suddenly, plaster fell from the decrepit walls. I turned my head to scan the dark corridor. Then a swish of frigid air as if someone had run past me. That's when I heard a childlike giggling. I stood frozen, realizing I was being watched. I felt it, I knew it. Then I heard what sounded like the pedaling and squeak of an old vintage bike. Like, the one rode by the predator in California!

"Oh no!"

I said as I looked about the tunnel. I resumed counting my steps—40, 41, 42, 43—to take my mind off my tension. Then, like usual, I was so freaked that I ran the rest of the way to the dorm.

When I arrived in my room, I saw a large roach on my only toothbrush. Damn! "Get off, get off, yuck!" I proceeded to take hot water with some soap and washed it over and over before I brushed my teeth. My limbs were heavy, and my mind was foggy from fatigue. Just as I was drifting off to sleep, my room lit up like daytime, and I heard multiple sirens. The warehouse across the street was on fire! Police, firemen, and their trucks were everywhere! They battled the flames for hours, while I watched out my window. It must have been around 4:00 a.m. when I finally fell asleep.

That night I had a nightmare. Strangely, it wasn't about the predator. I was alone driving when I came to the tallest bridge I've ever seen! This bridge towered multiple stories over a large body of water.

I'm not usually fearful of heights, yet in my dream I was panic stricken! As I hyperventilated my arm fell off the steering wheel, as if I had a stroke! My car suddenly and violently went out of control as if hit the median and flew off the side of the bridge! I bolted upright in bed and awakened before my car hit the water. The nightmare was so disturbing that I prayed it would never reoccur!

The next morning I was frantic when I realized my homework was due that day. Candy was knocking on my door.

"It's time for breakfast, Moe!"

I quickly jumped out of bed. "Candy, I didn't finish the homework!" She casually and calmly said, "Me neither. Get dressed and we'll put our heads together at breakfast!' Feeling more reassured, I replied, "Great! Let me do a TPA" (which meant a quickie sink bath—Tits, Pits, and Ass) "and I'll meet you in the cafeteria!"

The tunnel didn't seem so frightening during the day. Of course, there was more activity, and when I heard footsteps, I thought of student traffic. All the girls for the study group were seated at the lunch table. I went through the line for a huge stack of pancakes. My stomach was already growling at 4:00 a.m., and by now I was starved! It turned out all of us either had worked or gone out on dates, and no one finished their homework. Sandy, who was like the older team captain, said,

"Moe, you take question number one, Candy the second, Deanna the third, and so on."

Our table was quiet for a good twenty minutes.

I looked up when I finished my portion of the assignment and passed it to the others. I began pouring gooey syrup all over my pancakes. My mouth was starting to water like Pavlov's dog. I happened to glance up and noted a table of medical students facing ours. One was staring at me with this serious expression, no flirtatious smile. "Hmmm" I said out loud, while poking Candy, who was seated next to me. Like a ventriloquist, I attempted not to move my lips while whispering,

"Candy, look at that guy directly across from me."

My friend looked up. "Maybe you look like an "ex" or maybe he just has indigestion." The med student wasn't eating or drinking, just staring. Some of those at his table turned to see who he was looking at and grinned. I tried not to look up, as it was making me feel uncomfortable. It would have been different if he smiled and waved hello. I would have smiled and said hello, too! Sandy and the others were now ready to discuss our conclusions for each section. We were now all talking, writing, and gulping down food at the same time. Anxiously, I looked at my watch.

"Dang, we've got to leave now!"

I turned one more time, and his eyes almost pierced mine. As we stood to leave the table of medical students laughed. Yes, even the one who had the psycho-serious look. They just wanted to poke fun and intimidate us student nurses. I once again turned and smiled back at the pranksters

On returning that afternoon from a hectic day in clinical, the resident nurse called me to the desk. In her monotone voice, she said, "Moe, a woman dropped off this note to you." I was confused at first, wondering who it could be from. When I unfolded the corners, it read:

Dear Moe,
Thank you for caring. You will make a great Nurse someday.
Emma

"Wow, reading a letter like this makes me want to try harder to be the nurse she thinks I am."

Candy was reading over my shoulder, "Awe, that was sweet!"

In clinical, I'd had quite a challenging day, with a disoriented patient constantly climbing out of bed, another who refused her medications and one who had profuse vomiting.

I can tolerate many things—urine, diarrhea, blood—but I still gag horribly when someone vomits! It was embarrassing, and sometimes I wondered if I was made for this profession. This short note from Emma made me realize that I was.

I had a night off work and was excited that all of us girls were going out to eat at one of my favorite restaurants, called Calico's. They had the most incredible thick-crust pizza. Yes, thick crust with sausage, mushroom and onions! The salad was also delicious with provolone cheese and lots of dressing! I made sure to set aside some money to treat myself. It was also nice to just talk about something other than nursing. Kathy was a year ahead of us. We always shared our dating experiences, and Kathy never had a shortage of men.

"Yes, girls, you should have seen him...tall, dark, and handsome, but he had a pencil dick! I was so disappointed!" We always had a good laugh about her penile adjectives. Kathy then held up her pinky finger. "It wasn't even as long as this when hard!"

Candy, who was recently divorced, asked, "Kathy, was it my ex-husband?"

Oh, geez! We were bad that night, worse than men the way we talked! Sandy was talking about how male roommates were easier to live with than females. Deanna asked if she slept with all of them.

"Heck no! Do you think I want to ruin a good thing? I'm their female friend whom they consult when they need advice about women."

Kathy then turned to me and asked, "Moe, I never hear you talk about dating. Are you seeing anyone?" I kind of rolled my eyes and told her that all I did was work and go to school! But, I told them, there was one person that I had seen off and on for years. My friends all said in unison,

"Really?"

"Yes, he went to another high school, but I met him in my junior year at a party." I decided to discuss our complicated relationship with my fellow nursing students.

Mason Cunningham had these huge brown eyes and a thick head of dark blonde hair, a mane that went to the middle of his neck. He was handsome, six feet tall, with massive muscles and only 8 percent body fat. What attracted me to him at first was what I ended up resenting in the end. The man had so many friends, both male and female, because he was the life of the party. He took many extreme risks and lived each day as if it were the last. It was exhausting trying to keep up!

You always knew when he entered a room because he had this *big*, booming, gravelly voice. When we were dating, he had many girl "friends" that would ask him to go dancing with them or call to get his advice when they needed something repaired. Mason had a mechanical knowledge and could literally fix anything. What I truly liked about him most, though, was his family, mainly his mom. She was a trendsetter, with her fashion sense, and was the first woman I knew who had a spiked crew cut and looked amazing! Elizabeth—Liz—walked every morning; she was always tan, well-traveled, and a great conversationalist. We had a wonderful friendship, and I loved her vivacious energy. I wanted to be just like her when I was older. Mason's parents also always worked hard to make every holiday festive with great food, decorations, games, and laughter. So when we did break up, it was his family that I missed most.

The first time Mason and I broke up was because of tennis. We had been dating for six months or so, and Mason was determined to make me a better tennis player. I love sports, but tennis wasn't my forte. Geez, talk about competitive; he had no patience or mercy for starting out slow for me. The guy practically slammed the tennis ball down my throat when we started to volley. I yelled, "Hey! I thought we were warming up!" It turned more into some comical routine, with me running around avoiding being hammered by his shots. He sarcastically said,

"I'm here to play a competitive game, not volley all day!"

On one particular sunny day, I happen to mention that Mason and I were playing tennis at his old high school. One of my "friends," who happened to hear me, perked up when I mentioned Mason's name. Later, Mason and I were just about to start our game as scheduled when this annoyingly flirtatious brunette showed up, holding her tennis racket.

"Oh, I just happened to stop by, can I join you?"

Now, did I mention that the girl was on the tennis team, and this court was miles from her home? The girl barely knew Mason, but she liked what she saw. Unfortunately she didn't care if he already had a girlfriend. They eventually started making arrangements to play separate from me, and I broke up with Mason when I found out. We didn't see each other again until my senior year. Breakup number two was about his chronic tardiness for dates because he was with his guy friends. So it was on again, off again. He was a good person and a hard worker, but his friends were number one. I was ready to wait for someone who was more mature and willing to make me a priority in their life.

That evening I left the restaurant at around 10:30 p.m., and as I parked the jeep, my door suddenly was jerked open! I looked up frantically to see who was there. A disheveled older woman, with her blouse gaping open, screamed,

"Help! I've been gang raped!"

Before I could answer, the woman continued to ramble on.

"This man I was seeing, he left me at a house with these strange men. They started attacking me! Help!"

The emergency room was close, very close, so I got out of my car and walked her to the desk. The staff quickly took the woman to the back and called the police. My life had been far from normal the past year, with exposure to such chaotic and bizarre incidents.

Yes, I was ready for a slow, uneventful day, where the only excitement would be having enough money to go to Calico's for one of their salads topped with provolone cheese and house dressing and a big slice of thick crust pizza with sausage, mushroom and onion toppings!

The first year of school seemed to fly by, with clinical and classes Monday through Friday from 7:00 a.m. to 3:30 p.m. By the beginning of the second year, I started to work almost full-time hours to make enough money for tuition for the next two years. Mason and I would go out on the weekends I was home. His mom and I renewed our friendship and she treated me like another daughter. On several occasions, while she shopped during the week, she would buy me some much-needed clothes. I was awestruck at her kindness and generosity! Liz always had something to talk about and rarely ever was in a bad mood.

One weekend when I was home, Mom was gone; she left earlier that week to visit relatives in Wisconsin. I thought, *Awe, how lucky! Wish I could go!* It was strange, though, that Mom left without Big Al. *Oh well, good for her; it will be nice for her to visit Grandma and Grandpa McKinley.*

I returned back to school on Sunday to finish a nursing care plan. Back in the seventies, there were only two pay phones on each floor. I rarely if ever had anyone call me on it, until that day.

One of the students heard the phone ringing and answered. "Moe! Moe! Moe Bender! You have a phone call!"

I quickly jumped off my bed and ran out the door. I answered, "Hello?" I listened for a moment. "What? What's wrong? Did Grandma die?

It was Big Al on the other end, and he was so choked up that I could barely understand him. I was becoming more panic–stricken, waiting for him to clearly spit the words out. Someone knocked on the door, asking how long I'd be. I just flagged them away with my hand. When he finally told me why he was calling, I almost collapsed. "No, no! I can't believe it!"

I held the phone to my ear and let my dad finish telling me all he knew. I was crying as I left the phone booth. There were a couple of my friends waiting in line. "What's wrong, why are you upset?" In a trancelike state, I said, "I have to go, I have to leave. My cousin Bonnie was murdered."

CHAPTER 17

My cousin Bonnie was babysitting the two-year-old boy next door. The couple enjoyed having a night out with neighbors and routinely had Bonnie take care of little Ben. Later that evening the boy's parents returned to an unbelievably horrible sight. The couple scooped up their son and frantically ran out of the house. They were screaming wildly as they pounded on my aunt and uncle's door. They, too, had been out and got home just a short while before. The neighbors had found poor Bonnie, lying in a pool of blood on the kitchen floor. She had been stabbed more than a hundred times, while the child slept soundly in his bed. The back door was slung wide open, and bloody foot prints were still on the tile floor. Police from all over the county came to start investigating this brutal, senseless murder.

The next day, my whole family left together and drove almost the entire way in silence. I wondered what horrible monster murdered my beautiful, sweet cousin Bonnie? Why would he do such a thing? The weight of our incredible sorrow made our hearts ache. Once we arrived and saw my relatives, saw firsthand the extreme pain on my aunt and uncle's faces, it was almost more heartbreak than any of us could handle. There were reporters who came from miles away to cover the story about a popular high school teenager who was brutally murdered while babysitting. There were newspapers all over the country covering my cousin's tragic murder.

The funeral was a few days later. That same day, bloody clothing was discovered buried in a field not far from my cousin's home. The clothes belonged to one of the neighborhood boys who had a crush on Bonnie; he had been watching her for the last few months. Everywhere Bonnie went, Lenny was lurking nearby.

During the funeral, there were television station helicopters overhead that were covering the service.

The line of those who loved Bonnie wrapped around the entire building. There were hundreds, maybe a thousand that came to pay their last respects. There were so many tears that now freely flowed to the ground as everyone mourned the loss of this beautiful, kind, sweet girl.

Bonnie had so much to offer this world, such a bright future ahead of her. That is, if she had been given the chance to live a full life. Unfortunately, hers was cut short by such evil, by one with ice within his soul. It wasn't fair. I thought of the last time I saw Bonnie, when she came to visit us in St. Louis, how we were finding the different ways to sing "My Bonnie Lies over the Ocean." How beautifully she sang—she had the voice of an angel. Little did I know she would soon become one of God's angels. The image of my cousin singing that song played over and over in my head as I sat in the church pew.

> *My Bonnie lies over the ocean, my Bonnie lies over the sea,*
> *My Bonnie lies over the ocean, oh bring back my Bonnie to me.*
> *Bring back, bring back, oh bring back my Bonnie to me, to me,*
> *Bring back, bring back, oh bring back my Bonnie to me.*
> *Last night as I lay on my pillow, last night as I lay on my bed,*
> *Last night as I lay on my pillow, I dreamt that my Bonnie was dead.*
> *Bring back, bring back, oh bring back my Bonnie to me, to me,*
> *Bring back, bring back...*

Oh Lord, may our Bonnie rest in peace.

The police had sixteen-year-old Leonard Cobb in custody by the end of the week. That night, after Bonnie's body was discovered, the news had spread like wildfire throughout the neighborhood. Lenny's father immediately suspected his own son, due to his violent past. He was also aware of Lenny having stalked Bonnie the past few months.

Mr. Cobb went into Lenny's bedroom to look for his son. Lenny wasn't there; however, there were droplets of blood on the floor and bloodstained boots under his bed. Mr. Cobb was now violently trembling as he pulled out not only his son's boots but also clothing that was absolutely soaked with evidence.

"Oh, my God, *nooo! No*, Lenny, why?"

Mrs. Cobb now came into the room and screamed.

"*No*! Not our Lenny! He couldn't have done this!"

The boy was a loner, with a history of sudden violent outburst when provoked or teased. Bonnie was not only beautiful and popular but also sweet. She initially felt sorry for Lenny. She was always nice to him and everyone else at school. Lenny unfortunately mistook that kindness for something more, which led to his stalking Bonnie and eventually hunting her down like prey. Mr. and Mrs. Cobb scrambled to gather all the blood-soaked clothing and placed it in a plastic bag. A portion of their two acres had recently been plowed to prepare for planting a small crop of vegetables. Mr. Cobb ran to the field and started shoveling dirt like a madman.

"Lea Ann, Give me the bag! Give me the bag!"

Lenny's parents worked hard to conceal their son's boots, jeans, white T-shirt, and the kitchen knife found under his bed. When Mr. Cobb finished covering the bag in the two-foot hole, he collapsed on the ground and cried harder than he ever had before. Mrs. Cobb ran to the backyard, where Lenny was huddled under a willow tree. The police continued their investigation the next day, following the droplets of blood and footprints to the Cobb house. It wasn't long afterward that they found the clothes buried in the field.

This all seemed so surreal that I wanted to open my eyes and to realize that it was only a nightmare. The reality, though, was that none of our lives would ever be the same. There was a tragic void and anger we all felt, especially my aunt and uncle.

In one night, one senseless act of violence changed the life of hundreds and killed the dream of Bonnie's parents seeing their eldest child graduate from college, get married, and have children of her own. The world would never see how this caring, gifted young girl could have touched, healed, and inspired so many patients and people, the mentor she would have been had she lived long enough to fulfill her dream of becoming a physician. The light of hope grew dim, dark, sad, and cold that night, and ice started to freeze within so many souls.

The carefree world of the McKinleys, their neighbors, relatives, and anyone who read the paper or saw the news on this tragedy felt not only despair but also fear. Most households in their small town rarely if ever locked their doors during the day, but now they did. Parents were now fearful about leaving their children with babysitters. Parents wouldn't even allow their teens to babysit, unless they were accompanied by an older sibling, grandmother, or friend. The night of the funeral, the McKinley family and practically the whole community paid their respects at the house. My strong uncle and my beautiful raven-haired aunt tried to compose themselves and thank those who cared and loved Bonnie. Sadly, most of the time, though, they just sobbed on each other's shoulders.

At the end of the trial, everyone was horrified that this sixteen-year-old sociopath, who mutilated Bonnie with a hundred stab wounds, was tried as a juvenile. The judge gave Leonard seven years in prison. I thought, *My God, only seven years? Is that what Bonnie's life was worth?* My aunt and uncle and the whole community were filled with rage. But what I'm going to do is take you through a walk seven years into the future, the day that Leonard Cobb was released from prison in 1983.

Leonard had a jubilant skip as he pushed the duel prison doors open. He threw his head back and yelled, "Freeeeeedom!" while pumping both fists in the air. His parents quietly walked toward him, attempting to put their arms around him. Lenny swatted at their raised upper extremities while racing to the front seat of the car.

"C'mon! Let's get out of this hellhole!"

On the way home, Lenny's restless legs twitched violently, and a smug, wicked smile formed on his face. He felt that after seven years, he was smarter. He wouldn't make the same mistake twice. His "mistake" was getting caught—not the murder.

Once home, Lenny grabbed a six-pack of beer and closed himself off in his room. His mother wandered down the hall, placing her ear up against the door. She simultaneously tapped while opening, and then the wooden structure slammed back in her face.

"Get out! Leave me alone!"

The small, timid old woman covered her mouth with her hands. The harsh anger in Lenny's voice made her tremble. She wondered what he was plotting in his room. She stood there in silence as horrible thoughts filled her mind. He was gathering supplies and taking a mental note...masking tape, rope, knife...as he carefully placed the objects in his gym bag.

The first few nights after his release, Lenny got into the car to drive through the neighboring town. Slowly he drove through the parks and past schools, malls, or anywhere else he would find young, attractive women. There was one he liked enough to follow to her home. As the unsuspecting young girl went inside her house, Lenny smiled, as he could almost taste death.

Lenny was free for now. The next evening was the time he chose for following through with his plans. Lenny threw his gym bag in the back of his car and sped recklessly down the street. He decided to take the quieter, less traveled back roads to the next county. The music was blaring while Lenny was pounding wildly on the steering wheel. In his crazed state of mind, he would laugh out loud when he thought of what he would do to his victim. Then he started to experience some blurred vision. He was speeding at over ninety-five miles per hour as he began rubbing his eyes. When he removed his hands, his vision once again clear, he thought,

Damn dry eyes!

Then suddenly, and oh so clearly, a vision of Bonnie filled the windshield! Lenny screamed, and the car went violently out of control, rolled, and eventually came to a halt. Lenny was thrown fifty yards from the accident scene. An officer happened to be patrolling the area and saw the totaled car off the road. He had this uneasy feeling of dread as he noted a demolished car with no driver. The patrolman scanned the area in search of an accident victim. The weary officer happened to glance up toward the setting sun. He instantly gasped as he saw Lenny's body impaled high up on a tree. The thick tree limb penetrated Lenny's skull and exited his rectum. Ironically, the accident occurred at the corner of the rural highway and Justice Road.

Lenny's death wouldn't bring Bonnie back, but it did help calm the fears of the community. They felt it was just a matter of time before Lenny started looking for his next victim. After the funeral, it was more than ten years before I saw the Chicago McKinley family again. They had so many life changes, and so did the Benders. e all have good intentions of maintaining close family ties. We depart and say, "See you next time!" What we never really know is if there will be a next time.

The wonderful McKinley family struggled with the turmoil of losing Bonnie. Their lives were turned upside down, and sadness filled their lives for many years. Through God, they found strength and the will to move on, for Bonnie's sake. That's what she would have wanted. Their family became incredibly close, whereas others experiencing similar tragedy fall apart. It's a fight each day to prevent the ice from filling your soul; a fight to communicate when all you want to do is close down; a fight to be close when you're feeling cold inside; a fight to not act on your impulses and to be patient with the healing process. When you fight to stay close to those you love, in most cases you win by bringing the family even closer than before.

CHAPTER 18

It was around 10:00 p.m. when I pulled up to the dorm, and there were several men from the city neighborhood outside the dorm gates. They were all smoking cigarettes but stopped conversing when I walked up. Normally I would be frightened and just wait in my car until they walked away. Not now though; I didn't have time—I needed to get back to studying. I must've had this intense, "don't mess with me" kind of look on my face. My siblings tell me "it" (that look), can be pretty frightening. I guess the men thought so, too, and in silence they parted to let me through the gate. Fortunately, most of my friends were out when I returned to my room, where I unpacked and then went to bed. It was the first sound sleep that I had in several days. My eyes felt like dried-out prunes after all the crying at Bonnie's funeral, and it felt good to keep them closed.

The next morning I tried to get back in to my school routine. That meant putting on my super-starched, green-and-white nursing uniform and a wretched tall, pointed nursing cap that looked more like a witch's headdress. I can't begin to tell you how many patients' eyes I poked with that darn thing! What I can say about our uniforms, though, is that wearing them provided us with protection during home visits in the projects. We would frequently see elderly patients in high-crime areas without our instructors. That day, our first stop was to see Mrs. Bessie Barclay.

She had a history of hypertension, diabetes, and a non-healing wound on her lower leg. We made our visits in twos, and when my fellow student Lisa and I walked up to the door, the largest black man I had ever seen was on his way out. He had a long keloid scar that ran from his left ear to the corner of his mouth and several more on his arms. Both of our eyes were as big as saucers as he brushed past us. The large, jovial elderly woman laughed when she saw the look on our faces. "Girls, don't worry about safety here, 'cause no one wants to mess with Mama Bessie's nurses! There's jus' no way, child, especially not Lil Jerome."

In unison we both said,

"Little?"

Bessie sat in her wheelchair and explained,

Oh, Lil Jerome got the name when he was born two months early. It took him awhile to sprout, but once he started, the child just wouldn't stop! I practically raised him, so he's had his share of fanny paddling by Mamma Bessie."

I'm not sure about nowadays, but back then there seemed to be a respect in the projects for health care professionals who were helping those in their community. Yes, I believed Mama Bessie would keep us safe. She grew up in these projects and knew practically everyone, and many of them were related. The teens who were thrown out or homeless would frequently end up at Bessie's. She would, in turn, give them a hot meal and homegrown, street-smart counseling. Mama Bessie gave everyone a chance and often became the mother they never had.

The second visit for the day was at a dilapidated two-story home, where the mother and father lived downstairs and the mentally challenged adult daughter lived upstairs. The sixty-nine-year-old mother had just been released from psychiatric evaluation a couple of weeks earlier for chasing her daughter around the yard with an axe after finding her in bed with the stepdad. I turned to Lisa and said, "Whoa, I pray the daughter stays upstairs. I do not want to see any crazy jealous rages today, especially between a mother and a daughter—sad!"

We reached in through the large hole in the screen to knock on the door. We were surprised to see Mrs. Becker hobbling to the door with her walker. I wondered how she chased her daughter with an axe while maneuvering the bulky walker. The woman had a history of congestive heart disease, hypertension, peripheral neuropathy, diabetes...the diagnosed problems went on to page 2. We were there to repeat her blood pressure, count her medication (to check compliance), check her urine for glucose, make a notation of her mental status, and so on. Mrs. Becker slowly opened the door and let us in. She said,

"I made some fresh coffee for my nurses!"

She smiled at us as she poured coffee into three cups that were already set out on the countertop. Of course I accepted. Lisa and I realized it was Mrs. Becker's attempt to be hospitable and her way of showing her thanks. The weary old woman waddled to the table and groaned as she sank into the chair.

"Come over here, girls, and talk for a bit."

Mrs. Becker tapped on table with her arthritic, deformed fingers, encouraging us to sit and chat before her treatment. Her head still had a towel wrapped around it from her shower earlier in the morning. Her clothing had old dried perspiration stains under the arms, some tears, and a few buttons missing, but it was the best that she had to wear. My mind momentarily drifted as I thought about all the clueless pampered kids who never witnessed those living in the depths of poverty. Yes, maybe on television, but not firsthand. That day I had walked through the projects to a patient's dwelling; then now to this house, built in the early 1900s that had shutters falling off, no air conditioning, rodent feces scattered on the floor, and scant furnishings. This was a reality check for me, as I always complained about needing to work so hard for tuition, new clothes, and extra money for pizza. Most of the people we made home visits to barely had enough food to survive!

The touching part, though, was the fact they were all willing to share what little they had with us. Mrs. Becker revealed that she now lived alone, since her third husband moved upstairs with the daughter.

"I'm okay with that good-for-nothing man being out of my life. He's Elsie's problem now!"

We finished our treatment, and I asked Mrs. Becker if she wanted me to comb her hair. It had been wrapped in a towel for hours and stood straight up! Her little round face lit up like a light bulb, and she gave me the sweetest smile. "I'd like that, since I can't really hold my brush that well."

I thought a few moments while combing her hair, then tilted my head while the unedited words flowed out of my mouth. "Mrs. Becker, please excuse me, but how in the world did you hold that axe and run with your walker?"

She perked up and laughed. "Well, my good-for-nuthin' husband was running around with my daughter. Elsie's fifty years old, but he took advantage of her mental problems. No, I didn't want to hurt my daughter! I wanted to somehow teach that son of a bitch a lesson! My dang fingers are weak and messed up, though. I decided to put the axe in the basket on my walker. I gave them a pretty good chase with these fat old legs!" The elderly woman cackled like a hen as she walked us to the door.

That evening Sandy, Muriel, Candy, Deanna, Kathy, and I met at Calico's for pizza. I was absolutely starved; I had hardly eaten anything all day! We sat at the table, inhaling the amazing doughy scent of fresh pizza! I was like one of Pavlov's dogs, with drool forming at the corners of my mouth. Then I had a flashback of my home visits today. I thought to myself, *I'm so blessed. Thank you, God, for allowing me to have enough money to share this meal with my friends*.

The girls all wanted to hear the details of Bonnie's tragic murder and the funeral. It was tough reliving it all over again; however, it was comforting to have the support of my empathetic, close-knit group of nursing students.

CHAPTER 19

The following day at school went quickly, and I was pleasantly surprised that I didn't have any drama or wacky incidents. A stress-free day allowed me to have more mental energy for work that evening. After a couple of ICU nurses called in, I was pulled from the neurology floor to the coronary care unit. There was a new, handsome face in the unit that I'd never seen anywhere in the hospital. I thought the new guy looked more like a physician's assistant, as he looked close to my age.

He had this long, dark brown hair and intense brown eyes and looked like he fit better with a rock band than in a hospital. I wondered how he got away with wearing frayed blue jeans with his scrubs—and where was the lab coat? Several medical students were with him at the desk as I meekly walked up. He hastily looked up, and with and edgy, curt tone he said,

"I'm taking orders for Ted Drewes. Are you in?"

I looked puzzled and asked,

"Ted Drewes? What that?"

The new cute guy dared to roll his eyes at me! "Oh, geez, *you* are *not* from St. Louis! If you were, then you would know about Ted Drewes." I managed to be close enough now to read "Dr. Christopher" on his badge.

Then he managed to loosen up and give me a boyish grin.

"Okay, Ted Drewes has the most amazing custard in the whole city, maybe the state! In a nutshell, anyone who has been in St. Louis for awhile *knows* Ted Drewes."

The intensive care unit had each room filled—six patients, and two were on ventilators. One registered nurse was working that evening, and then there was me, a second-year nursing student.

Thank goodness there was feisty Dr. Christopher, who was a fourth-year medical student from Washington University, and another medical student from the St. Louis University side of the ICU. It seemed like I spent most of the time in the room of a critical patient who had meningococcal meningitis, a very serious bacterial infection of the thin lining around the brain.

The man, who was in his forties, had been drinking soda at a bar the day before when he suddenly passed out. The bartender, a friend of the patient's, stated he had complained of a horrible headache and blurred vision. By the time he got him to the emergency room, the man was comatose.

The patient never did regain consciousness during my shift, and his blood pressure continued to take a nose dive. Thank goodness the night RN came in early to help us out. The second patient was Mr. Paul, a fifty-year-old man with a history of Systemic Lupus Erythematosus. SLE is a systemic autoimmune disease that can cause tissue damage and inflammation to almost any organ. In Mr. Paul's case, his heart and kidneys were failing after living more than twenty years with the disease.

Mr. Paul was a sick man; however, he still maintained his sense of humor and flirtatious nature. He raised his head off his pillow and smiled. "Hey, Moe, I have a limerick for you!"

I chuckled and said, "Mr. Paul, is this it about the man from Blackheeth who sat on his false teeth?"

He laughed and replied, "No, Moe, that was yesterday's limerick!" The cute little man reminded me of a leprechaun, with his red hair and beard. "Today I made this one up just for you! Here ya go...

"There once was a patient at City (meaning City Hospital)
Who liked his nurses smart and pretty!
He himself was charming and witty!
Never complained like an old bitchy Biddy.

All alone wanting no man's pity,
Sittin' with a dang long tube in his ditty!"

I said, "Oh, my gosh, Mr. Paul! Does 'ditty' mean what I think it does? No, *no*, don't answer! What am I going to do with you?"

Mr. Paul was now slapping the sheets and laughing at his own humor. "I just made that up, Nurse Moe! I'm good, aren't I?" It was nice to have one patient who was at least alert and oriented with a crazy sense of humor. There were definitely times that he crossed my comfort zone with his innuendoes. He was right, though; he was all alone, and not one person came to see him while he was in the ICU. He wanted no one's pity, just someone to laugh at his goofy jokes...that's all.

It was now 12:30 a.m., and I was unbelievably happy to be leaving, especially as I still had homework to do. The only problem was that I didn't have enough time to talk to the cute doctor who dressed like a bum. As I walked out the double doors of the ICU, I felt a tap on my shoulder. It was Dr. Christopher, holding a small carton of Ted Drewes.

"Hey, you forgot your custard."

We made eye contact and smiled at one another before I snapped out of my giddy gaze. "Oh, yes! Thanks so much! Now I can really say I'm from St. Louis!" He grabbed his lab coat and accompanied me out of the chaos. Dr. Christopher cleared his throat and asked, "Hey, I thought I would walk you out to the car. It's not safe to be out in this neighborhood at any time."

I must say that I was truly flattered to have his protection. "Well, I won't be going to my car tonight, but I do have to walk through a creepy tunnel to the dorm."

We talked the whole way down the rickety iron-gated elevator to the basement and through the dark tunnel. It was the first time I made the trip without being frightened.

My new friend was Marc Christopher, born and raised in St. Louis. As we talked on our short walk, we seemed to have a lot in common. He had five siblings, and I had five siblings; he was also a Catholic; he seemed to be a financially struggling student, and so was I. We even had the same horoscope—my birthday was July 16 and his was July 8th. At the end of the tunnel, he gently grabbed my hand and asked me if I would like to join him for dinner at the family restaurant. The date was made for Friday evening.

I stood at the door and watched him turn back down the dark damp tunnel toward the hospital.

He was only several yards away when he jumped and quickly glanced back

"Moe, I felt someone give my backside a good kick! I thought it was you! No kidding!" Dr. Christopher eerily turned and scanned the peeling paint on the eerie tunnel.

"I'm freaked! Now who is going to walk *me* back?"

He then smiled, and waved at me with my phone number in his hand,

CHAPTER 20

The rest of the week seemed to drag by, as all I could think of was my date with a free-spirited, fun, gentlemanly young physician. It would be the first time that another man, other than Mason, intrigued me. The only problem was that my closet contained a few jeans, some sweaters, black slacks, and maybe one dress. When he called that evening he told me to dress casual, as it was "just the family restaurant." He said we'd probably take a walk afterwards in the park alongside their property. I had been running since the time I was fifteen years old and had been up to about thirty miles a week before I started nursing school. I was chronically a weight watcher, so the walk after dinner sounded great.

Mason called the next evening and asked if I was coming home for the weekend. He was an intelligent guy who, like his mom, had a photographic memory. At least that's what his mom said—but I wondered why he forgot so many of my birthdays. Whenever he discovered why I wasn't speaking to him, he would run up to Walgreens and get a milk carton box of chocolate malt balls. If Mason played trivial pursuit, though, he knew all the answers. He was not only smart but charming too at times. Yes, he had a real love for laughter and fun. I guess that's why I previously forgave him time and time again.

I informed Mason that I'd be spending Sunday afternoon with my family. My mom was making her famous homemade pizza, and I wasn't about to miss it. June's mouthwatering pizza masterpiece consisted of; a thick whole wheat crust that was soft on the inside with a crispy bottom. She had three different cheese toppings along with sausage mushrooms and onions. Doesn't get any better than that!

That Friday, Marc came to the dorm to pick me up. He had his dark hair pulled back and looked respectable with a nice beige cardigan sweater and... yep, frayed jeans. Oh well, like I said, money was probably tight for him, too. It's definitely expensive to pay for eight years of medical school. Marc stopped when he came to his old black '65 Chevy Nova. As we pulled out of the lot, his car started to knock so hard that I wondered if we were going to make it to his house at all. Marc looked up and smiled.

"Yikes, sorry, I should have looked into that noise but didn't have time!"

I reassured him that if we broke down, we could always walk.

"You live in the city, don't you?"

There were snow flurries as Marc turned off the street and onto the highway. He looked at me like I was crazy.

"Heck no, I live in unincorporated west county, not the city."

The snow started to fall so hard that Marc looked like an old man, leaning forward behind the wheel. We both actually struggled to see through the snow-covered windshield. After several miles, we finally exited off the highway and drove along tree-lined streets to the front of a quaint little restaurant. When we opened the thick mahogany doors, there was a comforting aroma of logs burning in a fireplace.

There were only a few patrons inside due to the inclement weather. Marc gently took my hand to lead me to the kitchen, where he introduced me to the staff. They had the same crew for more than ten years and were all more like an extended family to Marc. From there we went to the fireplace to warm up, and the bartender brought two glasses of hot spiced wine. In the corner of the room, an elderly woman set a cozy table, serving us a crisp tossed salad with warm homemade bread.

Marc pulled out my chair for me, and we began the most romantic evening I had ever experience. Yes, that is what it was, an experience where all my senses were taking in phenomenal scents of winter, wine, toasty fire, light sweet touch, and the sight of the incredibly amazing man in front of me.

After dinner the snowfall gradually stopped, and a thick blanket of snow glistening a bright bluish tone under the full moon. We walked hand in hand down the long, winding lane to his parents' home. It was a beautiful Colonial on several acres behind the restaurant. How sweet and polite to introduce me to his parents on the first date!

They must have been watching out the window, because they greeted us at the door with broad smiles. My first thought was what a handsome youthful couple they were, and how they still seemed truly happy after almost thirty years of marriage.

We all sat in their family room, which was filled with warm, inviting colors and a soft sofa situated by a stately brick and stone fireplace. The time flowed with friendly conversation. Marc and I had another hot spiced wine before we left for a walk through the glistening snow-filled park next door. The beauty of it all was breathtaking, with the scene looking more like a winter wonderland. We ventured off arm in arm, talking about everything under the sun from family, education, goals and friends. The time flew by so rapidly that I didn't realize it was past midnight. What was strange was that I had a feeling as if Marc and I had known each other forever, rather than it being our first date. There was now more than ten inches of snow on the ground, and needless to say, there was no going home now. That is, at least not until they plowed the major intersections. We sat by the fireplace, talking some more, until finally we shared a long, passionate kiss that seemed to last until the wee hours of the morning. I finally fell asleep on the arm of the couch when Marc left to gather logs for the fire.

At 6:00 a.m., I slowly opened each heavy eyelid and was momentarily confused when Marc's face was almost pressed against mine. What the heck? In my sleep deprived state of mind, I almost wondered where I was and who "He" was! I then looked down to make sure we both had our clothes on! Whew, yes! The clothes were zipped and intact! Then I recalled how we were snow bound for the night at his parent's house.

At that moment, I realized my mouth was like the Sahara Desert, and I wished I had a toothbrush—STAT! How comfortable this all was, and amazingly easy to spend so many hours with someone I hardly knew.

I found my way to the restroom to splash off my face and rinse my mouth with several swishes of water. I tiptoed back into the family room where Marc was sitting on the couch with his hands folded behind his head. When I walked into the room he gave me the sweetest smile; it made me grin from ear to ear. He said cheerfully, "Good Morning!"

" Good Morning to you too!" I replied.

I then looked out the window and saw the major thoroughfare by the restaurant had been cleared. There were now huge mounds of snow piled along the edge of the street. We quickly left before any other family members awoke; however, I was sure his noisy car engine would wake up the whole neighborhood!

That weekend it seemed like I walked with my head in the clouds with one thought only...my romantic new friend. On Sunday morning, when I was leaving my parents to head back to school, I saw this snowflake crystal hanging from my rearview mirror. The bright sun's rays were reflecting a brilliant variety of rainbow colors through the prism. One illuminated a little note on the dash. Marc must've researched my address and drove more than twenty miles to my parents' home.

"Wow!"

I said out loud. "He did this for me." I was touched more than words could say. I made up my mind that I was going to break up with Mason, once and for all. No more on again, off again. This time it's for good. Truth be told, having Mason as a mate was like trying to confine a wild stallion. He wanted to roam and be free, but he didn't want me to. Mason would probably be a better friend anyway than boyfriend; he had many loyal "girl" friends who really enjoyed his company. No matter what we did socially, Mason and I were rarely alone. Marc, on the other hand, seemed to enjoy being with me, one on one, as if nothing or no one else mattered.

On Sunday night I once again worked in the ICU. Oh, geez, I wondered when in the heck I'd have a chance to do my homework. There would be no sleep after work; I knew I'd have to study till dawn. What I wouldn't do for eight hours of REM! On my way up the elevator, I wondered what corny limerick Mr. Paul would have for me. It made me smile, just thinking about his humor. A couple residents were in his room when I turned the corner. The cardiac monitor was showing a supraventricular tachycardia that was racing wildly across the screen.

Mr. Paul's eyed were glazed and only half open. Slowly, I walked closer to touch his hand. Mr. Paul raised his head slightly to look at me. He weakly asked,

"Are you an angel?"

I patted his hand gently.

"Mr. Paul, it's me, Moe."

Mr. Paul had no recognition of my face or my name. He closed his eyes and mumbled,

"Angel, please tell the Lord I'm ready."

Mr. Paul died that night at the age of fifty. How could someone live fifty years and not have one person that cared enough to be with him when he was critically ill or when he passed away? In the short time I had been in nursing, there had been dozens and dozens of people who died without family or friends present. I momentarily reflected back to when I was eight or nine years old, when there was a stray cat in a field with a bluebird in his mouth. I chased the cat until he dropped the poor injured bird. Tears were streaming down my face as I gingerly petted the small blue bundle of mangled feathers. I stayed with him until he took his last breath and died in my hands. It was important to me then, as it is now, that all of God's creatures have someone to care for and comfort them in their final moments. Why do so many die alone?

When I came home that night, I found myself reflecting on my own life. The fact that no one ever came to visit Mr. Paul haunted me. It made me want to somehow leave my mark, make a difference, and surround myself with people who care. Unfortunately, the people who care aren't always members of the family. My own mother and I had grown distant, but I prayed it could be different down the road. It would be nice if I could have the relationship with June that I did with Mason's mom. Liz and I laughed, shopped, and took rides together to just enjoy the scenic views and conversation. Later that week I drove to Mason's house to end our relationship. His mom greeted me at the door with a warm hug.

"Oh, I missed you! How was school?" My heart broke that very moment. I knew it was going to be difficult to end it with Mason, because I would also lose someone who meant the world to me...his Mom.

CHAPTER 21

Marc and I went out throughout most of his last year of medical school. This summer he would be leaving for an Internship on the East coast. He did set the standard on what I hoped to find in my future husband. There was not only a physical attraction but also respect and friendship. Marc never missed a birthday, Valentine's Day or any other special occasion. He seemed to be perfect in all ways.

We hadn't made any plans as to what would happen when Marc moved away for his Internship program on the East coast. I guess I secretly desired to stay here in St. Louis. Marc also had family here and I knew he ultimately wanted to come back. Or at least that's what I thought.

The demands on Marc's call schedule kept him busy the last month of residency. I understood and took the time to apply for hospitals around St. Louis. Strangely, it had been a few days since we last spoke. Hopefully he remembered our date this Friday!

Late Thursday evening Marc finally called, His voice sounded enthusiastic and happy.

"Honey, How are you?"

I smiled at the sound of his voice, replying,

"Fantastic! It's good to hear from you!"

Marc proceeded to explain he needed to cancel due to a change in call schedule. Marc was clearly upset with the last minute mix-up.

"I'm so sorry! This is the third weekend in a row and I plan to raise Hell!"

I obviously was disappointed however reassured him that I had a couple finals.

"Don't worry I should probably be studying anyway. We can go another time."

That Friday evening, I prepared for intense book work. I scanned the room to see if I had all my supplies, coffee, chocolate candy bars, Cola and popcorn. As I plopped myself on the bed with my nursing manual, the door opened. Candy, Sandy and Deanna popped their head in with their purses in hand. Candy excitedly coaxed me,

"Come on Stranger, Get up and Go to Calico's with us! You have all day Saturday to study!" I popped off the bed and pulled my worn scrub top over my head.

"Give me a minute and I'll be ready!" I scurried around my room looking for a clean presentable top and counted the dollar bills in my purse. Over the last few months, my weekends revolved around Marc. My nights out with friends had become rare but glad they hadn't given up on me!

The restaurant was buzzing with activity by the time we arrived. It was eight o'clock and filled with patrons enjoying the atmosphere and amazing Italian fare. I was scanning the menu planning the perfect pizza; thick crust, sausage, mushroom and—suddenly, my thought process was interrupted with Sandy clearing her voice and Candy elbowing me. When I glanced up, Candy motioned with her finger towards the back corner of the restaurant. My stomach turned and I instantly felt ill when I saw the site. Marc was sitting across at a table for two with an attractive blonde. Each had an arm stretched across the table as they held hands. Marc had that same intense look of interest and smile that I'd seen many times before.

To my amazement, my Irish temper didn't flare nor did I go into an angry vocal frenzy. I was honestly too disappointed and hurt with the reality of Marc's betrayal. Despite my bruised and beaten ego, I stood upright with my shoulders back and head held high. I took slow deliberate steps as I walked toward their table. Damn, he even ordered my favorite pizza! Thick crust with sausage, mushroom and onion-Arrrgh! He didn't even like it until he met me! At that moment, Marc took a bite almost choking as he turned to see me.

The woman sitting across from Marc looked confused and unleashed her hand from Marc's. Marc instantly stood up.

"Moe, she's a friend and doesn't mean anything to me!"

His "friend" was royally pissed off and pounded on the table.

"What? "I" don't mean anything to you??"

The only thing I could say was a firm,

"Marc, I trusted you and now you lost that trust. Please don't ever call me again."

I turned to walk out of the restaurant with Marc close behind on my heels. To my amazement, his date re-seated her self at the table. Maybe she liked the pizza or was delusional enough to think he wouldn't cheat on her too. It was coincidental that a cab pulled up to the curb. I raced inside and slammed the door on Marc and any future we might have had together.

It was difficult trying to avoid Marc at the hospital whenever I worked or had my clinical training. Thank goodness he was in a different specialty rotation. The strange part of it all was that as much as I cared for him, I never could see Marc in my future. No vision of walking down the aisle as his wife or having children with him years down the road. Yet at the age of 16 when I first met Mason, I would frequently doodle over and over again, Mrs. Moe Cunningham.

Marc left that summer and it ended up being the last time he called St. Louis "home". The Northeast coast was where Marc was hired once he graduated from his residency. The first year he continued to send lovely, heartfelt letters that went unanswered. After a couple years he eventually found that special someone who became his wife.

That June, I graduated from my RN diploma program at St. Louis City Hospital and was ready to start my journey as a professional. My ultimate goal, however, was to have my BSN. When I initially applied for nursing school, I felt like I needed an intensive hands-on program like City Hospital. It was the way I learned—by flooding my senses with doing, seeing, feeling the hospital environment. That's what I felt like I needed to do to be a well-rounded nurse and truly learn the field. For three years I went to school during the day and several days a week worked from 4:00 p.m. to 11:00 p.m. Then in many cases, I studied until dawn

Now that I had my diploma, it was time to achieve my second goal...my degree in nursing. Right after receiving my nursing diploma, I applied to St. Louis University. That fall, I started taking a couple of courses each semester while I worked full time at a local hospital. Geez, my mind was always looking ahead to the future. I was barely into my BSN program before I started thinking about what I would do when I completed my degree. Thank God, I was blessed to have professors who made learning fun! Finally, after all these years, I loved school! No kidding! Maybe I'd eventually go to law school and be lawyer like Charlee or maybe take some journalism courses. Heck, like they say, you only live once! There's so much to learn, see, and do in this world that I wanted to explore all my professional options.

As a new nursing diploma graduate, I was able to find employment at an upscale suburban hospital, in the ICU. New grads typically think they know it all before they have a chance to even work in their chosen field. There's even a name for it, "RN-it is." If you are a new MD, then I guess it's "MD-itis"—or in Charlee's case, being a fairly new lawyer, "Lawyeritis." As a new nurse, I was ready to conquer the world, because I felt like I had all the answers! Once we were put on the floor along with the "old" nurses, who had decades of experience, we slowly came to humbly realize there was so much more to learn. It's ongoing, never stops; and if you are with the right crew or in the right stimulating job, you embrace learning something new each day while perfecting those skills that you already do.I unfortunately was assigned a bitch of a mentor, who was afraid to share her knowledge.

Yes, there was a small group of disgruntled RNs who were absolutely pissed that the newbies were paid almost as much as the more experienced staff. Heck, I don't blame them for being upset, but their anger should have been directed at administration. So needless to say, most of the new grads felt like they belonged in a leper colony. Don't get me wrong, the facility had some fine nurses! I'm just sorry my mentor was a "sour apple" who left a bad taste in my mouth.

Many of us new grads would seek each other out for advice or to vent our frustrations. It was during my orientation period that I started applying elsewhere. I ended up changing to the night shift for the next year. There was a more cohesive bond and team approach with the nurses, and it was a fantastic learning experience. However, the night shift was taking its toll on my mental psyche. I had been an early bird all my life and I *could not* sleep during the day. By the end of my night shift, I was so tired I became nauseated each night. I made the decision to leave when I fell asleep at a stoplight. It was the swishing of cars speeding by that woke me up! I had three days off before I started my new job in the emergency room at a northwest county hospital.

When I arrived home that morning, I pick up the phone and quickly dialed.

"Charlee, it's me! I had my last day in hell!"

Charlee laughed.

"Well, Sis," she said, "sounds like you need to meet me at work, so we can celebrate at Happy Hour."

Charlee's office wasn't in the best part of town, but she was as happy as a little lark, representing primarily poor, unwed mothers. Charlee could relate, because she was an unwed mother also. My four-year-old nephew was named Albert, after my Father. Later that afternoon I picked up Marie and Ann so they could join us. The rickety white front door of Charlee's office had a sign that read "Charlie Bender, Attorney at Law." I had to give the old door a good pull and when it opened it let out an ear piercing *creak*!

"Sheesh, Charlee, that's louder than Grandma's knees! Hello! Hello, Charlee?"

Marie, Ann, and I heard jovial, animated conversation coming from Charlee's office. All three of us once again yelled,

"Hello?"

We then slowly opened the door. To our surprise, Charlie was surrounded by a very tall Wonder Woman and four other...females? The tall one in red skin-tight wonder garb turned around. My gaze went directly to her, or rather *his*, groin! Oh my!

Ann and Marie must have had the same expression, because Charlee and her friends started laughing in unison.

"Moe! For Pete's sake, eyes up North...you're embarrassing Stanley!"

I immediately felt ashamed, like a lecherous male who ogled at large breasts.

"Oh, I'm so sorry Stanley"

Stanley winked and gave us a sly smile,

"That's okay, my Darlin's. It's part of the costume!

He then proceeded to do a little gyro dance as he reached down to tap the large hard plastic cup protecting and enhancing his groin. I caught myself just as my darn eyes started to wander below Stanley's belt again! I thought to myself, *what is wrong with me? As a nurse I see body parts all the time!*

One by one they gave Charlee a hug as they left the room. Charlee never discussed her clients; however, she told us she fought hard for the underprivileged in all forms. Charlee's practice was thriving, and she clearly appreciated diversity in her practice. The problem was that she herself was barely able to pay her own rent.

My sister was offered several jobs at prestigious law firms, but her mission was to devote her life to those who couldn't afford to help themselves. Her style was unassuming, but in the courtroom she was a barracuda to be feared. Oh, and did she ever hate those pompous, overindulged attorneys with high-priced suits. Charlee took great delight in having them for lunch. Not literally, of course—but they usually walked out of the courtroom with their tails between their legs.

Charlee started shuffling a few papers on her desk and was deep in thought. I motion the girls to follow me.

"We'll wait for you in the lobby while you finish up!"

Once again I coached Marie and Ann not to discuss politics during Happy Hour. Geez, Charlee is like a duck on a June bug and doesn't let it drop! "No R&D words, okay?" (Republican and Democrat.)

It seems like all I had been doing lately was work during the day and go to school at St. Louis University in the evening. Marc was in residency on the East coast and wrote every now and then. He just didn't want to give up on our relationship and hoped I would give him a second chance. Mason and I already resumed dating a month ago and his mom and I continued to have quality time going to lunch, or spending an afternoon shopping, and so on. She was my friend, my family. Elizabeth Cunningham was downright ' hilarious too! No kidding, she had a wonderful witty sense of humor. Mason did, too, but I think he focused more energy and desire on making everyone else laugh—and they did. I should have known that a relationship warning sign is when you cease to find your boyfriend's jokes funny.

The four of us girls opened the door to a noisy downtown pub called Duffy's. We all ordered our chardonnays and cheered to success in my new job. Marie was quite happy, working in the ICU at one of the older county hospitals. She enthusiastically piped up,

"Hey, did I tell you about the ghost we have in our unit?"

Oh, of course, everyone was aware of my fascination with the paranormal! Marie continued, "There is an unofficial paranormal incident log kept in our ICU. Would you believe that for decades, there have been reports documented by the staff? It seems that frequently, when patients have a near death experience or right before death, they see and hear children playing! The other day there was this elderly man who kept yelling, 'Who let all these children in the hospital?' I walked in to calm him down. He stated, 'Yes, those two little blond kids are right there smiling at me! Don't you see them?' Then it was about twenty minutes later that he had a sudden cardiac arrest and died! Isn't that strange?"

Ann replied,

"Those children were his angels."

I paused to reflect on my thoughts about people dying alone. Just maybe, even when there's no one there in the physical sense, there is always an angel by their side.

Ann invited us to tour her new banquet hall in North County. She had been married for over a year now and was in business with her in-laws. This was up Ann's alley, as she always cooked like she was feeding an army! Ann had a good heart, and it always gave her an excuse to invite more over for the meal.

Charlee then mentioned that she volunteered for a local Democratic party. There was silence for a moment. Ann, Marie, and I gave each other this wide-eyed look. Oh, geez. Gulp. Here we go! For the next hour, Charlee went on a passionate tirade about the Republicans. That is, until I held up a knife and asked her to please kill me. Charlee suddenly stopped and looked confused. "What? What are you talking about?"

I replied, "Sis, remember the Bender rule...no political discussions!"

My parents, Sam, T-Mac, and Alan were Republican. I would never divulge to the family how I was voting, because it depended on the candidate more than the party. Frequently discussions would escalate into arguments, where I would feel like I was in court defending my choice.

Charlee, her son Lil Albert and I were living together at that time but were so busy we had barely crossed paths the last few weeks. My bulldog Maggie previously stayed at my parents while I was in nursing school. She too moved into Charlee's with me. The next evening we were invited to our parents to have some of "Momma June's" amazing homemade pizza with whole wheat crust.

"Albert, are you ready to go to Grandma's house?" He jumped up and down, exposing his huge dimples!

"Yes, let's go now!" the little guy said as he pulled on my arm.

Maggie came waddling into the room with a piece of stuffing in her mouth. Charlee gasped! "Moe, did your dang dog chew up another chair?"

I quickly scurried into the living room. Over the past several months, I had become quite the expert at household furniture repairs resulting from Maggie's destruction—sanding down and re-staining chewed areas in table legs, sewing up pillows....One of the biggest challenges was repairing rips in a leather couch that we bought at an estate sale. The leather couch was like new when we bought it; however, my dog quickly put her "seal of approval" on the seat and several pillows. Have you ever tried to sew leather back together? It is tough! Most of the upholstery needles bent, and my veterinarian friend suggested a 2-0 straight surgical needle with a super sharp point that could almost penetrate bone!

Charlee continued to complain, "Damn, Moe, I didn't think I'd have to worry about an old dog chewing up the place!"

Then I saw little Al's damaged teddy bear with cotton protruding from his wound. Albert ran and picked up "Paco" (I have no idea where he got that name for his bear).

"Maggie's a *bad* bullie, Aunt Moe!"

I went up to Al and told him in my most empathetic tone, "Maggie the bulldog has a disorder called 'separation anxiety.' She's not able to communicate how she misses all of us during the day, so she acts out by chewing things up. It's her way of letting us know she's lonely. For now, I think we better take Paco-Bear for immediate surgery! Can you assist me?"

Al seemed to like the idea of helping to save his teddy bear. I cleared off the table and grabbed another sewing needle.

"Al, please pass me the thread. Thank you, assistant!" In less than ten minutes, his toy looked new again! Little Al was too busy giving Paco recovery hugs to complain about Maggie the mischief-making bulldog.

It was nice that all of the family was home this weekend. Sam was now married too and had two beautiful children, Steve and Avery. They were now residing in North County after they moved back from Florida. T-Mac worked designing packaging and always did art on the side. He was pursued by the owner of an art gallery; however, T-Mac just wasn't interested in following up on the opportunity. Today, T-Mac brought his wife and two children, Brina and Craig. Alan, too, was home from the army and wore his big boots everywhere, even when he jogged.

Then there was Abby, now was a teenager, who performed karaoke at each family gathering. Oh, geez, she absolutely loved Abba and Olivia Newton-John. We would all barely sit down when Abby would encourage us all to listen to a new song she learned. Growing up in California, we older kids had frequently used our clenched fist as an imaginary microphone. Abby had the whole setup with an actual mini plastic microphone.

"Come in the living room, everyone! It's time for the show...hurry up before the seats sell out!"

In Abby's eyes, there was always a grand audience for her performance. Oh, yes, and she was good, with just the right vibrato. At the precise moment when Abby ended her last note, Maggie released this loud, squishy fart. I thought, *Oh, my gosh, what timing!*

Sam howled with laughter and said, "What are you feeding that dog?"

Then June yelled, "What's Maggie doing in the living room?"

Then T-Mac hollered, "Oh, gawd, smell that? There's nothing worse than a dog fart!"

I gingerly picked up Maggie, who looked more like a mini manatee sprawled out on the rug. My nephews were running around, holding their noses. "Awe, poor Maggie's really getting a bad rap today! Let's go outside, so you can do your duty, okay?" Abby felt she needed to repeat her performance, as Maggie's gas had distracted ***her*** audience. Abby was literally pushing us all back down in our seats. "Hey, everyone, sit back down! I'm going to sing that last song all over again!" Under her breath Abby mumbled," I'd appreciate a little applause at the end, okay?"

I laughed when I heard that, because it reminded me of the time Charlee fired me from being her "audience" because I wasn't an enthusiastic clapper! "Hey, Charlee, does that sound familiar?"

The next day, Charlee, Little Albert, Abby, Alan, and I joined Mom and Dad for lunch at a family owned restaurant. We were only a few feet from the only bathroom in the joint. After we placed our order, Albert said, "I have to go pee!" Charlee got up and looked into the bathroom to make sure it wasn't occupied. Since we were right next door to the bathroom door, Charlie thought it was okay to let Albert go by himself.

"Okay, Al, go on in and call me when you're done going pee-pee." A couple minutes later, Charlee got up to check on her son. The little guy angrily shouted, "Close the door, Mom, I'm not done yet!" Charlee said, "I thought you were only going pee!"" A couple minutes after that, Charlee once again peeked in to check on Albert. He then quipped, "Take a picture, why don't ya!" The restaurant soon started filling up with hungry patrons. Then a little head popped out from behind the bathroom door, and Albert yelled (loudly) "Moooooooooooom, ready to wiiiiiipe!" Charlee, who usually wasn't afraid of anyone or anything, had bright crimson-colored cheeks and cowered down into her chair.

"Mom, can you get up and do it?" June and everyone in the establishment practically rolled out of their seats with laughter. June said, "He's your son!" Charlie timidly got up to wipe her son's little bottom as the crowd watched her enter the bathroom.

CHAPTER 23

The next afternoon I was off work but had to go on a home visit for a class at St. Louis University. Marie already had her four-year degree in nursing. Ann previously lost the banquet business in the divorce and completed her associates in nursing last year. We both decided to attend St. Louis University together for our BSN. Home health nursing was our first course together. Ann and I were driving back to the university in my old gray Jeep, and I unfortunately made a wrong turn.

"Ann, we might not be in the safest neighborhood. Do you notice all the bars on all the windows here?"

Just then my jeep sputtered and then stalled right next to a bar filled with men. To my horror, it was like I stepped on a fire ant mound with thousands of ants spewing out of the hole. In this case men came running out of the small door to see what two nurses were doing in this neighborhood. One man, who could barely stand, wobbled toward us, saying, "Just in time for a lap dance!"

Then a drunken cheer followed by the gang of males. At that moment, a big white Cadillac stopped and the door opened. In the front seat were two dark-haired men who had the Mafioso look—or maybe undercover cops? Hopefully! I sent up a silent prayer to God. The passenger asked, "What are you girls doing here?"

Ann and I frantically explained how we were nursing students at the university, and our car had broken down. The man said, "Get in; we will take you."

Well, I'd like to say, don't do this at home. Do not get in the car with strangers—*but* at that particular time, we had to weigh (quickly) the pros and cons of staying with a gang of rowdy drunk men or two Mafia dudes. This was before the time when everyday people had cell phones. It was almost dark, and no police officers were around. I felt either way we could be dead, but our chances were better in the caddy. As we scooted in the back, we nervously said,

"Yes, please take us to the university. We appreciate it!"

The two men were in their thirties, I'd guess, attractive in a gruff sort of way and despite the fine suits, looked like they had a questionable past. As they drove off, they gave each other a quick glance and a nod. I wondered if that meant we might not see our families again. Ugh! Why couldn't I have a normal, drama-free life where I go to school, work, eat, sleep, pee, poop and the next day it all starts all over again? The man on the passenger side asked,

"Have you ever seen the lovely east side of St. Louis?"

Ann and I almost gasped as we looked at each other. I replied,

"Umm...no, sir, and we don't care to. Could you please take us back to the university?"

The two men just laughed at their private joke. Ann and I almost held hands in fear as we rode in silence. To our amazement, they eventually took us back to school on Grand. We immediately called Ann's dad, who owned his own car repair shop. Yes, we got an earful about driving in that neighborhood, but thankfully we were safe. The next morning we woke up early, and he drove us back to my jeep and repaired it onsite.

On the way home, I drove down Highway 40 and turned off onto Spoede Road. As I drove down the lovely tree-lined street with spacious homes on large landscaped yards, I suddenly felt it all was familiar. There was this one ranch that was set up on a hill; it was the only unkempt yard, with grass that was knee high. There was a "For Sale" sign in front, and I parked in the circle drive to take down the information.

No one had lived there for quite some time. I walked around the half acre and smiled when I looked in the window to see a huge marble fireplace. Then I realized I was smiling as I visualized decorating the mantle with pine roping for Christmas, how I would take pride in doing my own landscaping. When I scanned the property, it was as if there was a fast forward video of me mowing, edging, and trimming the yard. It was so real and vivid. This neglected residence had an uncanny elegance, and I knew without a doubt that it would someday be my home.

The vision of the West County home stayed with me for six months after I first laid eyes on it. Mason and I decided to move in together to see if our relationship would work this time.

The home in West County was still available—and now more affordable, as it had been on the market for almost a year. On the day we closed, I put on my gym shorts, tennis shoes, and T-shirt and immediately started to work on the yard. That was when I first became aware that Mason was a hoarder! Oh, my gosh, I don't know where he found four broken lawn mowers, rusty engines, weird-looking machines, and televisions with tubes that he had great intentions of fixing-someday. On the first day we moved in, there was already no room in the garage for the car!

"Ugh! No more collecting crap, Mason! This is a home, not a junkyard!"

I was very particular about clean, clutter-free homes, and his hoarding was driving me insane! This was just the first of many arguments about his collecting and storing junk at the house.

Maggie was now almost ten years old. The old gal would attempt to waddle around the yard, trying to keep up with me. After a while she would retreat to her comfy pillow on the porch. She would take a nap until I was finished, then slowly waddle back in to take another long snooze. That first day I mowed the lawn, edged, trimmed, and planted flowers, and by the time I was done, it looked like a whole new house. It was just like what I envisioned several months prior. It was almost getting too cold, but I was out there painting the entire exterior of the home. When I finished the exterior, I attacked several layers of wallpaper in each room.

To me it was invigorating, doing hard physical labor. That was in addition to the long miles I was running, sometimes twice a day, and up to seventy miles a week.

All the activity helped keep me thin, but I had chronically chipped nails with all the scrubbing, painting, and so on...and my poor feet looked like hell with all the miles in my tennis shoes. Mason used to say,

"Don't think I'll ever marry a girl with feet like that!"

Of course it made me laugh because, in reality, I had ugly, itchy, sore, blistered, callused feet. I had what I called Franken-feet! Heck, I was on my feet as a nurse in a busy emergency room, and many times wouldn't sit down or pee until I came home. Then I'd run after work and work a bit more on the lawn. My feet were screaming for fresh air!

It was another six months before Mason, accepted my ugly feet and asked me to marry him. We went to both parents home to tell them the good news! My parents were having the family over for dinner, so it was perfect timing! June was busy finishing up dinner when we walked in the door. She was clearly perturbed and said,

"You are 30 minutes late!"

The smile remained on my face as I displayed my beautiful engagement ring. In a flat monotone voice and with out turning, my mother said-

"Nice."

That was it! My cheeks were fire red as I just started to boil with anger! Her cool detached behavior continued throughout dinner. We immediately excused ourselves after the meal and headed back home.

Mason and I married a few months later in a small neighborhood church ceremony.

I continued to work at the emergency room of a local hospital while finishing up my degree at St. Louis University. Mason worked two jobs, one full time, and started a home remodeling and repair business. He participated in numerous community sports leagues after work on a year-round basis. Between him working sixty or more hours a week and going to games afterward, we rarely saw one another.

Mason briefly came home from work o drop off more—you guessed it—junk! We now had one working lawnmower and six broken ones, along with a couple of malfunctioning air conditioners that were accumulating in the corner of the backyard. I let out an audible growl every time the pile grew.

Mason would look at me and say,

"What's your problem? When I fix them, it means more money!"

I would reply, "That's the problem, you're too busy to fix them, and soon we won't even have a backyard!"

The next week was going to be brutal, as I was scheduled five days in a row. It was rare to get out on time. An eight-hour shift would frequently turn into ten hours or more. I was the triage nurse; however, the ER was also short a nurse for the back rooms. Trying to do both was nearly impossible! Thank goodness we had a fantastic, experienced crew, who not only worked well as a team but were also all friends.

I never knew what type of day it would have in the ER but hoped it wouldn't be too crazy. Not long after I arrived the receptionist ran up to get me as I was taking a febrile patie

Now, I was wondering how badly a zipper could "cut" a penis. When I walked up to the front, there was blood covering the front of his pants all down the legs. I hurried to grab the nearest wheelchair. I thought, *This poor guy!* The real reason for the excessive bleeding was revealed to the physician suturing the deep laceration. Should drinking glasses now carry warning labels? "Warning: Glasses are intended for drinking purposes only, not masturbation!" One patient after another, hour after hour, huddled around the desk to sign in, one worse off than the next.

On my way out of work that day, I clocked out and attempted to leave three times! Each time I had to come back in as I escorted someone to the back. I desperately wanted to use the bathroom but needed to leave ASAP, while the doorway was clear. Traveling down the highway, I thought of exiting early so I could use the bathroom at a gas station or a fast food restaurant. Something just told me to go home, and I did, possibly a little bit faster than normal. I didn't even pull in the back; I parked in the circle drive in front and waddled to the door with my legs crossed.

The commode was a happy sight, and the stream of urine flowed as if there would be no end. As I left the bathroom, I looked for my lazy old bulldog. I said out loud, "I could be a burglar, Maggie! Where are you?" Like usual, she was sprawled out on my bed, looking more like a fawn-colored manatee. Then I looked closer and noticed—no snoring and *no breathing!*

"Oh, my God! Maggie! Maggie, don't die!"

I immediately picked her up and gave her CPR like I would my human patients. "No, Maggie, it's not your time, please, please, don't leave me!" I soon realized Maggie wasn't coming back. I sat there for more than two hours with my precious Maggie in my lap. I lovingly stroked her as I cried my eyes out. I wished I could have been there for Maggie. What if I left work on time? Would I have made it on time? Maggie was my friend, who had been there for me for the last ten years. When I was happy, she was happy. When I was sad, she was sad too and tried to make me feel better. It's impossible to recall all the times she made me laugh with her funny antics. How she loved my bras and would take them out of the laundry and bite holes where the nipple should be. How she would fart in a crowded room and then walk out. Oh, geez, I would get so mad, but then I'd have to smile, too. She gave me unconditional love, and she knew she was loved each and every day.

My precious Maggie's failing heart finally beat for the last time. She always had a piece of my heart with her. She was not alone. I phoned Mason, who raced home when he heard the news. It was the first time that I ever saw him cry. The pain of losing my loyal friend was almost unbearable; I often wondered why there wasn't a support group for people who lost their pets. No doubt there are many people who consider their pet an important family member. I called in sick a couple days and managed to find coverage for the next week. For several months I wasn't able to talk about Maggie without getting choked up and spilling some tears. I kept her favorite pillow for a very long time and would occasionally hug it when I started to mourn not having my friend with me. Time took away the deep pain of losing her, but the memories and life lessons of love Maggie gave me were there to stay.

Over the next year, I became more involved with the families in the neighborhood. Sandy Storm was an amazing, wonderful, warmhearted woman from New Orleans. If I was sick, she would bring over some awesome country cooking. My neighbor had an abundance of common sense and knowledge about homeopathic remedies for people and pets. She was a little younger than my mom and had three daughters. If I needed advice, Sandy always had time for me and was able to put me on the right track again. We became close, and I cherished her friendship. Behind our house on a little court were a few homes. The tiny neighborhood consisted of: two gym teachers and their daughters, the fun Irish O'Leary family, a recovery room nurse, and finally a retired elderly woman. We got together any chance we got, for any reason...

"Hey, it looks like we're getting nineteen inches of snow! Whose house should we meet at?"

On many occasions the O'Leary girls would come and perform their Irish Step Dance routine. Maura, Cassie, and Shanna all performed competitively in the St. Louis area. I was fortunate to have all these wonderful neighbors in my life.

On weekends Sam, T-Mac, and I participated in the local 10K and 5K runs. It was my goal to work up to a marathon, so I started to increase my mileage each week. My knees would kill me, and I'd just take ibuprofen and start my run. Of course, it's not recommended to jog with pain or mask it with medication. I was driven, though, and rarely went a day without a long run. It was like my valium and was a way I could keep my head clear.

Mason was athletic, too; however, his sports were usually fast and furious. He didn't have the patience for running. We would usually ski in Colorado each year. Late fall, we decided to ski in Tahoe, California. I'm thankful we usually went with other people, because Mason always looked forward to spending the entire day on the black diamonds. He stuffed his pockets with food and drinks, so there wouldn't be a need to stop at the lodge. I, on the other hand, appreciated the invigorating cool mountain air but wanted to stay on the intermediate slopes. We were there first thing in the morning and didn't leave until the lift closed. My husband and I usually didn't see each other until the end of the day. On one particular day I was experiencing a lot of muscle fatigue. Maybe it was due to the altitude. It was my final run down the mountain when I happened to come across Mason. The daredevil literally pointed his ski downhill and schussed with reckless abandon. He stopped on a dime, flinging a blanket of snow on me.

"Hey, come on down the last run with me!"

I looked, and most of the runs were closing down. I replied,

"They are shutting down for the night, and anyway I'm too tired!"

Frantically, he pointed to the only remaining lift and said,

"You can do it! Know you can!"

He pointed his skis downhill, and I followed. Well, to make a long story short, this particular lift started out as blue—intermediate—however, it led into a double diamond. When Mason saw the two black diamonds on the only slope down, he almost gulped out loud.

"Oops, sorry...really I am!" He added, "I thought there was an intermediate on this run!

I became frantic when I realized I'd have to tackle an expert slope with mega-moguls. Well, I did make it down but not without tumbling a few times. Mason cheered when I reached flat ground in one piece.

"See, you did it! Doesn't it make you want to do it all over again?"

That comment made me laugh,

"Ugh! No, no way!"

I personally looked forward to my leisurely intermediate runs. Later I'd join friends at the lodge so we could sip hot spiced wine by a roaring fire. Once I'm re-charged, I would enthusiastically inhale the crisp, cool mountain air and ski...slowly.

On the way home to St. Louis, we had to change planes in Phoenix. While we were at the gate, waiting to board, a man in a dark blue suit caught my attention. I was almost mesmerized, watching him consume his sandwich and a couple snacks. I watched him eat every bite! I really didn't know why that man fascinated me.

The flight was full, and there were plenty of people to observe. Airports are typically a great place to people watch when you're passing time. Our friends who accompanied us on the ski vacation were seated a few rows behind us. I buckled myself in while waiting for takeoff. My eyelids felt heavy and slowly closed. Yes, sleep is what I needed now. Time to take a few winks on the way home...then the stewardess swiftly passed us on her way toward the rear of the plane. The doors closed, and I thought we were prepared to take off any moment. Our friend Larry unlatched his buckle to come up to our seat. "Hey Moe, I think you better go back there!"

Puzzled, I replied, "Why?"

"I heard someone is nervous."

Shaking my head, I said, "Larry, I'm not a psychologist. What do you want me to do?"

He was always the nosey type and I felt he just wanted to get "the scoop." I unbuckled my seatbelt and walked toward the stewardess. She was in front of the passenger and turned to me, saying, "He's just shaking; I think he's afraid to fly!"

I looked over her shoulder to see a middle-aged man having a seizure. It was the same man who I watched at the gate. Urgently I yelled, "You need to call an ambulance!" Just then, the passenger suddenly stopped breathing. "He's in respiratory arrest!" This man had no pulse or spontaneous respirations.

I immediately started CPR, and the entire contents of his lunch came out of his nose and mouth. I turned him to his side, cleared his airway, and started back with mouth-to-mouth respirations and compressions. It was the first time I had to do CPR in the field without a team from the ER and all the advanced technology at my fingertips—oxygen, a monitor, defibrillator, IV, emergency meds, suction, and so on. Finally, a retired nurse anesthetist came forward to help me out. It seemed like forever, but the paramedics finally arrived. They resumed CPR while a couple others started an IV; then they scooped him onto a stretcher and swiftly sped away in the ambulance.

It all felt so surreal. What a nightmare! To my amazement, the crew and other passengers clapped in unison and thanked both the nurse anesthetist and me for coming to the passenger's aid.

It turned out that the passenger had a long history of uncontrolled hypertension, diabetes, and kidney failure. I later learned he died of a massive myocardial infarction. My mind replayed my first memory of the man. How could he be gone? He didn't even appear sick. He was just a man catching a bite before he boarded the plane. One second there, the next gone.

I thought about his family waiting for him at Lambert airport and wondered how long it would be before they received the bad news. This poor passenger was far away in another state. He probably thought he died alone, but he had the thoughts and prayers of every passenger on the plane.

CHAPTER 24

The year 1983 heralded the first of my greatest blessings—the birth of my daughter Laurel. During my pregnancy, I had visions of how she would look and what her personality would be like. I always visualized a baby with golden hair and the biggest blue eyes. I knew she would have the poise of Princess Grace. And those eyes could see to your soul. I felt she would have an intensity about everything—her education, friends, surroundings, and life in general. She was born August 24, 1983, and had the thickest head of dark brown hair. I was thrilled she was healthy, but a little surprised that her hair was so dark! Not at all like my vision. You can imagine my surprise when several months later months when the dark hair was replaced by golden locks. Laurel and I went everywhere together. We were as close as a mother and daughter could be. My vision was a reality.

Laurel was always mature for her age. Even when she was young I'd refer to her as my "old soul." One day, at about age of four, I asked her if she wanted to have a friend over. Laurel looked up at me, rather confused, and replied, "Why do I want to have a friend over when I have you?"

We then had a discussion as to why it's good to reach out to develop friendships with other people too. She was my little buddy. I could take her anywhere; she always had good manners and was well behaved.

Laurel was on the shy side. However, she started to open up a bit in kindergarten. She loved school and always wanted me to create assignments for her, even when she was at home. I was so happy when Laurel told me, "Homework is the best part about school!"

Sheesh! I sometimes couldn't believe she was mine. Laurel felt very mature, carrying in her armful of books while scurrying quickly to her room. I'd have a snack all ready and encourage her to sit down and tell me about her day at school. My dedicated daughter would poke her little head out of her room and say, "Remember, Mom? I need to do homework first!"

Wow, my father would have been overjoyed had he ever heard those words out of my mouth! That November, Laurel was voted president of her kindergarten class. She humbly walked out of the building wearing a tall red, white, and blue Uncle Sam hat. I cheerfully said, "Yippy! My little girl is now *the* president!"

I made a huge deal out of the occasion, which only embarrassed her. Most kids liked to be fussed over, but not Laurel. She even disliked huge parties on her birthday. Laurel would tell me in advance, "No parties, Mom, okay? Can we just have a nice dinner with a can of Dinty Moore beef stew?"

I'm laughing as I type this, because it became a joke to the family years later. Laurel ended up requesting Dinty Moore beef stew for her third, fourth, and fifth birthday dinners! It's tasty enough, but each year I'd encourage her to try something different like pasta or the Pancake House. Yes, I wanted her to try something new for her special day. It was on her sixth birthday that she finally had a new request. "Mom, this year for my special dinner, I want prime wib." Yes, that's how she thought it was pronounced... "wib" instead of rib. I almost gasped and said, "What? Prime rib? Where in the world did you have prime rib?" My own diet consisted mainly of pasta or other carbs, vegetables, and fruit—rarely any meat. She meekly replied, "At Grandma and Grandpa's house. It was soooooo good!" Laurel rubbed her belly as she described the flavor. That was the end of Dinty Moore beef stew and the beginning of Laurel's champagne taste.

Laurel had the most incredibly thick hair. She could have provided wigs for ten people. But her nickname was "Princess Tender-Head." I'd brush, and Laurel would let out a big yelp. She thought her hair was a curse but would later learn it was a wonderful gift. Seriously, I had problems finding a rubber band big enough to hold it in a ponytail! One day she came home from school with a big frown on her face. I could tell something was wrong, so I gave her a big hug and told her to tell me all about it.

"Mom, I hate my hair!"

My eyebrows raised at what seemed like a random statement, "Why in the world do you hate your pretty blonde hair?"

The sad blue eyes and cute pouty lip almost made me chuckle.

"Well", she said, "the kids were calling me marshmallow head! See how it sticks out real puffy *all* over?"

I cupped my hands around her little chin and said,

"Laurel, all I see is an adorable five-year-old who is my gift from God."

We decided though that maybe we would try a new hairstyle tomorrow, like a ponytail or a braid. That seemed to cure the name–calling, and the next time Laurel wore her hair down, the kids seemed to forget that it once looked like a marshmallow.

The second of my greatest blessings arrived on October 30, 1984, when I gave birth to my son, David. He and Laurel were only fourteen months apart. I was accurate with my vision of little David. He was a dark-haired baby with curious brown eyes. The day David was born, though, his skin was *so* dark that I thought he was taken from a mother of another color. His dad and I are both fair skinned, and David's eyes too were almost as black as night. My son was blessed with a darker Italian complexion like his sweet Grandma Cunningham. She laughed when she saw him and said, "The little guy looks just like me!"

My family eventually called David "Little Man," because he started talking at a young age and always sounded more like a Italian wise-guy. Whatever happened to baby talk? David was around three when he started extending his arm to shake hands when greeting men and boys. Marie and I would frequently bring her children, four-year-old Eva and three-year-old Kent, to play with Laurel and David. I used to call Marie's son "Lil Hugga-bunch." He would smile and give everyone a huge bear hug! As Kent would toddle over to David for his turn, David would start reaching for Kent's arm, saying, "Boys don't hug, they shake hands! Kent, give me your hand! I'm trying to shake your hand!" Of course, Kent was a very persistent hugger and squeezed his little friend until David grimaced, squirmed, and wiggled out of his embrace. Afterward, my son reminded him of *his* greeting protocol: "Remember, Kent, next time...shake my hand, dude!" Believe me, I hug everyone too, and I don't know where he got his "rule" from. David was a big flirt at a young age and certainly loved to hug the ladies! Yes, he loved to hug me, his teacher, neighbor girl, Grandma, and basically all ladies, but no men.

Marie and I wanted our kids to grow up as close as we'd always been. We encouraged them to talk on the phone. After Marie and I ended our conversations, I'd hand the phone to David so he could talk to Kent. For the first couple minutes, they would just giggle. Then, we'd here them calling to each other "poopy head!" over and over again.

"No, you are a poopy head!" "No, *you* are a poopy head!" They'd both giggle louder and louder, jumping up and down and roll on the floor like laughing hyenas. I would say, "Okay, give me the phone back. It's not nice" (but it was funny)" to call each other poopy head!"

David was very young when we noticed he had a weird fascination with the weather. When I say young, I mean racing up to the television as a baby in his walker when the weather channel was on. He would stop and just stare, as if he were in a trance. At first I thought it was the colorful weather chart, but the interest in forecasts and outdoor conditions continued for many years. As an older toddler, he'd asked about hail, hurricanes, lightning, or any bad weather he heard about on TV. One day, I turned around and little David was nowhere to be found. "David! David!"

Suddenly, I heard a tiny, muffled voice respond, "In here!"

"Where?" I replied.

"The closet!" My little three-year-old replied.

As I opened the door, I asked, "What in the world are you doing in the closet?"

In his little man voice, he anxiously yelled, "Shut the door! There's a tornado!"

Surprised with his response, I said, "What are you talking about, silly?"

He quickly said, "Look outside!" Then he reclosed the door.

I decided to look out the front window. I gasped as I pulled back the curtain. There was an eerie purple and green cloud shaped like a decrepit hand reaching toward the ground. There wasn't any rain at that moment, but that was definitely a funnel cloud. I picked up Laurel and David. Our house didn't have a basement, and second by second the sky was changing from yellow to green to purple. The wind had picked up to quite a blow. I raced out the door with my babies and ran towards the neighbor's house. She had a basement.

Laurel and David snuggled into my shoulder. The rain had started and was pelting us hard. The wind blew David's little baseball cap off his head. We were almost there when I leaped over some debris. While I pounded on the door, I turned to see what I had jumped over. To my horror, it was a downed power line! A tree between the houses had toppled over and tore the lines from the neighbor's house. *Oh, my gosh, we could have been electrocuted!* Sandy opened her door, and we all ran down to the basement. She quickly grabbed a couple towels and we started drying off the kids.

A tornado did strike the area, but fortunately no one was injured. It was then that I realized the TV wasn't on when David was in the closet. I asked my son, "David, how did you know there would be a tornado?" He innocently replied, "I just thunked it in my head." I said, "You mean the thought just came to you? He nodded, pointing to his head. "Yeah, it came to me here."

That was the first of many times when David would tell me, "I just thunked it." Like the time I purchased an antique 1920 Decker piano. I had ambitious intentions of teaching myself to play over the next several weeks. Then on his Mason's birthday, I was wishing I had the sheet music to play "Happy Birthday to You." At that precise moment, David started playing it on the piano! Once again I asked him how he knew the song, and his reply was, "I thunked it." At that point, David had never had a piano lesson! My son wasn't aware of it at his young age, but he was definitely intuitive and constantly saying what I was thinking—weird!

Before I had children, I never anticipated the extreme joy they would bring into my life. What was amusing to me was observing my kids interact and play. Laurel took her job seriously as a big sister. The little stinker turned out to be quite intense and rather bossy with her little brother.

"David, get my crayons! David, get my blankie! David, if you want to color in my book, you have to stay in the lines!"

Sweet little Laurel knew how to bark out the orders to her brother. Laurel loved to color and was very particular about using sharp crayons when outlining the pictures in her coloring book. We always had to have a steady supply of sharpeners for both crayons and pencils. Her lines had to be clean and sharply conform to the pattern.

"Mom, the ocean looks pretty using blue and green crayons together! Look at David's picture. Can you believe he's coloring his dogs purple? David, dogs are brown, black, or white, but not purple! Ugh!" I would chuckle at how precise and literal Laurel was with her art. As I snickered under my breath, I shared with Laurel that art was about expressing oneself in a variety of ways. "It's fun to be creative! In the art world, animals can be any shade, even rainbow...because it is your masterpiece."

Laurel carefully re-inspected her little brother's work and now patted him on the back. "Good job, David, very cweative". David in turn gave his sister a big smile, exposing his big dimples and chubby cheeks. He was proud that he had finally pleased "The Boss."

Laurel and David were my little buddies, and I took them everywhere. Occasionally we had surprise fun days. If one of their birthdays fell on a school day, I'd call the principal and ask if I could pick up Laurel and David, to take them for a picnic during lunch. It was priceless to see their happy, surprised faces when I arrived at school. What a treat to eat McDonalds under a big oak tree at Bierne Park! After lunch we would go on the slides and the swings for a while before I took them back to school. For days afterward I'd hear them gleefully tell their friends how they were able to leave school for a birthday picnic. It was a memory they still fondly recall now as adults. Isn't living life all about creating memories like that?

When David was three, we started calling him Bo-Bo or just Bo for his nickname. The kids and I would enjoy sitting on the floor for hours, drawing, coloring, or making our own books. That year I wrote a book for both of them, and T-Mac actually drew the pictures. Book number one was *Lil Laurel meets Mr. Max*, about a little girl who finds a stray golden retriever. The second book was *Bo-Bo's Bedtime*. Bo-Bo was active, and bedtime was always a fiasco, with him sneaking out of bed a half dozen times. In the book there was a magical song (which I made up) that would instantly lull the fictional "Bo-Bo" character to sleep. It was titled "Dream of Lollipops and Popsicles," and it went like this:

Dream of lollipops and popsicles,
parties and friends.
Just remember to dream of things
a smile brings!
Sleep and dream without the fears,
and wipe away those little tears.

Dream of lollipops and popsicles,
parties and friends.
Dream of lollipops and popsicles,
parties and friends.

Bo loved this song. He would say, "Sing it again, Mom! Just one more time, okay?" The problem was, it was always "one more time!"...a million times! I'm glad they both loved their books, though.

CHAPTER 25

In the summer of 1989, Lauren and David started playing on a variety of sports teams. Mason was now making an attempt to be home more to teach them how to bat, pitch, throw a football, or kick a soccer ball. The sports were what helped bond the kids closer to their father and he always volunteered to coach their teams. One afternoon I was watching them all practice ball in the back yard. I started counting the piles of junk. At that moment I deviously thought, *Tomorrow, yes, tomorrow is the day!* The day I would clear out all that crap!

The next morning, after Mason went to work, I started loading anything on the garage floor into the van, quickly, almost sprinting, because I knew he would be home for lunch! Luck was with me, because I saw a lawn mowing crew and asked if they wanted several broken mowers. "Sure!" they replied.

I almost gave them a high five! I said,

"If you want them, you must get them out of my backyard now...ASAP!"

I phoned someone with an air conditioning repair business and asked if he wanted several broken AC units....to keep. Yes! *I'm batting a thousand today!* I was getting dehydrated by the marathon hauling, clearing, and cleaning. By noon I once again had our backyard free of junk. The two-car garage was at the point where we could park one vehicle. I was thrilled and felt victorious! But when Mason came home, I felt frightened when I saw his blazing angry eyes.

"Where is everything? What did you do with my stuff? Those were mine and you had *no* right!"

His words came out like bullets from a machine gun. True, I *should* have asked, but it would have fallen on deaf ears. "See how you like it if I throw away your belongings!" Shit royally hit the fan that day, and things weren't the same for weeks. I never told Mason what I did with all the junk for fear he would go and retrieve it.

Our house had limited storage. Maybe if we moved to a larger home with a basement and land, things would be different. Oh, living in the country sounded like a dream come true! We could get back to nature, animals, family, and maybe have a barn for Mason's hoarder storage space.

I had looked in the newspaper for weeks before I found a five-acre property in rural, unincorporated West County. The past week it had rained hard every day. Oh, geez, I just hoped it would stop long enough for us to see the open house. The night before the open house, we went to my parents' house for dinner. We were just about out the door when my mom ran up to pin an angel on my coat. "This is to protect you!" I was pleasantly surprised by her nice gesture and thanked her.

The next day Mason complained about seeing a house that was so far away. "Do you know it would take me almost an hour to get to work?"

I defensively piped,

"Let's just look and see, okay? The house has dropped almost fifty thousand in the past six months!"

At the time, we had an enormous conversion van, so we packed up the kids and headed to the house. It seemed like we kept driving and driving, and just before we were ready to turn around we saw "Open House." We followed the signs winding round and round up the massive hill.

"Geez Louise! Where the heck is this place?"

We no longer were on a paved road; it looked like a sea of mud. Mason sarcastically said, "Is this rural enough for you?"

Our search for this hidden residence was becoming ridiculous. "Oh, my gosh, I'm sorry for the goose-chase. Let's just go home!"

It was then that we saw the old farmhouse, high upon the mountain with a great view of the countryside. Mason, said, "We're here, so we might as well look."

The tires started spinning and spewing rocks and mud half way up the hill. We heard our tires squealing. Then suddenly, without warning, the van was spinning while rolling backward down the mountain. At the bottom of the driveway was a bluff that dropped more than fifty feet. It happened all so fast that we didn't even have time to scream. Laurel had her hands covering her eyes, and Bo yelled, "Mom, I'm jumping out the door!"

"No, Bo, don't open it!"

That's when the van turned on two wheels, ready to topple over the edge. I was so filled with absolute paralyzing fear that I couldn't talk, but I did pray. It was as if time momentarily stopped, and suddenly everything became quiet.

Then it was as if someone pushed the van, against gravity back onto all four wheels! The owners from up above were staring at us with absolute disbelief and horror in their eyes. Once we had all four tires on the ground, I screamed, "Let's get out of here, go, go now!" My heart was beating wildly as I asked the kids if they were alright. Laurel asked, "Mom, how did that happen?"

Yes, even a young child knew that only a miracle could prevent us from toppling over the bluff. Later that, night when I retold the story to my friends, I started to cry and became traumatized all over again. It was months, or maybe more like years, before I could retell the incident without getting emotional. The mere thought that my kids could have been killed that day choked me up. No, certainly no farms for me now. How strange it was that my mom happened to pin the angel on my coat the night before. I'm convinced that all of our angels were with us that day.

It was now a glorious, bright, sunny October in 1993. The kids and I were driving to Grandma and Grandpa Bender's house for Sunday dinner. The air felt invigoratingly cool, and I almost wished I could be running rather than eating. Maybe Laurel, Bo, and I could go to the junior high track after our meal. Laurel enjoyed trying to race me or climb the monkey bars. Bo always brought his camouflage case filled with army men and played in the sand. Many years later we learned that open sandboxes were not ideal places for young kids. Back then, mothers didn't realize children could come into contact with hookworm larvae, roundworms, and other parasites from dogs, cats, and other animals that have excreted in the sand. Children could accidentally ingest the roundworm larvae, which could cause blindness. Parents of the twenty-first century are generally more aware of potential environmental hazards, and many diligently read the manufacturing labels to ensure sand is safe and doesn't contain asbestos or other contaminants.

If they purchase sand for home playgrounds, they cover it. Bo loved sandboxes, and thank God he never had any residual effects from playing in open boxes in his youth. It reminds me of my own youth back in the '60s; it was common for all the neighborhood kids to follow the toxic plume of smoke from the mosquito fogger truck. We were unknowingly breathing DDT!

No adult told us to stop or told us about the toxic smoke spewing out the back. Parents weren't aware of the dangers back then; most didn't seem to consider that if the smoke could kill pests, it was probably not good for humans, either.

The kids and I drove up to the white ranch style home that now had several cars parked out front. "Hi, Big Al!" I said as I gave my dad a big hug. Laurel and Bo ran up to also give him hugs. My dad was in the living room, watching television. "Laurel and Bo, there's a good Western on now! You know old Westerns are Grandpa's favorite movies! Do you want to watch it with me?"

Laurel and Bo looked at each other and laughed.

"No Grandpa, it's in black and white; we like color shows!"

My Father then let out a hearty laugh saying,

"Kids, many of the greatest classics of all time are black-and-white movies!"

Big Al also loved any military programs.

"Moe, one of my favorite movies is next, *The Enola Gay*. It's about the super B-29 bomber that was the first aircraft to drop an atomic bomb on Hiroshima, Japan."

I perked up and said,

"Oh, yes, I've seen that before!"

Big Al continued, "Did you know that the bomber was named after the pilot's mom? Her name was Enola Gay Tibbets." Laurel and David started to glance out the windows at the kids playing outside. They had no interest in the Enola Gay or old Westerns. I'm certain, though, that many years from now, the sight of an old Western will surely bring a smile to their faces as they remember their Grandpa Bender.

My dad was the eternal educator, and I did enjoy hearing his fun facts. Just in not too much lengthy, drawn-out detail! Big Al was good for giving you more info than most brains wanted to absorb. Bo hopped up on his grandpa's lap to show him his new army trucks. Laurel and I went to see what Momma June was up to. The wonderful scent coming from the kitchen made me hungry.

"Oh, Mom, you are absolutely the best cook! No one makes mostaccioli or pizza like you do!" Mom always looked like she was in pain when she was cooking; sometimes you could even hear her groan.

"Having fun yet, Mom? Need any help?"

June wiped the perspiration from her brow.

"Ugh, it's too darn hot in this kitchen! How about preparing the relish tray and slicing pickles?"

Now that's a task where I ingest half of what I prepare. I love pickles! Laurel piped up and said,

"I'll help, too!"

June looked up and asked, "Where's Mason?"

Without looking up from my slicing and dicing assignment, I replied,

"Oh, he had a football game at Forest park. He will be joining us later."

We all looked up when Charlee pulled up with her fiancé, Ray. It was the first time he was meeting the family. "We will have to tell Alan not to reveal embarrassing Charlee Bender moments or secrets. He's good for that!" At that moment, Charlee and Ray walked in the room with his two daughters, Leann, age eleven, and Christy, age ten.

The first thing I noticed was the absolute glow on Charlee's face and the sparkle in her eyes every time she looked at Ray. Here Charlee was a petite five feet two and Ray was almost six feet five. I walked up to shake her fiancé's hand.

"Hey, Charlee, do you need a ladder to kiss Ray?"

She replied, "Haha! Funny, very funny!"

They always say opposites attract, and in this case it was a nice complement of personalities. Charlee was high-strung, outspoken, fiercely loyal, and devoid of a verbal "edit" button. (Now that I think about it, most of the rest of us Benders didn't have one, either!) Ray was somewhat quiet yet charming. I could tell he was proud to be at Charlee's side, with his arm draped lovingly around her shoulders. It had been a long time since Charlee had someone special in her life, and I could tell Ray would make a great stepfather to her son.

My little sister Abby was now twenty-three years old and in travel school. She had matured into quite the beautiful young lady. She looked more like Mom, with her fair complexion, pretty hazel eyes, and silky soft light brown hair that fell just above her shoulders. Abby had always been a real lifesaver for me. She was the one who was most often there to help me take care of Laurel and Bo. She frequently came over when they were babies so I could get some sleep during the day when I was working at night. June used to say, "I raised my kids; now you can raise your own." When Bo was a baby, he had his nights and days mixed up for the first five months. It was Abby who would come to my rescue when I couldn't take another twenty-four hours without sleep. It was also Abby who Laurel and Bo looked forward to seeing each and every time to came to visit.

"Who wants to hear me do some Abba Karaoke?"

I had to chuckle under my breath, because Abby still loved an audience for her family performances. There were too many Benders to be seated at the same table during dinner, so the kids ate in the second kitchen in the finished basement. They thought it was cool, being away from the parents where they could be more rowdy.

It was during dinner that my dad suddenly started eating a bit slower and using more effort to swallow. I thought to myself, *Oh no!* Whenever my dad showed any sign of discomfort or illness, it usually ended up being a doozy!

"Dad, are you okay?"

Big Al continued to attempt to swallow and replied, "I don't know what's going on. It seems like I'm having some difficulty getting the food down. It's like I have a spasm in my esophagus." Big Al was bug-eyed but continued to slowly yet more forcibly try to swallow.

I asked, "Dad, how long has that been going on?"

He shrugged his shoulders "Umm, I don't know, maybe a year."

The answer definitely alarmed me.

"A *year*? Dad, you need to be looked at ASAP! Why didn't you ever have it checked out?"

Big Al always minimized any symptoms and wasn't all that crazy about being a patient.

"No kidding, Dad. If you can't get that food down your esophagus, you're going to the hospital!"

June sarcastically piped up, "I told him to go months ago, but you know you know your father."

Then all my siblings were chiming in and scolding Big Al for waiting so long to have his symptoms checked out. My little brother Alan was now six feet one and had filled out over the years. He had recently moved back to St. Louis from California. Alan firmly stated, "Dad, if you aren't at the doctor's by Monday, then I'm coming over here and carrying your ass to the office!"

Big Al grimaced. "Don't be disrespectful, son. I'm still your father!" He then reassured us that he would make an appointment the next day.

The Bender tradition was for all the boys (my brothers) to head for the living room to attempt to find sports on the television. June complained, "C'mon, why don't you stay and play some cards for a while?"

Sam, T-Mac, and Alan were all patting their guts. T-Mac even had the capability of expanding his abdomen to make him look nine months pregnant. He usually did it after meals to make everyone laugh and let Mom know he enjoyed her dinner. T-Mac started doing his pregnant boy routine and said, "Ugh! Mom, I can't fit at the table. I ate too much!" June then looked at us girls, asking,

"Anyone up for going to play bingo?"

My immediate thought was to cringe. I hated being exposed to cigarette smoke, and the Hall was always filled with plumes of smoke.

It was also difficult for me to sit after a meal; I always needed to move to help digest it. My mom loved to play bingo, however, and spent several days a week at the Hall with her friend. Sam and T-Mac's wives stayed to play rummy with my mom. June was happy now, so the kids and I decided to go with Abby to walk to the track. We stopped in the living room to chat before we left. Charlee and Ray were on the couch, and he was massaging her back as they watched TV. I said, "Geez, you two, get a room! I feel like I'm watching foreplay!" Charlie protested,

"What? I have my clothes on! Ray's just massaging my weary back."

It was at the Haywood Junior High track where Abby had broken her arms when she fell off the monkey bars several years earlier. She had been up there playing while T-Mac did some Farklet (interval) training on the track. Abby said to, "I won't be up climbing on those anymore!" Then she showed me her surgical scars and how she still had some residual weakness in her hands after all that time.

"How about you walk with Laurel while I run some laps?" Bo started sprinting and yelled back. "Mom, race me, okay?"

I acted like it was an effort for me to catch up. "You're just too fast for me, Bo!"

When we came home, the family was all passing buttered popcorn in the living room. My dad was now watching a Clint Eastwood movie. Big Al chuckled and looked at Bo. "I remember the time Bo was about three years old and I told him twice to stay in his car seat. The third time, Bo looked at me, pointed his finger as if it were a magnum, and said, 'Go ahead, Grandpa, make my day!" Dad was laughing and slapping his knee. Oh, geez, the little bugger said it just like Harry Callahan (played by Clint Eastwood), in the movie *Sudden Impact*! What was even funnier was that my dad continued to retell that story about Bo for many years

When the kids and I returned home that evening, Mason was carrying his duffle bag from the car to the house. I asked, "Where were you?"

He replied, "I decided to have a few beers with the guys after the game."

Mason didn't miss all the family gatherings, just the ones when games were scheduled. Laurel, Bo, and I didn't mind, because we functioned as a happy little team on our own. Not long after we came home, Laurel and Bo started to play a game. Laurel threw a blanket over Bo's head and twirled him round and round, saying, "I hate you, Willow!"

They both giggled as Bo became dizzy and unsteady as he attempted to find Laurel with the blanket over his head. I was puzzled and asked,

"Why do you say "I hate you, Willow'? Where did you get that from?"

By this time, Bo had put the blanket around Laurel's head and was spinning her round and round. There was a muffled sound from under the cover. "I don't know, Mom, we just made it up! I shrugged my shoulders and said,

"Okay, whatever makes you happy!"

Then it occurred to me that they enjoyed making up new, sometimes weird games, just like I did when I was young.

Mason was now settling in from football and carefully examined my attire.

"If you're not wearing your gyms shorts, you're wearing your scrubs. You ought to change it up every so often."

In defense, I replied, "That's because if I'm not working at the hospital, then I'm mowing the lawn, edging, trimming, running, painting, cleaning house, and taking care of the kids. I'm comfortable in these old shorts!"

It was my first indication that my husband desired to see a wife who looked more feminine and sexy. Then later I thought about my granny panties under my gym shorts. My nightgown drawer consisted of a variety of free T-shirts from community races. There really wasn't anything sexy in my closet or drawers, but I didn't feel like being sensuous, either.

That Monday, Big Al went to the doctor, as he promised us kids. The doctor scheduled a battery of test from an endoscopy (scope to examine the esophagus), CAT scan, biopsy, and PET scan. When I first saw Big

Al struggling to get food down at the dinner table, I knew at that precise moment it was bad...and it was. When all the test results were in, the physician called my mom and dad in his office to give them the unfortunate news. Big Al was about to have the biggest battle of his life. My father's goal was to grow old with my mom, and he felt responsible to make sure he was there to take care of her for many years to come. Now he didn't even know if he'd be here next Christmas. There was a tumor the size of a baseball at the junction of his esophagus and stomach. Big Al was diagnosed with stage 3 esophageal cancer. My dad reassured us that everything would be okay and not to worry. Statistically, I knew we had a lot to be concerned about, and the prognosis wasn't good.

The next several months were not easy for my father, with the surgery, chemo, and radiation. The strange thing was that my friend Ann's father-in-law was diagnosed at the same time as Big Al. He was ten years younger than Big Al and passed away two months later. My father was a fighter, though, and he insisted that he was going to beat this curse. One Sunday, after he was discharged from the hospital, his favorite past time was to review his medical bill from the hospital. Big Al's glasses were dangling at this tip of his nose. He grimaced as he looked at one charge.

"Oh my gully, they've billed me for a damn Kotex! I didn't use any feminine pad!"

That certainly made us all laugh. Unfortunately, Big Al was always finding a discrepancy on his hospital charges.

I said, "Well, maybe they used it as a bandage."

He shook his head and said,

"Absolutely not! I watch their every move!"

Al was detail oriented and reviewed anything—contracts, bills, homework, everything—with a fine-toothed comb and a keen eye.

One family Sunday, Laurel, Bo, and I were coming over for the usual family dinner. As I opened the door, I was shocked to see that Big Al was sitting on the chair, cyanotic. He had the look of death hovering over him, and I started to panic.

"Dad! What's wrong? Are you having trouble breathing? I'm calling an ambulance!"

He yelled, "*No*! No, you're not, and I won't go if you call!"

I said, "Yes, you will!" Just then my other siblings were walking through the door. I yelled,

"Dad needs to go to the emergency room!"

Big Al was still being a stubborn ass, said,

"No, no, I'm not going! Do *not* call an ambulance!"

My brother Alan walked up to Big Al, who was now not so big after all the chemo and radiation treatments. Without saying a word, he scooped up Big Al in his arms and hastily carried him out the door. My father screeched,

"Alan, put me down!"

Alan was determined to get Dad to the hospital ASAP.

"Dad, if you won't go by ambulance, then I'm carrying your ass there, whether you like it or not!"

Thank God he did at that moment, because Big Al ended up having a pericardial effusion with more than a liter of fluid in the sac around his heart. This would have eventually restricted the heart from beating, and death was waiting right around the corner for him.

Big Al went for immediate cardiac surgery and spent several days in the ICU. I knew they wouldn't let Laurel and Bo back to see him, but they wanted to come up with me anyway.

I scanned the waiting room and saw Charlee and Ray. I asked,

"Charlee, where's Mom?"

Charlie sighed and informed me that she had gone to play bingo.

"What?" I exclaimed. "She just played last night!"

I was irritated and felt she should be here at the hospital with Dad. However, Mom felt like she spent most of the year with Dad at his multiple hospital visits. She said, "I just need to have fun sometime and to get away now and then." Yes, true, Dad had been in and out of the hospital almost every other month for the past year. I guess it's not for me to judge unless I've been there, but know I'd want my husband to be there for me through good times and downright awful moments, too.

Another six months passed by, and Mason's business was booming. The list of clients was growing and they were all happy to have someone who was prompt, knowledgeable, and able to troubleshoot any household problem. Seriously, he was a genius and amazed me with his ability to fix almost anything under the sun. The only thing we both seemed to have difficulty fixing was our marriage. It was in 1995 that we both decided to take the first step in consulting attorneys. It wasn't until 1996 that I decided to take the necessary steps to finalize the divorce. This was tough, leaving someone I had known since high school.

In hindsight, I reflected on what brought us together in the first place. Sure Mason was good-looking smart and had a sense of humor too. In all honesty though, it was the strong sense of *family* I felt whenever I was around *his* parents. The Cunningham's, were such a loving couple who made any holiday or get-together a festive occasion! The more the merrier to the Cunningham's! There were many Friday night's that my choice would be to hang-out with them. They made me feel so loved, as if I was their own daughter. It was because of Cunningham's and the kids that I stayed so long.

My Dad continued to fight a valiant battle with cancer. I chose not to think about him ever dying, and deep inside I thought he would win! In reality, Big Al was no longer "big"—he was fading away to skin and bone. When my father was first diagnosed with esophageal cancer, the doctors gave him a matter of months, a year at most. But Dad's intense will to live, was fueled by his inner strength. By gully, he wanted to prove them all wrong! It had been years since he was first diagnosed. Day by day, it was clear the cancer was taking its toll on his health.

There was yet another disease not being addressed by our family: Mom's growing anger and depression. She was not a bad person or a bad mother, but she refused to acknowledge the family was in turmoil. I remembered the happier days, when June was always there to greet us when we came home from school. I truly loved to see her pretty, smiling face after a hectic day. June proudly displayed our artwork or good grades on the refrigerator and listened to stories of a hectic day at school. She made sure we had food on the table and clothes on our backs, signed us all up for sports, and attended all of our games. June was a good Mother going through some difficult times.

Mothers are not all from the same cookie cutter mold; no one teaches you how to be the perfect mother—there is no such person. I never walked in my Mom's shoes and I imagine the road wasn't always easy. Over the years though, June seemed to develop a negativity that loomed over the entire family.

Whatever we did do was never enough, and the demands seemed endless. We needed her to be strong at a time when she felt weak, but refused help from professionals. We in turn started to distance ourselves from dealing with her verbal digs and tactics of putting one sibling against the other. My choice at the time was to throw my hands up and run in the opposite direction.

Laurel and Bo were now thirteen and twelve years of age—an age when teens think they are old enough to care for themselves and be independent. The thought of their parents divorcing was something they didn't want to face; they felt they had teen worries of their own. My friend and neighbor, Sandy offered her home to us as a temporary place until the divorce was final. To the kids it wasn't as if we were apart at all, as we lived next door! They just ran back and forth between the two homes and honestly thought it was pretty cool! To me, living next door to the ex–to-be was a little too close for comfort.

We had been living in Sandy's home for a week and unfortunately I had several nightmares. It was a nightmare that I had once many years ago. In this nightmare, I was in my car driving to the top of the tallest sky-bound bridge I had ever seen. Like before, it towered high above a body of water. When I was almost at the top, I began to feel dizzy as I proceeded to have a stroke. My arm fell limp off the steering wheel as the car went out of control and off the bridge. Needless to say, I bolted upright before my car hit the murky water several stories below. I was still shaking when I woke up and realized it was all a bad nightmare. A nightmare that I wondered why would randomly reoccur again and again.

Laurel, Bo, and I would occasionally change up dinner and have theme night. That basically meant sometimes we would have breakfast for dinner, food that Indians and Pilgrims ate in the seventeenth century, or whatever else they were studying at school. One particular we decided to have a night in England. Our dinner was in honor of Great-Grandma and Grandpa Bender from Manchester, England.

My Grandma Bender was ninety-six years of age when she passed away in the mid-'80s. She was a spunky, outspoken Englishwoman who was raised in Liverpool. She loved to share stories about how the Bender family was distantly related to the owners of Manchester United.

My Granny "B" would get out a big brown box of Manchester United memorabilia and enjoyed showing us signed programs she collected at the games.

She proudly displaying pictures of our "cousin Louie," telling me he started out as a butcher. This tiny lady seemed so proper, yet she had a love of bullfighting, soccer and rugby. I told her that I preferred football. Granny would throw up her arms and exasperatedly shout,

"Oh, American football is for sissies! Now, rugby is the game for *real* men!"

Her comment made us all laugh. What my granny was known for, though, was her amazingly yummy English scones. In 1981, we made our last trip to see her before she died. I asked her if she could give me the recipe to her famous scones. She said in her haughty voice,

"No, absolutely not, but you *can* watch me make them. Watch and learn! Watch and learn, so scurry on over here."

Laurel, Bo, and I had previously checked out a book from the library that had a number of traditional English recipes. While looking through the book, Bo started laughing and said,

"Look, Laurel, English people eat Spotted Dick!"

I looked up from writing down our store list to see Laurel covering her mouth. I said,

"What? What are you talking about?"

Bo pointed it out to me and said,

"See, it says Spotted Dick right here in this book! Hehehehe!"

I started to read the recipe and informed my silly kids that "Spotted Dick" was a name for a traditional English dessert. Laurel, who was as curious as her brother asked,

"But why do they call it Spotted Dick? It doesn't look like one in the book."

I rolled my eyes and flipped the pages to see if it noted an explanation.

"Geez, I don't know! Let me see...hmm, well, there is something about "spotted" representing the raisins or currants. Oh yes, then there's more about the dough being called 'dick' back then. Hey, how about we settle for some of Great-Grandma's English scones with butter and jelly? Then we'll make some fish 'n' chips, too!" That seemed to satisfy the kids, and we soon headed to Dierbergs, our local grocery store, for the ingredients. While I was locking the door, Laurel and Bo ran to our red 1979 MGB.

"Mom, it's a British car! Can we ride in this with the top down?"

Shaking my head, I said, "No, absolutely not! It's not safe. We will ride in the Laredo with your seat belts." I had sold my canvas-topped CJ5 and now had a four-door Cherokee Laredo. The two-seat MGB was rarely driven and was going to be sold. While we were at a stoplight, I noticed a shiny black car alongside of us. I mentioned out loud,

"Oh, that's pretty!"

Laurel piped up,

"That's a 1987 BMWi with leather sports seats! The car behind it is a 1985 Mercedes Benz 300d, turbo diesel!"

My eyes were as wide as saucers!

"What? How in the heck did you know that, Laurel? You're only fourteen years old!"

Laurel rolled her eyes back at me and said,

"Mom, I'm going to be a luxury car saleswoman when I grow up! I have to know those things!"

Bo, who was now twelve years old, chimed in,

"We have a luxury dealership on Olive; don't you pay attention to the cars?"

Once we arrived at the store, Laurel wanted to take charge of the grocery list. Laurel was a responsible little shopper and asked if she could check off items placed in the cart. Like usual, I gave Bo a "pre-warning" about not asking for comics or candy while in line. He seemed to take it much better if I reminded him ahead of time, before we even entered the store.

He still tested the waters by giving me a sly smile and looking up at me as we passed rows of chocolate bars and chewy treats. He'd say, "Oh yeah, no candy, right?"

I would say, "Very good, you remembered! Right! No candy!"

Sometimes Bo would reach out and act like he was grabbing a package and start chewing his imaginary sweets. "Oh, yum, this is good!" He'd blow air into his cheeks, making it look as if his mouth was full of candy. "Want some, Mom?"

I watched both Laurel and Bo as they walked ahead of me in the parking lot. The two were close enough so I could hear Laurel instructing Bo that he would set the table while she helped me with the scones. Yes, she was a born teacher and acted like a second mother to her brother. No doubt I was blessed to have such a wonderful relationship with the kids. They truly made me happy, but I knew tides would bring change to their lives and mine. It was just a matter of time. I prayed that we would still hold tight and remain a close family.

What had been on my mind was a growing desire to relocate out of Missouri. There were several RN positions available in the Tampa/St. Pete area in Florida. The kids and I could move there that May, stay for the summer, and return before the school year if they didn't like it. Yes, the kids and I will be talking about the move.

My father's last several hospitalizations were not a due to cancer but a fractured his hip. Big Al fell on the third step in the basement. A few months later, he was hospitalized for a postoperative infection from his hip surgery. In the last several years, Big Al was at death's door more than half a dozen times, but he'd always manage to bounce back.

June was growing weary of being in hospitals and was absolutely brutal to the nursing staff. I'm sure they cringed every time they had to come face to face with Mom's icy glare.

"Do you know I had that light on for more than fifteen minutes?"

As a nurse I knew firsthand that there was a huge nursing shortage. The staff frequently had to deal with more than twice the normal load. The young nurse apologized,

"Oh, I'm so sorry! We had a call in tonight. I'll be right there with Mr. Bender's pain medication!"

June proceeded to huff and puff, letting the poor nurse know she still wasn't off the hook!

I shook my head,

"Mom, please try not to be so hateful and demanding."

June rolled her eyes. "You're always sticking up for *them*!" she said, meaning the hospital staff. "Yes, you do! Oh, and did it ever occur to you that I could use your help at home? Instead, you're thinking of moving more than a thousand miles away!"

I now rolled my eyes and wondered why we had to have this conversation over and over again.

"Mom, first of all, you and I could never live under the same roof for *any* length of time! I'm sorry, but we'd murder each other. That's all there is to it!"

Anytime my mom and I start to argue, I'd slowly start to squirm in my seat. Like the floor nurses, I now couldn't wait to leave the room.

"Well, I better go for now. Love ya, Big Al!" I then walked over to my mom and gave her a kiss on the cheek. It seemed that I was always leaving Mom feeling worse or regretting even making the visit. "You didn't eat enough, stay long enough, come early enough, visit enough..." nothing I did was ever "enough."

Now I had several months to prepare for the move and spend time with my siblings. I welcomed a new beginning and a journey to the unknown.

Charlee and Ray were now living in the Kansas City area and had a beautiful three-year-old daughter named Courtney. My sister was busy raising a toddler and starting a new practice. I missed her companionship and meeting each other at Happy Hour for some girl talk. My little sister Abby came over every chance she had and was anxious to see Laurel and David as much as possible before we all left for Florida.

It was just a matter of six more months before our move would become a reality! It was nice to have Sam and T-Mac in town as my race partners. We were now participating in local races almost every weekend, weather permitting. A first for all of us was the St. Louis Marathon. I had worked up my mileage to the point where I felt I was able to finish running 26.2 miles. I positioned myself in the crowd with those who averaged 7 minutes per mile. Sam and T-Mac were faster and positioned closer to the starting line. I happened to glance at the fairly attractive male runner stretching next to me. The man seemed like he had a professional background, maybe a banker, stockbroker, or attorney type, with a neatly trimmed beard. My new male companion and I had a good pace going for the first ten miles of the marathon. Then out of nowhere, he said,

"I am *so* cold, *really* cold!"

We both had on nylon tights with the long-sleeved race T-shirt. I replied,

"I'm not too bad, but my hands are a bit nippy."

Once again he repeated himself,

"Oh, I'm sooo cold!"

At that moment, my new friend suddenly had this goofy look on his face. He then reached up to grab the knit beanie off his head and stuffed it down his tights to cover his penis! I thought to myself, *What the Heck?* The big balled-up hat made it look like he was running with a humongous boner!

I took the opportunity to sprint the hell away from him. I believe I made record time, only momentarily looking back. "Eat my dust!" It was around the eighteen-mile mark where I suddenly felt miserable, with the urge to stop. I definitely slowed down but never ceased running, not even for a moment. I ended up finishing the race in four hours. No doubt I wanted to finish with a faster time, *but* I finished, that's what's important! Another plus was that I didn't have to worry about limiting any calories over the holidays! Yes, hand over the mashed potatoes and gravy, and *yes*, I'll take a slice of apple crumb pie and piece of pumpkin too!

Four more months passed, and it was a beautiful spring morning. My daughter Laurel was now fourteen years old. She started to try to work on increasing her mileage too. I couldn't wait until we were all down in Florida, running on the beach along the gulf coast. Bo had the need for speed, though, and loved to sprint 440s with me but wasn't into distance running. So one morning we ran several miles and came home to mow our neighbor's lawn, which was almost an acre. I felt that was the least I could do after all she had done for us. Laurel came out to the yard, asking me if I would help her work on cartwheels.

"Laurel, when I was a cheerleader, I used to practice my routine, pikes and flips, in the backyard. And the yard is perfect, with no poop piles; it's flat and newly mowed!"

It occurred to me that I hadn't tried a handspring in years, and I wondered if I could still do it! Laurel cheered me on, "Try it, Mom!" I started running, flipped, and miraculously landed on my feet!

"Whoa! Scary! I don't know if I'll do that again!"

Just at that moment we heard laughter behind us. It was fifteen-year-old Maura O'Leary, who had witnessed the whole flip routine. While Maura was still doubled over with laughter, I asked,

"Maura, what's so funny?"

The young girl looked up, still snickering, "I didn't think *old* people could do that!

"That" meaning a hand-spring.

My eyes opened wide. "*Old?* Maura, I'm only forty. I'm not *old*!"

We were all laughing by then. I figured it did look a little ridiculous, if not crazy, for a woman my age to be doing handsprings in the backyard.

That evening Bo had his good buddy Wilson stay overnight. Those two had been almost constant companions since kindergarten. Wilson's mother Penny and I were also friends, and she even went to the same Catholic grade school as my ex! Penny was starting a new business venture in Florida. She was the one who gave me the idea to check out the Tampa/St. Pete area, as her family used to spend summer vacation there. I was watching television when Bo and Wilson came in. Bo announced, "Mom, Laurel just walked out the door?"

I shot up from the chair. "What do you mean? She walked out?"

Bo said, "She's sleepwalking!"

We all ran to the door to find Laurel mumbling while walking down the steps. Her eyes were open, but she had an empty, glazed stare. I gently put my arm around her to redirect her back to the house.

"Laurel, you're walking in your sleep. It's time to go back to bed." The boys thought it was funny; I could hear them giggling behind me.

Laurel had been up late for several days; maybe it was her chaotic schedule, lack of sleep, or the stress of our upcoming move causing her to start sleepwalking again.

These episodes had occurred a couple times a year when she was much younger. I stayed up a while longer to make sure Laurel stayed in bed.

My own sleep that night was extremely elusive, and once I did fall asleep, I had that horrible nightmare again. This time it was more detailed.

In my dream I was in a car, driving in a horrible storm on a highway. Then there was a bend in the road that led to the tallest bridge I had ever seen in my entire life! This bridge was over a large body of water and continued as far as I could see.

Strangely, in my dream there weren't any other cars on the bridge. When I was almost at the top, the strong wind seemed to keep pushing my car toward the edge. In my nightmare, I suddenly started to experience weakness in my arm. My repeated, panicked attempts to regain control of the car were unsuccessful. My car crashed through the guard rail and I found myself airborne off the side of the bridge. It was then that I woke up, gasping from the nightmare. This was a reoccurring nightmare for many months now. It got to the point where I would start to fear even the smaller local bridges. Maybe subconsciously I had a fear of losing control of my life, worrying if I could make it on my own as a single mom. When I was visiting a friend in the St. Charles area and had to cross the bridge, I repeatedly kept saying to myself, "Stop being irrational, focus on the beauty of this bridge and not some stupid nightmare!"

Laurel said, "Mom, why do you always hold your breath when crossing a bridge?"

I looked at my beautiful daughter and smiled, not wanting to alarm her with my thoughts.

"I guess just a habit!"

One morning when Laurel and I went on a run, we came across an enormous fawn-colored dog, sitting noble in the middle of a sprawling green lawn. The dog had black mask markings on its face and must've weighed around 150 pounds! The owner came out to call his gentle pet into the house.

Laurel asked, "What type of dog is that?"

The owner replied, "English mastiff, and she is as sweet as they come!"

Laurel couldn't wait to research the mastiff breed in our computer. Like mother, like daughter.

Laurel was a huge animal lover who repeatedly asked if we could live on a farm someday.

"Laurel, I don't know how I could work full time, take care of you kids, and run a farm too!"

The English mastiff breed intrigued me, though, and I agreed to consider one for our next pet.

The kids were still finishing up school, so I made arrangements to spend the next weekend looking for places to rent. My friend Penny was moving to an Island off of St. Pete Beach and suggested I check out that area for the kids. She told me the neighborhood had more full-time residents with children. The hospital that hired me for the temporary position was in St. Petersburg. It was my first trip to the area, and I was excited to explore to see if it felt like home. I rented a car while at the Tampa airport and ended up downtown Tampa. Unfortunately, I took the late flight in, and it was too dark to see much of anything. I was never very good at directions but was told I could get to 275 from 75 once I was in Manatee County. I was in my little car, wanting to absorb all the sights of the new city the kids and I would be living. Hopefully, I wouldn't get too distracted to follow the signs to St. Pete Beach. Suddenly, I noted the signs and said out loud, "Oh, geez, the woman at the gas station said 275 to St. Pete."

I veered off to the left. I could smell the salty air of the Gulf Coast. "This is heaven! Yes!" My head was turning left to right trying to take in all the sights, until I suddenly felt impending doom. My heart started to pound wildly in my chest, and I frantically gripped the steering wheel when I saw the tallest bridge that I'd ever seen in my entire life. This was Not a nightmare but a reality! I was now next in line to pay my toll and was in a full-blown panic attack!

"I can do this, I can do this, I *can* do this!"

The bridge before me was the majestic Sunshine Skyway Bridge, connecting the Pinellas and Manatee Counties. It was the bridge in my nightmare.

In the nightmare I lost control over my car after having a stroke, my car broke through the bridge barricade plunging down, down, down deep into Tampa Bay. This was it! The woman in the booth reluctantly took my toll money. She gave me a leery glance, as if I looked crazed and may be another potential "jumper." This was where I would die! I had no choice but to go over to the other side. Higher and higher I climbed, until I finally reached the top and...closed my eyes! Then I opened them and took a *really* deep breath while slowly heading down to the bottom of the bridge.

I realized this panic attack was absolutely ridiculous. "Yes, get a grip!" I said out loud.

My heartbeat now slowed, no longer pounding like a basketball dribbling hard and fast on a gymnasium floor. Look straight, don't look down... *swish! swish!* The other cars honked and swished by as they passed me on the bridge. I was driving like a Northern Q-tip on a lazy Sunday afternoon (Q-tip, referring to teeny-tiny elderly driver who can barely see over the steering wheel. From the back you see is a mound of round fluffy white hair.. like a Q-tip). I finally made it safely to the other side of the bridge. Now back on level ground, I yelled out loud, "*Whew!* I did it! No problem," and then laughed like a lunatic.

I later learned that this incredible structure was the world's longest cable-stayed bridge and designed 190 feet above Tampa Bay! It spans more than 5.5 miles and is 431 feet high!

Sadly, there had been approximately 130 people committed suicide by jumping from the bridge since it reopened in 1987. By 1999, the State of Florida installed six crisis phones on the center span of the Sunshine Skyway Bridge. The phones lead directly to a twenty-four-hour crisis hotline.

In May 1980, a freighter called the *Summit Venture* rammed into the bridge during a violent storm, causing more than one hundred feet of roadway to tumble into the bay below. Tragically, thirty-five people were killed that day. In 1987, the current bridge was constructed, now able to withstand the impact of an eighty-seven-thousand-ton ship. The bridge had an incredible mysterious, majestic beauty that captured me—yet also scared me to death!

The first small two-story house I looked at won me over with the lovely Mediterranean architecture and little turret on the second story. I quickly put down a deposit, and the kids and I would be moving in just a week or so. Of course, it wasn't on the beach; however, Fort DeSoto Park was only a mile or so away. Fort Desoto Park became my favorite part about the whole trip to St. Petersburg. This was the largest park in Pinellas County, and it had three miles of pristine sandy beaches and miles of trails to rollerblade, run, or bike. On one end were the waves rolling in from the Gulf, and on the other side there was another view of the amazing Sunshine Skyway Bridge.

From this view I wondered how I could have been so afraid, as it was now one of the most serene, beautiful sites I had ever seen. To end this most glorious and, yes, momentarily chilling trip, I put on my rollerblades and skated around the park to the gulf side. Then I watched the brilliant orange sun settle into the horizon.

Once back to St. Louis, I was anxious to share my Florida experience with Laurel and Bo. We would be moving down in less than two weeks to make Florida our home. They certainly thought it sounded cool but were more focused on checking out mastiff puppies. Laurel said,

"Remember, Mom? You said you would think about us getting a puppy in Florida? Well, why wait when we can have one now? Can we stop by the home that needs to get rid of the mastiff? It's on the way down to Florida!" I looked in the newspaper, which had a classified ad saying English mastiff puppies needed homes ASAP. The current owners weren't able to keep them due to an illness in the family. I sighed and said, "Hmm, well, okay. We can do that." I thought to myself, *What did I just say? Oh, great, let's add a little more stress to the move and get a puppy! And not just any puppy—a super-sized one!*

CHAPTER 28

The next two weeks flew by, and I kept busy, making arrangements to have furniture and other belongings shipped to Florida. That Sunday I missed an early scheduled lunch at my parents' house, what with all the last-minute packing. I picked up the phone to call June. "Hi, Mom, the kids and I will be over in a couple hours."

There was a brief silence on the other end. June was quite cool in her response.

"I'm sorry, but we already have plans."

Confused, I said, "What? You know we are leaving for Florida tomorrow right?"

My mother replied, "Yes."

To clarify, I asked again, "So you're too busy to see us this evening?"

In another icy tone, she replied, "You were only going to stay a short while anyway, so we made plans." Wow, maybe the reality and distance of the move hadn't hit June yet. The kids would be coming back and forth quite often, but I might not be able to. As they say, you need to walk in someone else's shoes to understand why they respond a certain way. My mom's and my relationship hadn't always been strained, but it had been for almost a decade. For the life of me, I don't believe I would ever miss an opportunity to say good-bye to my children. You never know what the future may hold, and it may be the last good-bye!

Well, needless to say, it was going to be nice to have a fresh start and get away from some of the tension. I desired to have healthy relationships with my kids, friends, future boyfriends, and eventually my mom.

The day had come when we were finally leaving for Florida. My friend Marie was accompanying us for the move, as her own kids were vacationing with the ex-husband. Laurel was now almost fifteen and Bo almost fourteen. We were finally all headed to our new Southern home. Laurel handed me a newspaper.

"Remember you said we could stop to look at mastiff puppy on the way?"

I thought, *Ugh! Ohhh, yes!* I looked at her and said, "Did I say that?" and laughed.

Laurel and Bo replied in unison, "*Yes!* Yes, you did!" I acted like I was hitting my head on the steering wheel to knock some sense into myself. As I had agreed a couple of weeks earlier, Marie, Laurel, David, and I decided to take a short detour to "look" at Mastiff puppies.

The winding country road lead to a neatly landscaped property surrounded with white board fencing that went on for miles. Laurel, Bo, and I could see cows and horses grazing in the rolling green pasture.

"Wow, this is one beautiful farm!" I said. "I'm really enjoying our little ride to 'look' at mastiffs!"

Laurel repeated, "Yes, *just* look!"

The owner opened the gate, and we parked right out in front of the house. The elderly woman told us, "Come right on back, and I'll show you the puppies. I'm afraid we will be selling this farm, as my husband had a stroke. We just don't have anyone to help us out anymore. There are only two pups left; one is apricot-colored and the other is fawn." The pups were kept in a separate building by the barn, which was like more like a carriage house. We walked through the door, and two big, clumsy puppies came running up to Laurel and Bo. I said, "Oh, my gosh, how old are these pups, and how much do they weigh?" The woman replied, "Well, the girls are three and a half months and almost forty pounds!"

Laurel attempted to lift one and laughed. "I can barely pick her up!" The fawn-colored mastiff stayed with Laurel and Bo, while the other kept running back and forth between them and the owner.

The puppy won us all over, and I knew we wouldn't be leaving without the new furry member of our family. We had a long talk with the owner, who gave us information on the breed. The parents of the pups were on the premises, with the adult male weighing 190 pounds and the female 165 pounds. The kids and I were tossing out ideas of names that we thought fit our new pup. Laurel finally said, "Mable! Mable Moo Cunningham!"

Our new pup then licked Laurel, as if she approved of her new name. Moving a thousand miles away was going to be hard enough without taking a puppy the size of a calf. I glanced in my rearview mirror at her adorable fuzzy face and smiled. *Awe, we'll be okay; it certainly won't be the most difficult thing I'll have to face in life.* Mable had excitedly and willingly gotten into the backseat with the kids. Unfortunately, with all the suitcases, we didn't have room for a humongous kennel too. Mable loved all the attention from her new human siblings. They were now in charge of making sure to tell us if she looked like she was going to have an accident.

David said, "Mom, Marie, Mable makes a great pillow! Try it when it's your turn to be in the backseat!"

Laurel chuckled, "Yes, a pillow that drools!"

It was nice to have Marie here with us on the big move. No doubt it comes in handy having another driver over the thousand-mile trip. Thankfully, our friend Ann (the third Amigo) would also be flying down to join us after a couple of days. We not only had our super-sized puppy Mable, but also David's gerbils, both named Gerbs. Marie and I took turns driving, trying to make the trip in eighteen hours, but we just couldn't do it. We were both so exhausted, and all we wanted to do was sleep.

The problem was that most all of the hotels South of Valdosta, Georgia, were sold out! How could that be? No kidding, we were desperately struggling to keep our heavy lids open. One motel did have a room but was right next to a twenty-four-hour strip club. *No way I'm taking the kids there.* So we drove a bit more, and one very out-of-the-way motel, with most of the lights burned out on the sign, had one vacancy. Oh, so wonderful to see the back of my eyelids! REM sleep, here I come! But...guess what happens to gerbils at night? Those critters come to life and are *very* active—*ahhh!*

All I heard the entire night was the pitter-patter of gerbil feet, playing, running, and scratch, scratch, scratch, and more scratching! Bo thought it was quite hilarious; however, he had been able to sleep for hours in the backseat while Marie and I drove from St. Louis to northern Florida. I finally was able to get in a few winks by dawn, after the "gerbs" decided they had enough play time.

By 11:00 a.m., Marie and I decided it was time to get back on the road. We all were quite excited that we only had a few hours before we were in St. Pete.

The strange thing about our new pup Mable was that she willingly got into the back of our SUV when we left the farm where she was raised. Unfortunately, after that, she never wanted back in the car again! Most dogs enjoy sticking their heads out the window and getting dry eye from the wind...Mable did not. So every time we'd stop to let her out stretch or go to the bathroom, the kids and I needed to round her up like livestock to put her in the vehicle.

"What's going to happen when she's over a hundred pounds?" "I can barely lift her now!"

Marie laughed, saying, "That's it, Laurel and David, you can never leave your mom in case she needs assistance putting this moose in the car!"

For two days, all of us worked very hard to move our belongings into our new place. The kids loved the tile roof and turret. David said, "Hey, this house has a lookout tower!" David and Laurel ran into the house to pick out their rooms. Laurel said, "I get the room with the little porch!"

David yelled, "I get the one with the secret room in the closet!"

My friend Penny from St. Louis had moved down to the area less than a year before. Penny had one daughter and three boys, including David's best friend Wilson. They went to elementary school together before his family moved to this area. His mom, Penny, was the one who initially tuned me into nursing job opportunities here in Florida. Her family used to vacation at St. Pete Beach, and she moved down to their estate home a year ago. The home was right on the bay and equipped with Jet Skis, a Sea Ray boat, and a kayak. David was thrilled that he would already have a buddy in the neighborhood that also had cool toys! Penny was having several friends over later that night at her magnificent home. She thought it would be a nice opportunity for us to meet our neighbors.

Marie, Laurel, and I had to pick Ann up at the airport. She would also be visiting for a few days and flying back to St. Louis with Marie. Marie combed her beautiful, thick, wavy dark brown hair after she put on her Jimmy Buffet T-shirt, shorts, and sandals. She then put on the festive straw beach hat. The vibrant colors made her eyes look even brighter. Leave it to Marie to always dress for the occasion! Marie, Ann, and I had been friends now for more than two decades, and it was nice to have them here with me at my new home. At the airport we all rushed to meet Ann, who walked out of the gate looking like a glamorous Barbie doll in her bright floral sundress. She said, "It seems so strange that you're living in Florida now, but I'm glad we have a cool place to visit!"

Later that evening, Marie, Ann, the kids, and I headed for Penny's house party. Marie instantly jumped into the refreshing pool by the bay. Penny's big Labrador puppy swiftly jumped in too and was in hot pursuit of Marie. This sixty-pound pup was pissed off that someone else was swimming in his territory! I almost heard the theme song of *Jaws* as he forcefully swam toward Marie and placed his enormous puppy paws on her shoulders! Marie yelled,

"He's trying to drown me!"

The sight was hysterically funny but at the same time potentially dangerous. The big yellow pup finally gave up and allowed Marie to swim without being accosted.

We were all sipping our drinks by the pool, admiring the Sunshine Skyway Bridge out in beautiful Tampa Bay. Ann and Marie noticed a kayak by Penny's dock.

"Hey do you think Penny will mind if we Kayak tomorrow?"

Penny overheard and said, "Sure, feel free to use it!"

Laughing, Marie asked, " Moe, are there sharks in the bay?"

I said, "Oh definitely! I heard the best hammerhead fishing is right by the Sunshine Skyway pier. And a neighbor said he sees lemon and nurse sharks off his dock all the time. Anyway, there's only one kayak, but you and Ann can go while I continue to unpack."

Marie and Ann were discussing how they would leave the next morning, shortly after breakfast. I suggested that later in the afternoon, we could have a picnic lunch by the beach. I added, "Oh, and Marie, Penny mentioned a hole in the kayak, but to just keep paddling and you'll stay afloat!"

Marie turned to me and said, "Okay, we will keep paddling."

That night at the party, Laurel met Bell, who was fifteen years old, and her thirteen-year-old sister Regan.

They were also neighbors from down the street. I immediately knew Bell would make a great new friend for Laurel. Bell and Regan had classic poise, long wavy brown hair, and porcelain complexions. They were not only lovely young ladies but also extremely sweet, like Laurel. Regan and Bell's father was a pro golfer, and their mother was an attorney, like Charlee.

Little did Laurel and Bell know that night was the beginning of their close bond and a friendship that would last many decades.

The next morning Marie and Ann woke up around 6:00 a.m. to a breakfast table with a variety of huge muffins from the 7-Eleven down the street. I cautioned the girls, "Be careful when selecting your muffin! Laurel is notorious for eating the tops and leaving the stumps!"

Laurel and Bo snickered when they heard my accusation. Laurel replied, "Guilty as charged!

We sat huddled around the table, leisurely talking, and refilled our coffee cups several times. Afterwards I dropped them both off at Penny's to kayak.

"Hey, how long are you two going to be out?"

Marie reassured me it would only be a couple of hours or so. The two gung-ho women put on their life jackets and headed out toward the Sunshine Skyway Bridge.

Later, the sun was high in the sky, and the girls were still not back! I phoned Penny to ask if she had seen Ann and Marie. "No, I haven't seen them since this morning!" I then walked behind her house to get a better look at the bay—but no kayak. "Damn! Where are you two?" I walked back to the house and looked inside to see if they were home.

"Marie? Ann?" Then as I was once again walking out the door, I saw my two friends walking in the middle of the street, barefooted, in their bathing suits and life jackets. I yelled,

"What happened?"

while running toward them. Marie looked absolutely dehydrated; Ann was red from the sun and absolutely drained. Marie explained, "What happened was we stopped paddling! Yes, Ann and I were awestruck with the beauty of the Sunshine Skyway and stopped rowing. Then suddenly we started to take on *a lot* of water in the kayak!"

I raised my hand to my mouth. "Oh, no!"

Ann chimed in, "All Marie and I could think about were all the hammerhead sharks you talked about yesterday and how we would be shark bait!"

Marie then added, "We started to paddle like to ever-ready rabbits! No kidding, a mile a minute, but it didn't help. The kayak sank into the bay!

We then had to swim the kayak to shore, but all we could find were steep, barnacle-covered sea walls! I cut myself trying to get out."

They ended up grabbing onto the kayak and swimming to someone's dock on the other side of the neighborhood. Their shoes were lost when the kayak sank, and they had to walk home barefoot. Marie and I then drove to the house where they left the kayak, and we kayaked back to Penny's. Later that night, after they were fed and rehydrated, we all had a good laugh about their day. It seemed like we ended of many of our days watching the sunset on the gulf at Fort De Soto Park. We would all be mesmerized by the bright orange glow of the sun and how it seemed to slowly melt into the green flash off in the horizon.

In the morning I was filled with sadness at the thought of taking Marie and Ann to the airport. *They are headed back to St. Louis, and I am staying here in Florida.* We would no longer be able to quickly run over to each other's houses for coffee or a bite to eat. Charlee, Ann, Marie, and all my friends that I'd known for most of my life were almost a thousand miles away. Florida was now my new home and I had to shake off all my old insecurities about being on this journey as a single woman. *I can do it and I will open myself up to new adventures.*

It was almost midnight when Mable quickly hopped off the bed and ran to the back door. We were having a horrible storm with winds strong enough to blow the screen open on the turret. It slapped violently open and shut, *bang! bang! bang!* Mable was whining as if she had to go to the bathroom. There I was in my pajamas, I also whined, "Ugh, Mable, not now!"

Mable frantically scratched on the door. She was normally the type of dog that stayed in the yard without a leash. The rain blew in as I opened the door to let her out.

"Hurry up, Mable!"

I partially closed the door to prevent the rain from saturating the house. When I opened the door again, no Mable! *Darn!* Laurel was overnight at Bell's, and Bo was staying over at Wilson's!

"Mable! Mable!" Still no Mable...

I quickly ran to the car then drove around the neighborhood in my pajamas.

"Mable! Mable!"

At the other end of the neighborhood was Mable, munching on a hibiscus bush! I got out of the car to open the back of my SUV. Darn Mable started to run off again! She was still afraid of car rides!

I ran up to her then started to pull Mable toward my vehicle—without success. There was definitely no way to pick her up since she was almost sixty pounds! So I drove the car home to pick up the leash, then I sprinted in the pouring rain in my pajamas to get Mable. Now that the car wasn't around, Mable enjoyed our little walk in the rain. Yes, another one of those situations that you laugh about later, but not now!

That afternoon, I had to take Mable in for her examination and vaccines at our new vet's office.

I put Mable on the leash and put treats in my pocket to lure her to the SUV. Darn, Mable didn't buy it one bit; she started to pull away as we neared the car. After the escapade the night before, I was too exhausted to play games or pull this stubborn moose alone! Laurel was at Bell's house, so I ran back in the house to get my phone.

"Laurel, I need you to come home to help me put Mable in the car!" Laurel replied,

"Awe, Mom, don't make *me* the bad guy! I don't want to be the bad guy!"

I was getting frustrated now. "Darn it! I'm in a hurry to get to the vet's office and don't give a darn who is the bad guy!" I then made another call to David, who was at Wilson's house.

"Bo, please can you, Wilson, and his brothers help me get Mable in the car?"

It was only five minutes later when I saw Bo and the three Wagner boys running down the middle of the street. It was a comical sight to see!

"Here we come to save the day!"

The youngest one was flexing his muscles, saying,

"It takes someone strong to pick her up!"

Mable knew what was in store for her, so she playfully galloped off to the other yard. David yelled,

"Catch her!"

I opened up the back of the SUV, and we finally put Mable Moo in the back. The worst was yet to come. On the drive to the vet's office, I heard Mable retch several times followed by a flow of fluids, and the most sickening smell wafted throughout the car! If there was an orifice, there was something awful pouring out of it.

Mable had diarrhea, vomited, and urinated in the back of my SUV! The whole area was covered with a massive amount of everything! When I arrived at the office, I ran in to ask if they had paper towels. Then I ran back out to wipe up whatever I could and to clean off my poor dog. Then I couldn't get Mable out of the car and had to ask for help. No one was available, and they acted like I was an idiot, not being able to get my dog out of the car. I was totally unimpressed by my new vet office; it would be my last visit there. When I checked out of the office, I needed help *again* putting Mable back in the car! Unfortunately, it took several minutes before someone was willing to help me out. I adored this super-sized pup, however was beginning to think I took on more puppy than I could handle.

My friend Penny stopped by on her way to a business meeting. She kicked off her uncomfortable shoes as she headed for the kitchen for some coffee. After an hour, Penny headed to the door, looking for her shoes. I scanned the room and cringed.

"Umm, were you wearing shiny black heels?"

Penny looked up and said,

"Why, yes! See them?"

Slowly and sadly, I pointed over to what my mastiff pup was chewing.

The first month in our new home, we went through almost half a dozen pillows, a hole in the carpet, and even a hole in the wall! There was nothing she wouldn't chew! You'd think I'd be used to it, after my bulldog; however, the damage was much bigger, given Mable's much larger size. I took a couple rollerblade wheels and plaster to fill the hole in the wall, then primed and painted it. That was the first time I wondered if I actually made the right decision to buy Mable. I went to the pet store to buy a lion-sized crate. While I was there, I saw a man walking his ever-so-lazy older English mastiff. He reassured me that someday, my Mable would be that calm too.

CHAPTER 29

Since my divorce, I dated an unfulfilling assortment of men. One was a middle-aged physician, who told me he had been divorced for a year. There wasn't really a big physical attraction; however, I thought he was nice. I told myself to give him a chance. Well, the truth came out, and in realty he was having one of those divorces like the movie *War of the Roses*. It wasn't pretty! My date *eventually* told me the wife had been arrested for trying to run him over! He wasn't really divorced yet, either-ugh! Yes, I crossed him off my list fast! In reality, it felt more like work to go out on dates. I thought it would be healthier to wait for the right one.

I had to work ten-hour evening shifts in the emergency room. The staff was nice, though not as cohesive as the one I worked at in St. Louis. Whenever children would injure themselves, I would try to see who their favorite superhero or cartoon character was and then draw it on their dressing or bandage. One seven-year-old cut himself falling off his bike. The cute little guy told me he loved the Ninja Turtles. I said, "Okay, how about I'll draw Leonardo for you?"

He excitedly said, "*Cool!* I'll never take it off!"

We had some slow periods filled with a variety of cuts, flu, GI bleeding, and minor auto accidents. It was around ten o'clock one night when the ambulance brought in an eighteen-year-old who had attempted suicide. These were always absolutely gut-wrenching cases for me to deal with in the emergency room. The paramedics were still doing CPR on this boy when they whisked him through the emergency room doors. The physician and all of us nurses then worked to revive him until we were exhausted. After a long while, the code was called, and this fair-haired eighteen-year-old, who had so much to live for, was pronounced at 10:58 p.m. His parents were waiting just outside the room. One of the paramedics handed me a sign that read "I Am Nobody." He sadly said,

"This is what we found taped to the boy's chest."

A knot formed in my throat and in my stomach as I slowly walked to the deceased young man's side.

I gently stroked his hair.

"You were somebody to someone. Oh, how I wish you knew."

I left momentarily to call the kids but didn't want to reveal the tragic case I had just dealt with.

"Hi, Laurel!"

She sleepily said, "Is everything okay?"

I smiled at hearing her voice. "Yes, I just wanted to tell you both that I love you very much."

I woke up early, cherishing the thought of having a large cup of coffee. To my surprise, the phone rang around 6:00 a.m. It was my sister Charlee, whom I spoke to almost every other day—but not usually at the crack of dawn.

"Hey, Sis, what's up?" I asked.

There was a long pause on Charlee's end; then, sounding rather perturbed, she said, "I just wanted to know when you were coming home from Florida? You know, I've had the brunt of taking care of Mom's endless needs and visiting Dad almost every weekend for months! I'm just tired of it and need help from my sibling!"

I was wide-eyed at her anger, as Charlee and I always had a strong sibling bond.

"Whoa, wait a minute! I am a single mom, living here a thousand miles away! It's not like I can even afford to go back and forth twice a month, or even once! Besides, Mom couldn't even spend an hour with us before we moved. That's inexcusable—and I know I shouldn't take it out on Dad, but I was hurt!"

Charlee quickly retorted,

"Why the hell did you move so far away when Dad has cancer?"

Yes, I felt guilty, and in my mind I never thought my father would actually die from cancer. He was diagnosed years ago, and I honestly thought he would beat it.

Charlee said, "Dad doesn't look good, so I hope you didn't sign yourself up for too many months!"

I cleared my throat,

"Sis, I'm sorry I haven't been there to help, but I honestly couldn't take it anymore. I had opportunity here, David's best friend relocated here, and it just made sense. Charlee—"

"You're just so damn selfish!" she shouted.

Charlee didn't call back, and I didn't call her either. I made a brief visit to see my parents that weekend. I realized that those with ice within their souls aren't just murderers, pedophiles, or other hardened criminals. Unfortunately, it can also include everyday people, whose only crime is to build a senseless defensive wall following arguments, miscommunication, or misunderstandings. Everyone is capable of having ice within his or her soul. Instead of openly addressing "issues," they allow the frustration and anger to build, gradually distancing themselves from loved ones for months, years, and sometimes forever.

I once worked with a male nurse who hadn't seen his mother for more than fifteen years! I asked him what had happened. His reply astonished me. He said,

"Well, she kicked me out after high school and told me to get a job. I haven't seen her since."

My mom and I had butted heads for more than a decade. This was the first time I put my foot down and just left. In a healthy relationship, you should willingly and naturally want to bring out the best in each other. It involves not only taking but giving too. I like to give the example of a rowing crew, where every member has a role, whether it's a two- or eight-man team. It's magnificent to witness everyone functioning in harmony, and the union is a beautiful sight.

You may not have smooth sailing or row rhythmically all the time, but you try to evaluate what went wrong and get back in the boat again. When someone ignores a problem or stops trying, the relationship boat is bound to sink. My boat was going in circles, so I had no choice but to get out for a while—but not forever.

CHAPTER 30

Hurricane George was a powerful storm that formed about four hundred miles from Cape Verde. At one point George packed 150 mph winds and was classified as a category 4 hurricane. It slowed to 100 mph as it crossed over Puerto Rico, causing horrific damage to the island. By September 24, 1998, the hurricane was just off the coast of Cuba and headed for Florida. The concern was that the storm would once again intensify as it hit the warmer waters of the Gulf. By September 25, we were alerted that we needed to vacate the island we lived on off of St. Pete and seek shelter on higher ground. I had been dating someone who always complained about Mable's slobbering, so I stopped dating him. You like me, you like my dog. So going to his place wasn't an option. Thankfully, Penny invited us to come to her business to wait out the storm.

We left early the next morning to get back to the island and maybe catch up on some sleep. The kids went in to snooze for a bit, and I decided to look up a new veterinarian on the computer. Mable needed her shots, I needed advice eliminating her fear of cars and also getting her to stop eating the house and all its contents. I came across a Florida vet who was online for questions concerning pets. I thought, "Oh, fantastic!" And I started to type away. My screen name, XL, was a shortened combination of words, "Excel in Life" and my name.

XL to Vet: Hi, do you have time for a couple questions about my dog?

Vet to XL: Sure, XL! How can I help you?

XL: There are a couple concerns, but the biggest one is Mable's fear of getting into our car. It takes rounding up a posse of neighborhood kids to help me get her in the SUV.

Vet: LOL! You probably shouldn't have bought a dog that's bigger than you are! <grin> Most dogs absolutely love their car rides, but there are those pets that truly panic attack at the thought of getting into a vehicle. You probably first need to rule out any medical condition that would cause your dog to want to avoid car rids. Like carsickness.

XL: Oh yes! That was a problem on the way to the vet's office! Oh my gosh, it came out of both ends.

Vet: We certainly need to address the issue or prescribe a medication for Mable.

XL: I agree.

XL: I wasn't too happy with my vet's office, and I'm looking for a new one that can help me, help Mable.

Vet: Once the carsickness is addressed, you can work with your pet on calming her fears. If Mable was from a shelter, she may have some issues with abandonment or a history of something negative that we're not aware of early on. They can be alleviated with time and consistency. I would try opening up the back of the vehicle, take some treats, and sit there with Mable. Don't go anywhere. You two will just sit, look at the scenery, eat treats, and give her a lot of loving pats. Make it fun for Mable! Do that for a week, and gradually progress to very short trips, maybe around the block. You can't start out forcing her to get in the car, or she will develop a deeper aversion to the rides. You will need to be patient, but in the end it will pay off with a pet that will enjoy her car rides.

XL: Well, where are you located? I'm new to Florida and am looking for a new vet. Mable will need her vaccines in another month or so.

Our conversation continued for an hour or so, and I was impressed that he took so much time with me. Dr. Hopkins' office was an hour or so away, but maybe it would be worth driving to a vet and office that cared about their clients. When I signed off the chat, I found that I was still smiling at the computer—so goofy! I finally felt like there was hope in dealing with Mable.

The next day the kids and I all took turns taking toys, treats, and a comfy blanket and sitting with Mable in the car. We didn't go anywhere, just sat as instructed by Dr. Milton Hopkins. The neighbors all thought it was hilarious, seeing a big, goofy-looking mastiff sitting in the SUV with a jowly canine grin.

We didn't take Mable anywhere for two weeks. The neighbors—Bella, Regan, the Wagner boys, and their sister—would all come up to the SUV, bringing treats. Mable would stick her mega head out like an eel from a rock to retrieve food. It got to the point where she expected treats from every human that walked by.

When someone wasn't aware of our mission and obliviously meandered by, Mable would look at me like,

"What's his problem? Did you forget to tell him the rules? No treat, no pass!"

Mable thought that this island was her kingdom and she was Queen Bee! At the end of the week, I thought I'd write Dr. Hopkins on Mable's progress. We ended up typing back and forth for another hour or so. I discovered that his middle name was "Albert," the same as my father. His first name, Milton, is the same as the Wisconsin town I was born in and where Big Al went to college. Awe, heck, maybe I was just fishing for strange coincidences, but I enjoyed chatting with him online.

Laurel completed the first month of her sophomore year at the local high school. Bell was quite popular and introduced Laurel to all of her friends. What a blessing! I couldn't afford to send David to the same private school that Wilson was attending. It was more difficult for him, not knowing anyone at his new school. No doubt, I felt guilty about the move. On one hand, Laurel was flourishing more here in Florida than Missouri, and on the other hand, David was not. He loved being here with Laurel and me, but not in this educational program. David was used to having quite a few friends, and now he had to start fresh. David was my social butterfly, and I just assumed it would be easier for him. *It's only been a month in school, though*, I reasoned to myself, *and it's just a matter of time before he will meet more kids in class*.

As parents we all want our kids to have smooth sailing every day. Not to ever have to experience pain, rejection, loneliness, sadness. I told myself it's a part of life that we all must experience—I wanted this move to not disrupt their life, but make it better.

They had a father, though, and they missed him. It may be necessary to move back to St. Louis, for the sake of the kids. Yet, one is doing better than ever and one is not. I prayed for guidance in making the right decision for all of us.

Mable was good for the kids, and they adored seeing her happy face when they came home from school. Wherever they were, Mable was there too. Thank heaven, she slowly but surely started to overcome her fear of car rides. Unfortunately, we found Mable Moo had another new fear, and that was of the beach!

Mable cheerfully hopped down from the SUV at Fort De Soto Park. I'm sure she loved inhaling the scent of hot dogs from the pavilion! This was at the end of our third week of making short trips. The first few were just around the block. Mable frolicked in the sand until we walked down the path between the sand dunes to the beach. When Mable got a glimpse of the rushing waves, she broke away from us and ran all the way back to the car! *Oh geez, this dog is going to give me grey hair!*

That evening Laurel, David, and I went to see Bell cheer and watch the football game. David enjoyed checking out the other cheerleaders and looked forward to being in the same school next year with Laurel, Bell, and Regan. My fingers were crossed that he would not want to leave and move back to St. Louis.

It was late by the time we came home, as we stopped off for some ice cream cones. I then went to the computer to check e-mail and found a short, sweet note from Dr. Hopkins. By this time we had been chatting with each other almost every other day for over a month. The subject for the first month was advice about Mable, but it gradually included family life too. What was refreshing about Dr. Hopkins was that he was an absolute gentleman. We both had no idea what the other looked like, but at this point I didn't care what outer package he came in. I knew he was a wonderful man with a kind, gentle heart. That's what was most important to me. I had just recently told him that I was divorced mother of two teens, and he then revealed he was a single father of two as well. The first time we chatted was September 26, and now it was the first week in November.

Each morning I excitedly ran to my e-mail. To see if I had a note from my new friend and I did. It read: "Dear XL, Would you be willing to have dinner with me on November 16? The Don Cesar has a beautiful restaurant on the beach, and I can pick you up or meet you there at 7:00 p.m. If you feel uncomfortable, I certainly understand.

What a strange thought, going out on a date with someone I didn't know or even have a clue as to what he looked like! My gut, my intuition told me it all felt right with him. I immediately responded and accepted his invitation.

It was a few days until the date, and Milt and I thought we would exchange pictures on the computer. He wasn't real familiar with sending photos online, which made me believe he was an older man. It was a couple of days before he could find a recent photo and figure out how to send it. I was like a wide-eyed kid in a candy shop as I waited for this *huge* file to download. Oh my, it was a painfully slow process, only downloading millimeter by millimeter, starting from the top of his head. I was surprised that Milt had a head full of dark brown hair. I thought, *Okay, he's not bald!* Then, snail-slow, a few more millimeters exposed a forehead. After about five more minutes, the most amazing brown eyes were staring back at me from the computer! They were intense, intellectual, soft brown eyes. His dark brown hair fell boyishly on his forehead, and he had the sweetest smile on his face. Dr. Hopkins was forty-two years old, six feet three, with a slender, athletic build. His face mesmerized me as I smiled back at him.

It was then my turn to send my picture to Milt. It was one that I had taken less than a year earlier, with a bright green tree in the background. My stomach turned, and I was anxious about disappointing him. You never really know what image a person develops from conversation.

"Okay, here goes!"

I pressed the button and waited for him to respond. And I waited awhile longer, then twenty minutes went by, and he finally went offline!

Oh, my gosh! Maybe we won't be going out on the sixteenth. My heart sank at the thought of how, for the first time in years, I was actually excited about dating. I had grown accustomed to talking to him every other day for the past month, and he felt comfortable, so familiar. It was then that my phone rang. On the other end was a sweet, gentle Southern accent, and the first thing he said was, "You're absolutely beautiful, XL."

Just then Laurel and Bell came into the house, all rowdy and rambunctious, which was unusual for them. I gave them a "shush" sign with my finger and closed the door. They were so loud that I could hardly hear Milt's soft voice! I responded, "Thank you, I thought I scared you away when you signed offline."

Laurel and Bell poked their heads in the door,

"Mom, we're hungry. Can we go up to BK? Aren't you hungry too?

It's past two, and we haven't eaten yet. Guess what Bell told me..."
both girls started laughing.

I politely said,

"Can you hold on for a minute, Milt?"

Trying to compose myself, I put my hand over the phone and said,

"Come on, you two...wait in the other room, okay? Please! I'm on the phone!"

Now, Laurel and Bell were most always such proper, sweet little human beings. A couple of minutes later, the door opened again.

"Who are you talking to? You think you'll be ready in five minutes?"

I thought, *Oh, gees! A minute please?"*

Milt could sense a little tension in my voice and asked,

"Is there anything wrong?"

I hesitated then replied,

"My household isn't usually this crazy when I'm on the phone. Maybe the girls can tell it's someone special."

From that point on, the noise level decreased, and we went on to have the most phenomenal conversation. We just seemed to click immediately. It was a connection that I had never felt before, ever! We had several strange coincidences.

- Big Al reviewed F-4 jet contracts
- Milt's father was an aeronautical engineer
- Both worked in the same government building in St. Louis, but in different years
- My dad went to "*Milton*" College
- I was born in "*Milton*", Wisconsin
- Milt's middle name was Albert, the same name as my Father.

The following day Laurel, David, and I were having professional pictures taken at Ft. De Soto Park, right on the beach. That evening we all wore blue jeans and crispy starched white shirts. I had always loved the sunset and wanted to capture it on our family photo. The photographer took several shots on the sand, then suggested one closer to the water. Well, feisty David took this as an opportunity to be mischievous. "Hey, Mom, let's get your hair wet!" Then David started splashing water before we were done with our shots. Lauren began splashing too.

"Ugh! Hey! Heeeeeeey!" I protested.

The photographer had fun with it and started taking pictures. I had images that would remind me of looking like a wet rat for many years to come. *But*, I must admit, we had fun and had a laugh...we needed one. We finished with the pictures and continued to watch the sunset over the Gulf of Mexico. *This has to be the best, most therapeutic treatment for stress,* I thought. We became one with the calm vision of serene artistry. All three of us sat there in silence as we gazed at the brilliant green flash and the end of a beautiful day.

Laurel and David were full of questions about my upcoming date with Milt. Laurel said, "Mom, where did you meet him?" David asked, "Does he play sports? Does he like animals?" I gave them a brief synopsis of how we met.

What was funny was that Mable sat and waited by the door, as if she knew he was coming over. I normally wouldn't have met him at the house; however after a month and a half of conversations and checking him out online (yes, he actually *was* a veterinarian), I felt safe. At no point in that span of time had he ever been fresh or suggestive.

I chose a black sleeveless shell with a gold and black skirt, with a stretch belt that had a gold clasp buckle in front. I thought to myself that it wasn't too revealing or too cautiously restrained. I thought the outfit looked nice. Mable loved both shoes and feet; she momentarily left her perch at the door to dart for my black sandals. I yelled, "Oh no, Mable! No, you don't!" I quickly put them on my feet. Mable went back to her guard duty by the door. Then I saw an old, rusted, maroon-colored SUV forerunner pull in our driveway.

Laurel and David shouted, "He's here Mom!"

My heart was beating a mile a minute, and the palms of my hands started to perspire. Then *knock, knock, knock!* I was almost beside myself with excitement when I opened the heavy mahogany door. Mable and I both looked up to a tall, wonderfully handsome man. Milt had soft, deep-set brown set eyes with a dark masculine brow.

His high cheek bones and nose reflected an Indian descent. The white starched shirt was buttoned to the very top, looking quite conservative, like a banker. On his classically handsome face, there was something else I noticed...no laugh lines. I thought that if he were around this family long enough, we would surely give him a few.

Milt gave me an ear-to-ear boyish grin and leaned forward to give me a big hug. Just then, the stretchy belt I was wearing snapped off my waist and flew across the room, hitting the wall—bang! Just like a supersized rubber band! I was really embarrassed, but we both laughed so hard that I didn't think we would stop. Mable took to Milt immediately and excitedly jumped around him like a 150-pound Chihuahua. I guess she could tell that Milt liked mega-dogs. He was sweet and took an interest in my kids by asking them a few questions about themselves. I could tell Lauren and David approved.

The conversation just flowed so naturally as we had our seaside dinner table at the Don Cesar. It was as if we'd known each other for years. How could this be? I found that one of his favorite pastimes was to watch the sunset! Wow, another bullet point for what we had in common. Our hands were one as we continued to talk about life work family. We paused just long enough to watch the setting sun. After the most amazing, romantic dinner, we walked the beach, arm in arm, listening to the waves rushing onto the shore. The weather conditions were perfect with a gentle sea breeze, and we walked under millions of stars in the sky.

"Tell me more about your parents in St. Louis."

I then went into more detail about my dad's esophageal and gastric cancer and his incredible will to live and to do whatever it took to continue to grow old with my mom. I shared with him how my mom was a housewife and as a child I loved coming home to see her smiling face after school. I continued, "She's an Irish Finnish woman who is also an amazing Italian cook! The best pizza ever! How about you, Milt?"

He looked at me with sadness in his eyes.

"My mother passed away when I was eighteen years old of a heart attack. She was only forty."

I empathetically replied,

"Oh, I bet that was so difficult for you!"

He continued to share with me how his mother had previously been diagnosed with systemic lupus and had been in and out of the hospital since he was five years old.

"Yes, on my first day of kindergarten, I had to take a cab to school. My dad was at the hospital with my mother."

Our conversation made me lose all track of time but soon realized it was getting late. It was the end of a truly marvelous date and hoped there would be another!

The next day I received a beautiful bouquet of two dozen roses from Milt! *Does it get any better than this?* He called later than evening, and that was the beginning of his "count downs" to the days and minutes until we see each other again. He would say,

"Only three days, eight hours, and twenty-three minutes!"

That weekend we went to Ybor City, a historic district located in the Latin quarter of Tampa, Florida. It was around I-4 and North Twenty-Second Street and was one of the oldest sections of the city. Ybor City was considered to be the cigar capital, so it only seemed fitting to find a cigar museum there too! The streets were lined with art studios, quaint shops, multicultural restaurants, and a variety of night clubs. It was a popular hot night spot for the college crowd; however, there were all ages, shapes, sizes, and backgrounds at Ybor.

Milt and I once again walked hand in hand throughout this exciting community. We chose a romantic Italian restaurant to have dinner, and once again the conversation flowed throughout the whole evening. The slender, well-groomed waiter came to take our wine order, and Milt recalled that I liked white Zinfandel. Milt, in his deep southern twang, replied, "We'll have a bottle of Zi-an-*fan-dayle*."

It might not have been too polite; however, I started to snicker. He looked at me, rather puzzled. "What's so funny?"

I replied,

"Oh, the cute way you said Zinfandel. Zi-an Fan *dayle*! Sorry for laughing! I actually enjoyed the Southern pronunciation."

He then smiled too. The waiter gracefully walked up and poured *red* Zinfandel into each glass. The red Zinfandel was a deep red, robust, semi-sweet wine. I realized the reds were healthier; however, I much preferred the lighter taste of white. Additionally, the white or light blush whites tend not to turn teeth a bluish color, as the red ones do. It's all personal preference, but I must have hesitated to pick up the glass. I said,

"Ohhh, I thought he was bringing *white* Zinfandel."

My date replied,

"If you don't like it, I guarantee that each glass will taste better than the first!"

Milt's sassy response made us both laugh. We both said "Cheers!" and he added,

"To many more dates like this one!"

CHAPTER 31

Laurel was taking driver's education in school and was excited about me taking her out on the roads. The thought of having my daughter behind the wheel for the first time scared the heck out of me!

"Laurel, how many times have you driven with your instructor?"

She momentarily looked up,

"Hmm, maybe a couple."

Her response made me panicky and wide-eyed. I replied,

"A couple? Is that all? Whoa, Laurel, I don't know if I'm ready to be a driving instructor!"

After a lot of coaxing, Laurel and I went to the far end of a park so she could drive in an empty lot. She was going around and around. Then Laurel asked if she should turn. I thought she meant turn between the lines in the parking spot. I nodded and said,

"Right." I meant, "Yes."

Well, a warning out there to amateur parent driving instructors. You can say "Yes" or "No," but never "Right"—unless you mean for the driver to turn that direction. Laurel, sitting ever so erect in the driver's seat, proceeded to turn *right* out of the parking lot into traffic. I was literally grabbing onto the dash, trying not to get hysterical.

"Laurel, I meant right as in okay, not to turn out into the street traffic!"

She said, "Mom, chill, I'm doing okay."

Laurel drove a bit further, while I bit my nails. She pointed to the left and asked,

"Should I turn?"

Habits die slowly with me, and I once again said, "Right! *No*, I mean yes! Turn left! The way you pointed!" We only drove around another mile before I told Laurel we had to call it a day. The truth was that I was ready to have a heart attack, at least but I felt like it.

It was now January 1999, and Milt and I were now seeing each other almost every Tuesday and, if possible, each weekend. His sweet, calm nature was a good complement to my hyper side. Thank goodness he accompanied me on Laurel's driving lessons. I, of course, sat in back while Milt gave her instructions. Over time I became more comfortable seeing Laurel behind the wheel and didn't panic so much.

Milt and I decided to rollerblade and bike on a sunny Saturday afternoon at Fort DeSoto Park. By this time, we had been dating almost three months. I had on my gym shorts and bathing suit top while rollerblading while Milt biked behind me on the beautiful palm-lined thirteen-mile path. A car with a few young men whistled and hooted out their window when we turned the corner. I laughed, saying, "Milt, even the men honk at you!" To me, he was the most handsome man alive, with his sleek, athletic long legs and toned arms poised in a racing position on the bike.

He now pedaled his bike alongside me and turned his head to face me.

"No, they were honking at you. I just have to put a ring on your finger and take you off the market."

I thought, *What? Was that the wind in my ears, or did he just propose to me?*

I stopped suddenly, and he stopped in the middle of the trail. I cocked my head and looked at him.

"Milt, maybe I heard you wrong, but...did you say you want to put a ring on my finger?"

He gave me a big boyish grin again.

"Yes, that's what I said. Will you marry me?"

This was amazingly spontaneous and totally unexpected!

"Of course! Yes, I will marry you.

We kissed as if we were the only ones in the park. Someone rode by and yelled,

"Get a room!"

I laughed as I recalled saying that very thing to Charlee and Ray. They were so in love, they could barely keep their hands off one another, and now Milt and I were the same way.

That evening we watched the sunset as we had done many times before. But this time I was watching the last beautiful moments of day with my fiancé, the man I was going to marry.

Merging our two families was going to be quite the learning experience for us. In the months following our engagement, we attempted get our kids together as often as we could.

Milt's ten-year-old son Jason was a cute, lanky, blond-haired boy with blue eyes and freckles across the bridge of his nose. He was quiet, intelligent, and reserved like his father. Now Ester was a pretty fourteen-year-old with strawberry blond hair, braces, and deep–set, almond-shaped blue eyes. She, too, was quiet; however, it may have been due more to distrust than to shyness. I realized it wasn't easy for kids when their parents divorced and then had plans to remarry. David, though, seemed to bring out the silly side of Jason with sports, wrestling, and head noogies! I enjoyed seeing Jason smile more as he slowly became comfortable with the thought of being in a blended family. Several months after everyone had the chance to get to know one another, we took the kids to stay overnight at a resort in Sanibel. Much to their dismay, David and Jason had to share a fold-out couch. David drew an imaginary line down the center and said firmly,

"Now listen up, Jason. Remember, no going over the line, and I certainly better not wake up to you snugglin' on me!"

I thought we were all going to bust a gut with David's rule.

No doubt this would be a slow process and transition for kids, who may feel like the other parent is being replaced. Laurel, David, and I were an affectionate family with lots of hugs and I-love-yous. I found my future stepkids to be sweet, good kids, but not as open in their verbal or physical expressions of love. But Milt and I were in this as a team and for the long haul. We would do whatever it took to make it work, and we would never give up on making us all a family.

It had been several months since I had spoken to Charlee. She actually did phone once; however, I unfortunately allowed weeks to go by before I returned her call. I finally left a message for her and never did hear back. Our defense wall was built, and now a barrier was between us. How is it that we allowed something so small to escalate, like the metaphor—a mountain out of a mole mound. That's what we did. I set about making plans to be the one to contact her with an apology. Heck, she didn't even know about Milt or that we were engaged to be married. I need to call her, not today but sometime soon and break the ice between us.

CHAPTER 32

It was summer break, and the kids were spending a month in St. Louis with their father. Milt had a week off, so we decided to take a trip to New York City and then drive to the Finger Lakes Region in upstate New York. This was actually the first trip that we'd had all alone. It would be a good test to see how we handled so much togetherness, as our previous trips were shorter and with kids. From sunup to sundown, we were walking, whether it was through Central Park, Times Square, Broadway shows, or comedy clubs. Being together was easy; it was a harmonious flow, so synchronized in our likes, desires, and dislikes. There were so many police officers on horses patrolling the streets that we felt fairly safe.

After a few days we decided to explore Upstate New York. It was unbelievably scenic, with the rolling mountainside along the interstate. There were lush green valleys covered with colorful flowers in the meadows. The Catskill Mountains continued to frame the interstate, and our ears popped like we were in the Colorado Rockies. After a few hours, NY-17 became I-88 and eventually passed a little sign that read "Chenango Bridge." Before I asked if we could turn off, Milt already had his blinker on. I exclaimed,

"Hey, you better stop reading my mind!"

He turned with a surprised look and smiled.

We pulled down a road that followed the winding Chenango River. It was called; Wisconsin drive. A few acres of land exposed the flowing river beneath the mountains. We both stood admiring the beauty of this quaint Valley town surrounded by foothills.

"Milt, isn't it funny we ended up on Wisconsin Drive? That's where I was born!"

We started to walk in the tall grass green that had a colorful array of wild flowers. I felt a tickle on my arm and saw a ladybug. I carefully raised my forearm to show Milt, then burst into laughter when I saw he had two on his head!

"Well, I guess this means we will have good luck!"

I couldn't help but to recall my incident with Leslie and the ladybugs back in 1962. In the scope of life, that brief period of time seemed so insignificant. Yet, almost four decades later, those" *trifle"* moments from long ago were very significant in forming who I am today. So many connected incidents that lead to your destiny. Milt and I smiled at each other as we left Chenango Bridge and headed to Finger Lakes.

The trip reassured us that we were a good match, not only in the love we had for one another but also the friendship we shared. Once back in Florida, it was Milt who drove over the Sunshine Skyway Bridge. I didn't think I was quite ready yet to tackle the challenge. Not yet at least.

CHAPTER 33

Milt & I had only been home a few days when I had a phone call from my Mom. I somehow knew it wasn't good news.

"Mom, what's wrong? Is Dad okay?"

She replied, "Well, he's as good as he can be, but Charlee came to visit and ended up in the hospital! She had a severe asthma attack and had all kinds of breathing treatments! Don't worry, for now she is stable."

No doubt, I wanted this silent war to end. Most importantly, I wanted Charlee to know I cared.

"Mom, Milt and I will try to catch a flight tomorrow."

There was only one thing I could do that might soften the strangeness of popping in on my sister after not seeing her for almost a year. I had to go to the grocery store! When I pulled into the parking lot, Milt asked,

"Where are you going?"

I said, "You'll see!"

Then I ran to the vegetable section to pick out the biggest carrots with large shoulders long, leafy green tops. Then on the way out, I picked up two magic markers. Once back in the car, I picked out the largest two carrots in the whole bunch and began to chisel like I hadn't done for years! There were little flecks of carrots all over my rental car! Then I worked on the second carrot, which was much taller than the first.

We picked up Laurel and David, but I was careful not to expose my creation in the bag. Laurel said, "Wow, Mom, it's been a long time since I've seen Aunt Charlee. I miss her!"

David said, "Yeah, me too!" All three of us took the elevator to the fourth floor to Charlee's room. We rounded the corner and could hear laughter and flamboyantly expressive voices coming from one of the rooms. I said out loud, "That voice sounds familiar! I've heard it before!" It sounded as if they were partying! David said,

"Are we in a hospital or at the casino?"

To our surprise, the noise was coming from Charlee's room. There, surrounding Charlee's bed, were her old clients from the district—*and* Stanley, again wearing a red, skin-tight wonder woman outfit!

I looked at him and smiled. "I remember you! I met you at my sister's office several years ago!"

Milt, Laurel, and David stopped to take a second look at Stanley. I thought to myself how boring this world would be if we were all the same. Stanley had been a loyal, dear friend of Charlee's, and he was here for her now at the hospital.

"Charlee, it looks like company is the best medicine! You look great!" My sister, now wide-eyed, cheered,

"Whew! I can't believe it's my little sis from Florida, my niece and nephew and...who is the tall handsome man? Give me a hug!"

My sister may not have been wealthy, but she was rich in those who loved her. She was surrounded by friends, her loving husband Ray, and my parents. Big Al looked so small in the big hospital chair next to Charlee's bed. My Father was busy scanning his own hospital bill from his last admission.

"Damn, can you believe they charged me for *another* Kotex?"

My mom was angrily pressing the nurse's call button.

"When are you discharging Charlee?"

In the midst of everything going on, I meekly said to my sister,

"Um, Charlee, I don't know if this is the best time, but I made you a little gift."

I pulled out my two anatomically correct Charlee and Ray carrot people. Charlee's eyes were as big as saucers and smiled so big, I could count every tooth in her head!

"Wow! Carrot people! I used to make them for my little sis!" Her curious, flamboyant friend Stanley grasped the big Ray-Carrot out of my hand. He then laughed hysterically!

"I've never seen anything like this before...Ray and Charlee carrot people!?"

Stanley checked out Carrot Ray's "package,"

"Hey Ray, you're carved like a Ken doll!"

Curious, Ray grabbed it from him, saying,

"Give me my Carrot Man, Stanley!"

Charlee grinned as she admired her personalized veggie person,

"Awe, you made me a pretty carrot face! Oh and Look at my pretty long green hair!"

Laurel and David were cracking up at witnessing such a crazy chaotic scene.

Thankfully, Charlee was discharged that day, and we all headed for June and Big Al's house. I introduced my soul mate to the entire Bender clan, one by one. My mom was personable and warm and genuinely seemed happy to have all of us back together. Funny, you know, I never realized how much I missed them all, until I was back home. The longer I was away, the easier it was to maintain distance. The pang of missing the Benders gradually diminished. Now that I was home, yes, I missed my family! Well, except for my brother Alan going on and on, telling my future husband all the goofy, embarrassing things I did as a child. Like how I used to pick on him by using a wrestling move called, The Pretzel! It was a great way to restrain Alan's long arms during a fight. I'd spin him around like a pretzel so he couldn't hit me back. Oh no, now Alan was demonstrating, *The Pretzel*, on Milt!

In large families, there will always be someone you'll be butting heads with at some point, especially when the personalities are as strong as those in the Bender clan. One minute you love them, and the next minute that same person will make you want to tear your hair out. I sat there quietly on the couch observing Milt, my kids, Mom, Big Al, Charlee, Abby, T-Mac, Sam, Alan, and their spouses and children.

There was a musical flow of conversation as I felt the warmth of love inside the room. Big Al was now much weaker than the last time I was in St. Louis. I just wasn't sure how much longer he could fight his battle with cancer. For the time being, I wanted to cherish this moment with my father. A tear suddenly ran down my cheek with the realization that it could be the last time we were all together. That night our house truly became a home filled great food, festive dialogue, laughter—and yes, even an old black-and-white Western.

When our return flight landed in Florida, I asked Milt if I could drive home. Milt, well aware of my fear of bridges, looked at me rather surprised.

"You mean you want to drive over the Sunshine Skyway Bridge?"

I nodded and said,

"Yes, of course!"

As I passed the toll bridge, I started to feel an uneasy feeling of panic. Milt grew concerned at the look of fear on my face. I momentarily clenched the steering wheel after I paid the toll. I started to squirm in my seat, feeling panicky. Then I absolutely freaked out when I realized, *there's no way back!*

My car slowly proceeded up, up, up, as if I would run into the bright full moon in the sky. To my amazement, there wasn't another car on the entire bridge! *How is that possible?* My heart started to beat so hard that I wanted to pound my chest to make it stop. It was as if I was on the tallest roller coaster in the world, and I was about to go down! In a split second, my arm felt so weak that I wasn't sure if I could steer!

It then went limp. My car quickly veered out of control and crashed into the guardrail. I heard a crunch as my head hit the steering wheel. Blood spattered onto the windshield. I heard the windshield break and quickly looked to where Milt had been sitting. He was gone. *Oh, my God, where is he?*

My broken teeth seem to whirl and dance in front of me. The airbag did not deploy! *No, no, not now! Please, God, help me!* There were fragmented pieces of glass flying in all directions. The SUV became airborne over the guard rail. There were no sounds at that moment, just total silence as the car descended in slow motion. *Will I find Milt in the deep, dark Tampa Bay, or will we both die alone?*

That's when I saw a white haze through my windshield form into the shape of a young girl. It was Leslie Ward. In a sweet, calm voice, she said,

"Moe, I never had a chance to live my life. Please don't be so afraid of death, that you won't live yours."

The car suddenly stopped in midair, and I woke up. Yes, I woke up—however, I felt someone gently holding my left hand, and I knew Leslie was there with me. As I turned, I saw Milt next to me. He was sleeping soundly, with a peaceful, sweet expression on his face.

Later that day, when we landed in Tampa, I asked if I could drive home. Milt looked puzzled, just as he had in my dream.

"You want to drive over the Sunshine Skyway Bridge?"

I looked at him and smiled,

"Don't worry, I will be fine now."

I told Milt about my dream the night before and he laughed as he shook his head.

"I don't know what's sillier, your irrational fear of the Sunshine Skyway bridge or all your ghost stories!"

The smirk on my face was evidence that I didn't appreciate my fiancé making fun of me! He was the type of person who needed double blind studies for everything! To Milt, the world was black or white with very few grey areas. He squeezed my hand three times as he grinned at me. I thought to myself, I'll let it slide *this* time. Needless to say my life was good and I was happy. I found myself smiling as we drove south on 275 towards home. It was getting late and I could see the stars sparkling overhead.

We drove a mile or so past the toll booth when Milt suddenly yelled,

"Pull over, pull over!"

Instantly, I glanced to the right. I saw a young thin blonde woman in soaking wet t-shirt and jeans! Her drenched locks fell just above her waist. By the light of the moon you could see large water droplets fall from her hair and clothing. The woman anxiously waved her arms overhead.

Quickly, I glanced at my rearview mirrors. I then veered off to shoulder of the road. Milt and I quickly exited the car and ran towards the woman.

"Are you Ok? What happened? Do you want us to call the police?

She crossed her arms over her thin shoulders, shivering as she raced to our vehicle.

"Can you take me to the other side of the bridge? I need to go home."

In unison, Milt and I said,

"Yes! Of course we can!"

I draped a towel around her that we kept for impromptu beach days. My concern mounted as I asked,

"Are you injured, are you sure you're Ok?"

Milt opened the door to the back seat and the woman climbed in. I was checking for oncoming traffic before I pulled out. Milt, looked down as he fumbled to reach for his phone that fell between the seats.

"Here you can use my cell to call your family or we can call ...."

Milt gasped as he turned to face the woman! The woman was no where in site, yet the seat and towel were soaking wet!

Milt's eyes were now as wide as saucers,

"Moe, I think I just saw my first ghost!"

My SUV then went up, up, up to the very top of this amazingly magnificent structure. I now had a renewed appreciation for this cable-stayed bridge that towered 190 feet above the bay. The moon's bright rays were reflecting a silver light on the tower above. The midnight blue water below looked like Tampa Bay was filled with millions of sparkling diamonds. I thought the Sunshine Skyway Bridge was truly the epitome of awe-inspiring beauty. *I will fear you no more.* As we crossed the central span of the bridge, I whispered,

"Thank you, Leslie Ward."

It was only a few months later, on a cold, dreary, bone-chilling January day, that my father lost his long battle with cancer. Big Al's doctors once called him "The Miracle Man." In the last several years, he had been at death's door many times. Amazingly he always seemed to stabilize and bounce out of the ICU. Not this time; sadly, not this time.

The day of my father's funeral, St. Louis recorded one of the coldest subzero temperatures in over a decade. The sun slowly peeked out of the clouds as "Taps" were played at his beautiful military funeral. The bright rays now shone brightly onto the glistening snow that gingerly draped the thousands of tombstones at the Veterans Memorial Cemetery. My father lived like a hero, and he died like one too.

Three weeks after the service, I was still in a depressed slump. I was home now in Florida, alone, up in my second-floor office. I was tearful as I created a memory card to honor my dad. As I walked downstairs, I suddenly felt a chill and a gush of icy cold wind. Very much like what I felt outdoors at Big Al's funeral in St. Louis! I stepped down off the third step and out of the cold. I walked back up...into a blustery, frigid wind! I ran to check the air conditioner; it was off. We did have some cool weather in Florida, so I checked the windows: closed. I walk back to the third step and into the fleeting burst of winter. I stood in the midst of the strange whirling wind. Then it went away as quickly as it began.

I excitedly ran to the phone to call my mom.

"Mom, I think I just felt Dad's presence!"

She responded with confusion,

"What?"

I explained what just occurred with the icy presence on the third step. Then I anxiously waited for her reply.

"Sheesh, Moe, now why in the world would your dad fly all the way down to Florida to haunt you? Why wouldn't he just haunt me here in St. Louis? I haven't seen him yet, so why would he go to Florida first? You know, he really wasn't too crazy about Florida's weather. It's waaaay too hot and so humid!"

Mom went on and on until I said,

"Mom! Please, don't ice my soul!"

June puzzled, stopped midsentence.

"What? Do what to your ice? Moe, what have you been smoking?

I chuckled at her response to my own private joke. "Never mind Mom, I love you."

Yes, my thoughts on ice within the soul, wasn't something I shared with many people. Despite the years spent butting heads with my mother, I realized there were more decades of love between us. The ice within all our souls slowly melted and allowed us to once again be a cohesive family.

Later, I walked into the den and was surprised the television was on. There on the screen was an old black-and-white John Wayne movie! Strangely, the channel then changed to... *The Enola Gay*!

Ha! Yes! I looked up toward heaven and smiled. Big Al does like Florida after all!

www.ladybuglady.com

interstate275florida.com/ssb.htm

www.sharingflorida.com

bridgehunter.com

The author and her husband, admiring the beauty of the Chenango River.

Made in the USA
Charleston, SC
13 July 2012